LOVE ALL

A STEAMY SPORTS ROMANCE

LIZA MALLOY

CHAPTER ONE

- Olivia -

Stupid global warming.

It shouldn't have been so humid in late September. I wiped the sweat off my forehead and adjusted my grip on the racket.

"Lean into the serve," I shouted across the net for what had to be the thirtieth time the past hour. He didn't, of course, but the ball still sailed over the net. *Thank God*. I returned it with ease, let the volley play out, hitting the ball until, finally, the kid tried his backhand and lobbed the ball straight into the net.

I checked my watch then walked forward to meet him at the net. I modeled how to hold the racket for a backhand hit, then praised his efforts.

"Practice against your garage," I suggested as he left to pack up.

I glanced to the court at the end of the row where Nate, another member of the varsity tennis team, was also teaching a private lesson. He seemed to be showing his student a proper backhand grip, too, but he was doing so by pressing his groin against the girl's backside and wrapping his arms around her waist.

I rolled my eyes. "Pervert," I mumbled.

Not that the girl seemed to mind. She was giggling and leaning into him like they were on a date. I couldn't exactly blame her. On the surface, Nate was perfect. Thick brown hair that always fell right into place, big brown puppy dog eyes framed by dark lashes, perpetually bronzed skin, and an athletic build that made every girl drool.

Until he opened his mouth and you realized he was absolutely aware of his own perfection. In Nate's mind, he was God's gift to women.

Barf.

Really, if you Googled 'preppy rich guy,' Nate's picture would probably pop up. I'd never known guys like him actually existed before starting college, but true to the stereotype, the prestigious university was chock full of Nates. They were all the same— never worked a day in their lives but still thought their plight mattered or that their challenges could somehow even compare to anyone else's. They expected—no, demanded—validation from everyone around them. And they didn't show an ounce of gratitude when life handed them gift after gift.

They were the type of guys that would take advantage of drunk freshman girls at their frat parties and convince themselves they were doing a favor to the girl. The type of guys who threatened to call Daddy if a professor didn't change a B to an A. The type of guys who didn't need to work to support themselves in college.

So...why was Nate teaching private tennis lessons?

I was doing it for the money, obviously. My tennis scholarship covered full tuition with a stipend for textbooks, but student loans funded my rent and other living expenses. Since I needed to keep my grades up to ensure I could snag the type of career that could eventually pay off those loans, I didn't have a ton of time for an actual job during the school year. But since I basically lived on the tennis courts anyway, teaching worked.

A shadow fell over the green acrylic court, and I squinted at the sky, wondering how long I had left before the inevitable downpour began. My apartment was less than a mile away, but with my luck, it'd start pouring before I even left the courts.

Nate jogged towards me and grabbed a hopper to start collecting stray balls. I turned to him, just in time to see his eyes widen with glee as his student bent down to grab her purse, flashing a little more of her cutesie bloomers than appropriate.

I groaned. "Pedophile."

"She's seventeen," he replied. "That's a full year past the age of consent here."

I winced, although the fact that he knew consent even mattered actually impressed me. "So that's why you teach—to meet potential dates?"

He grinned, revealing perfectly straight, white teeth. No doubt Daddy had spent thousands on that smile.

"It's going to rain. Need a ride?" he offered.

"Nope." I walked away to grab the balls from the furthest corner of the courts, reaching my hand under a crack beneath the fence to reach one that had snuck out. "Ouch!" I scratched the top of my hand as I pulled it back.

"Want a bandage?" Nate asked, making me jump.

I glared, not having realized he was right behind me.

It was a small scrape, but a smidge of blood was already trickling out. I really didn't want to ruin one of my bright white tennis skirts by inadvertently wiping my bloody hand on it, so I followed Nate over to the pro shop. I let him open the first-aid kit and select the bandage, but when he started to unwrap it, I snatched it away.

"I can open my own Bandaid," I insisted, painfully aware that I sounded like a petulant child. Normally, I could open and apply my own bandage, but since this cut was on the top of my dominant hand, it was trickier. The Bandaid folded over and adhered to itself while I attempted to stick it on using only my left hand.

"Are you always this stubborn?" Nate asked, ripping open a second Bandaid and clutching my hand firmly. He'd pressed the bandage into place before I could protest. Then, as if on cue, a giant clap of thunder shook the small pro shop and announced the arrival of the rain. We peered out the window just as the skies erupted, dumping buckets of water on the courts.

I swore under my breath.

"Wow. Where I come from, ladies don't talk like that," Nate teased.

I rolled my eyes. "Where you come from, money grows on trees and people think polo is a real sport."

He cracked a smile. "Do you make this many assumptions about everyone or just the people you like?"

"It's not an assumption. I've seen your car."

He followed my gaze over to the parking lot. His cobalt blue BMW was the only remaining vehicle in the lot.

"Let me guess—graduation present from Daddy?"

"It's like you know me!' He chuckled and nodded towards the car. "Come on, Stubborn. I'll give you a ride."

Reluctantly, I agreed, unable to stomach the possibility of trudging home through the deluge. We sprinted to the car, soaked despite the short distance.

Laughing, Nate reached into the back seat and retrieved a small hand towel. He handed it to me. I dabbed at my arms and legs, suddenly self-conscious about dripping all over the pristine, beige leather interior. My eyes followed Nate's movement as he grabbed for another rag in the back. A new iPad lay on the back seat.

"Has no one ever told you not to leave valuables in plain sight in your car? Someone might steal it."

He shrugged. "Stuff can be replaced."

My jaw muscles tightened at his nonchalant tone as I fastened my belt. "This car even smells new." I said, wondering how he'd managed that if it was nearly four years old.

Nate started the ignition. "Well, I would tell you that it is new, that it was actually a present for my twenty first birthday and not for high school graduation, but I'd hate to burst your know-it-all bubble."

That explained it. "Same difference," I mumbled.

Nate shifted the car into reverse, then back into park. He turned to face me. "Why do you hate me?"

"I don't hate you. I just think you're an overprivileged entitled snowflake."

"Wow. How do you really feel?"

I crossed my arms and stared pointedly. Sure, it was harsh, but it was good for him. I was possibly the first person ever to speak the truth to Nate.

Nate didn't budge though, and after a moment, it became clear that I may never actually get home if I didn't say something else.

"Oh please, I'm sure you have some opinions about me."

He gave me a quick once over then shook his head. "Not really. I hardly know you. We've played tennis together for over two years now and I literally don't know a single thing about you."

"We haven't played together," I said, but even I knew that was nitpicky. Technically the men's and women's teams were separate, but our practices were usually back to back and most of our matches were at the same location. Nate was a Senior, a year ahead of me, but that didn't matter since we both played varsity.

"You're stubborn," he finally said. "I know that. And you're a badass on the courts."

I had to smile at that. I *was* sort of a badass.

He tapped his chin in thought. "What else do I know about you? Hmm. You're a hard worker, you hate men, and you sometimes forget to breathe."

I was going to protest his assumption about my feelings towards men, but then the last part intrigued me more. "I forget to breathe?"

Nate pointed to my arms, which were currently crossed over my abdomen. "Your tattoo says 'Breathe,' doesn't it?"

I did in fact have the word "breathe" tattooed in script along the inside of my left forearm, but it was tiny and most people didn't notice it. "I don't *forget* to breathe," I said, forcing myself to stop trying to read into why he'd noticed the tattoo anyway. "It's just a good reminder, when I'm overwhelmed, to just take a breath and keep going."

"You don't seem like the type to get overwhelmed."

"Now who's making assumptions?" I asked.

Nate grinned again, and I couldn't help noticing a small dimple on his right cheek. I turned abruptly to my window as he pulled out of the lot. I told him my address and the closest intersection, but when the car rolled to a stop a few minutes later, it wasn't in front of my apartment.

"I don't live here," I said, staring blankly at the old-fashioned diner before us.

"I figured as much, but I'm hungry, so it stands to reason that you, too, might be hungry. Plus, I wanted to hear more about this snowflake theory of yours."

"I have homework to do." The lack of control I now faced was precisely why I shouldn't have accepted a ride in the first place. The rain, of course, had already died down to a light sprinkle, but now I was probably closer to three miles from my apartment.

"You'll think better with a full stomach," he said, killing the ignition. "My treat."

"You know this is kidnapping," I said, reluctantly climbing out of the car. "Telling a girl you'll drive her home then forcing her someplace else."

"Let me guess, you're pre-law?"

I shook my head.

"Pre-med?"

"Why do you assume I'm going to graduate school?"

He shrugged and held open the door to the diner. "Are you planning to go pro with tennis?"

I snorted at that.

"What, if anyone could it's you."

My lips curved up at the unexpected compliment. Maybe I was a tad hungry.

CHAPTER TWO

- Nate -

Olivia fidgeted with her skirt as we slid into the booth at the diner. She didn't wrinkle her nose at the sticky menu or squirt hand sanitizer all over the table like the last girl I'd brought here. Not that I'd expected her to do either of those things. I also guessed she wouldn't ask about gluten free buns for the veggie burger. Of course, I couldn't say any of that aloud, because then Olivia would know I was just as bad as her with my assumptions.

Her bold blue eyes peered up at me. "You're not going to look at the menu?"

"I eat here a lot. I already know what I like."

Olivia quirked an eyebrow and folded her menu. "Okay then, what's good?"

"Patty melt, fries, chocolate shake."

She held my gaze for a moment, then nodded.

"You're going to eat that?" I didn't even attempt to hide the disbelief in my voice. Olivia didn't look like she ate a lot of red meat, fried foods or ice cream.

"If you say it's good," she said. "Vanilla shake though."

"You don't like chocolate? Are you a sociopath?"

"I like chocolate. I just prefer vanilla," she said dryly.

The waitress came to take our orders before I had a chance to mock her preference any further.

"So what are you studying?" I asked once we were alone again.

"Business administration."

I wrinkled my nose. The only thing that sounded duller or more tedious than classes in business administration was a career in the field.

My response didn't go unnoticed.

"Okay, what titillating major are you pursuing?" she countered.

"Finance."

Olivia laughed. "Gonna be a stockbroker like Daddy?"

I chewed the side of my mouth. My father was a stockbroker, and he did plan for me to follow in his footsteps. I suspected Olivia didn't so much know that as assumed it, but it still annoyed me that she was correct. I opted to flip the question instead of answering her. "What does your father do? Let me guess...beat cop?"

Her eyes twinkled as a bemused grin crossed her face. My heart thudded harder at the sight of that smile, almost like I was proud. Maybe I was.

I'd never been close with Olivia, but I'd seen her lots over the past couple of years. She smiled with her mouth often enough, but it never looked authentic. Even after a victory, the curl of her lips seemed forced, like her accomplishment didn't actually bring her joy. Olivia was a master of that type of smile that looked beautiful but didn't actually reach her eyes.

I was certain that, for whatever reason, she wasn't actually as happy as she pretended to be. If I were a betting man, I'd guess Olivia Roberts hid a lot of pain under that beautiful smile. And damn if it didn't make me feel like Santa Claus when I helped her forget it, even if only for a moment.

The waitress returned with our shakes, distracting us both. I took a sip from my straw, desperate for anything to cool me off after a couple hours in the brutal humidity. Olivia delicately plucked the cherry from her shake, popping it into her mouth as she pulled the stem loose. Her eyes closed as she chewed, so I took the opportunity to stare.

Her long, sandy blonde hair was pulled back into a ponytail, but a few strands had escaped and framed her smooth face. Olivia's hair looked soft, and I was tempted to reach out and touch it, just to tuck it behind her ear. She'd probably slap me if I did that, though.

I suspected that was what intrigued me so much about her, the fact that she was so completely disinterested in me. Most girls seemed quite receptive to my charms, but Olivia was down-right annoyed.

"What?" she asked, and I realized she'd opened her eyes and caught me staring.

"You were about to tell me what your father does," I said, struggling to think about anything other than the way she licked her full, rosy lips after devouring the juicy fruit.

"I don't have a father."

"Divorce? Or like a two mommies, sperm donor type of thing?"

She made a face. "Neither. I have one mom, heterosexual, not that it's any of your business, and I don't know who my father is. My parents were never…involved."

"Oh, so your mom," I began, about to spout a flip comment about the type of woman who slept with so many guys she didn't even know which one knocked her up. I stopped abruptly when Olivia twirled a steak knife in her fingers like a trained assassin.

"Keep talking and I'll stab you in the eye," she said.

From her expression, I guessed she meant it.

I cleared my throat and focused on my milkshake, trying to recall why I'd wanted to spend more time with this girl. It was much easier to appreciate her on the tennis courts, where I could admire her grace, athleticism, and off-the-charts body from a distance, where she could neither stab me nor overload me with snarky, judgmental comments.

"What's your mom do?" I asked finally.

"She's a waitress," she replied. "At a place pretty similar to this."

That alone told me a lot about Olivia. Well, namely that she was broke. It also explained why she worked so much.

"What about your mom?" she asked.

I laughed. "You already know everything about me. Why don't you tell me what my mother does?"

"I'm betting she majored in English, never got a real job, and spends her days flirting with the pool boy and spending your daddy's money."

"She was a psych major," I corrected, finding no fault with the rest of her guess.

Olivia shrugged, remarkably unimpressed with the accuracy of her assumptions.

Our food arrived, so we busied ourselves with ketchup and napkins for a minute. When I finally dared look up again, Olivia was scowling.

"Are you this standoffish with every guy that takes you out to dinner, or just me?" I asked.

She sipped her milkshake before answering. "I'm not the type of girl that guys take out to dinner."

I tried to decipher the possible meanings of that, but was stumped. Olivia was gorgeous, and not in an eye-of-the-beholder type of way, but in the factual, indisputable sort of way. She had the long, shiny hair from shampoo commercials, show-stopping bold blue eyes, perfectly symmetrical and delicate facial features, and the long, tanned legs of someone who spent hours playing tennis. I didn't believe for one minute that she wasn't constantly fielding invitations from interested guys.

"Bullshit," I finally said. "They're asking, you just aren't going."

A wry smile crept onto her face. "You are the first guy to actually kidnap me."

"So why don't you date?"

"This is not a date."

"Agreed. Answer the question."

"I guess I don't see the point," she finally said. "I didn't come to college to meet a sugar daddy. I came here to get a degree so I can get a decent job and not end up in a shitty apartment working second shift into my forties."

"Lots of people date during college and still earn a degree and get a job after graduation."

"I don't have time for dating. Between tennis and studying, I barely have time to sleep and eat, let alone engage in meaningless banter with frat guys who secretly just want to hook up and then brag to all their bros."

I chewed slowly while I thought about that. "You think I'm one of those frat guys?"

She shrugged then reached for another fry, drowning it in ketchup before nibbling the tip. "You tell me. What were your expectations for this? Did you maybe think you'd buy me a delicious five dollar sandwich and then I'd eagerly blow you in the backseat of your BMW?"

I leaned away from the table, literally speechless.

Olivia continued to stare unabashedly, as though she hadn't just made incredibly offensive assumptions about my character. *Again.*

"Wow. Just wow," I finally said. "First off, counting the milkshake, this will be close to eight dollars, plus tip. Second of all, I would never risk damaging the interior of my car by doing that in the backseat. Thirdly, how dare you even assume I'd let that dirty mouth of yours anywhere near my precious—"

"Can I get you anything else?" the waitress interrupted.

I glanced at Olivia.

"No thanks," she said politely.

I accepted the bill, retrieved a twenty from my wallet, then upon better thought added a few more dollars just so she wouldn't dare accuse me of being stingy on the tip.

"You know," I said as we continued eating. "Some people like to give others the benefit of the doubt. Get to know people before assuming the worst."

Olivia boldly reached across the table and snatched the cherry from the shake that I'd set on the edge of my plate. "Some of us prefer to avoid disappointment. I'll keep my assumptions until people prove me wrong."

At least she was honest, I thought, oddly envious of the cherry stem as she pressed her tongue against it. "Challenge accepted."

When we left the diner, I drove at a snail's pace to buy time to think of a witty comment. Or at least something else to earn another sincere smile. But I came up short.

"Thank you for the ride," she said, already clutching her racket and duffel bag before I even slowed to a complete stop in front of her apartment.

"And for the excellent meal, right?" I added, incapable of just letting it go.

She stared dryly. "I'll thank you for the food when you thank me for not pressing charges on the whole kidnapping front."

I bit back a smile. Even pissed off, Olivia was captivating. "This was fun. Why haven't we hung out before?"

"Because we have nothing in common."

"Not true. There's tennis, lame business majors, and douchebag fathers."

Olivia gazed back at me and for the briefest of moments, I thought she would say something meaningful, but instead she just shook her head, dismissing whatever idea had crossed her intriguing mind.

"You can't possibly want to spend more time with me. I've been a total bitch to you all afternoon."

I wasn't about to deny that last part, so instead I pushed my luck with a bad joke. "We could move into the back seat and you could make it up to me," I said, wiggling my eyebrows seductively.

I'd hoped for a snarky comeback, but instead she just rolled her eyes and chuckled. "I'll see you at practice," she mumbled, climbing out of the car.

I watched as she smoothed the pleated white skirt over her gorgeously rounded ass and walked up to her door, not sparing a wave or a glance back. I waited until she'd shut the door behind her before I drove off, questioning myself.

How had I gone so long without pursuing her? I'd noticed Olivia the day she'd made varsity, the same day, ironically, that Coach Aaron had given his annual speech about the unwritten rule that we were not to date any other tennis players. Too messy, he'd declared. I tended to agree. Convenient, sure, but then when things went wrong, you'd be left dealing with the drama when you needed to focus on the game. So maybe that was why I hadn't given her much subsequent thought. Olivia was hot, sure, but she probably wasn't worth the trouble.

Except now, for some reason, I knew Olivia was worth whatever effort it would take to crack that hardened exterior of hers.

I needed to get to know Olivia, to figure out why she was the way she was. I needed to know what made her so sad. I needed to cure her loneliness. I wanted to fix whatever was broken in her.

CHAPTER THREE

- Olivia -

"Ouch!" I shook my hand then bent to retrieve the elastic band that had snapped against my skin as I tried to fix my ponytail. Stupid cheap bulk purchase hair products. I made a mental note to bring a backup elastic or two for all of my matches.

"I have an extra if you want," Mia offered, approaching the net.

"Thanks, but I'm probably okay," I said. Practice was almost over, and since Mia was really my only friend on the team, I didn't want to be indebted to her.

She shrugged, then returned to her side of the net. We exchanged a few more volleys, and Coach Katelyn paced behind us shouting pointers and corrections. Before long, she shouted for everyone to bring it in. We ended every practice with a brief team meeting, so there was nothing surprising about the occurrence. And then she dismissed us to the locker rooms.

I hadn't planned to wash my hair when I showered, but since it had been flat against my neck the last half hour, I now needed to. Still, I didn't have time to dry it before class so I simply combed it and hoped for the best.

"Good luck on your test," I said to Mia as she headed out.

She smiled and crossed her fingers.

Alone in the locker room, I swiped on deodorant and applied a minimal layer of makeup. It was stupid not to take the hair tie from Mia. I wasn't sure why I still couldn't accept that she was actually kind. I guess part of it was the fact that Mia was pretty much the only one on the team who was nice to me right off the bat. When I'd joined the team as a freshman—a year younger than most of the other varsity players— the coaches immediately singled me out, noting my potential. At first, most of the girls had snubbed me, almost like it was a traditional, passive-aggressive hazing ritual. But then when I started playing well, they all warmed up. It just wasn't authentic with anyone but Mia.

Mia was a Junior and an English major. She wasn't the best on the team—far from it, actually—but we were paired often because she excelled at playing to my weak spots. Playing her gave me a better workout. Plus, she was funny and lighthearted and kind to everyone. Really, we were exact opposites in that respect.

I swung the door open, too focused on my social inadequacies to realize there was someone standing outside it until he grunted.

"Shit. Sorry," I mumbled. My guilt disappeared when I saw who it was.

"Stalking much?" I asked Nate.

"I'm here for practice, not you," he said.

I pointed to the door. "You're practicing in the women's locker room now?"

He rolled his eyes dramatically and I couldn't help but notice his thick, dark lashes.

"Truce," he said, holding up a massive glazed donut wrapped in a thin piece of deli paper. "I come baring carbs."

"You brought me a donut?" It was a dumb question, since I

was close enough now that its excessively sweet odor permeated my nostrils, causing my mouth to water.

Nate smiled. He started to hand it to me then paused. "Admit I'm a nice guy," he said.

I crossed my arms over my chest. "Nice guys don't put conditions on donuts, especially when the intended recipient just played tennis for four hours."

He held out the donut. I hesitated, afraid if I reached for it, he'd yank it away. But he didn't.

"Thank you," I said. I wanted to storm off to eat my pastry in peace, but he was standing so close to the locker room door that I'd probably have to touch him to walk around it. So instead, I stood there and began nibbling it.

"How was practice?"

I shrugged, unable to answer with my mouth full of sugary goodness anyway.

Nate pressed his lips together in a failed attempt to bite back a smile.

"What?" I asked after I swallowed.

He reached his finger out and delicately brushed my top lip. "You got some glaze there," he said. His eyes focused so intently on my lips then that I felt my face flush. I couldn't possibly eat with someone watching me so closely.

I licked my lips in case any crumbs remained. Nate's eyes flared.

"Oh my God," I mumbled, pressing a hand to his chest so I could walk around him. "Seriously?"

"Seriously what?"

"Is the donut like foreplay for you?"

His lips parted but he looked truly confused now.

"Did you think if you bought me a donut, I'd hook up with you in the locker room or something? Is that your grand plan? Seduction by sugar?"

I shook my head and held the donut out for him to take.

"Nevermind. If you're expecting something in return, I don't even want it. I can buy my own donuts."

"Olivia…" he began.

I clutched the pastry back to my chest, realizing how dumb it was to give up my donut. "No, you know what? I'm keeping this. I'm going to eat this donut and enjoy it, but not with you staring at me. I don't know what you might think of me, but I'm really not the type of girl you can buy over with cheap baked goods."

"I wasn't trying to—"

I held up my hand, silencing him. "I should go."

He looked like he wanted to say something, then just shook his head and started to follow me.

I took another bite, and as delicious as it was, that only annoyed me more. Clearly, Nate was trying to flirt. I realized that much. But guys like him tended to buy girls jewelry, expensive theater tickets, or even fancy floral bouquets. Did he really think I was so easy that a simple donut and a cheap diner-meal would win me over?

I stopped and turned to face him again. "Look, I know what you must think of me, but I'm not that girl. I have standards, okay? I'm not just going to drop my skirt over a donut. And the fact that you even think I'm like that is insulting."

I swiveled away and made my way back to the courts, stopping abruptly when I saw the entire men's tennis team standing around the edge of the court eating donuts. I stared down at the donut in my hand, confused.

A few of the guys cheered when they saw Nate, and a couple even patted him on the back and thanked him for the donuts.

I wished I could melt into the courts. I couldn't even muster the energy to keep walking away, let alone to turn and face him. *God.* I was an arrogant, presumptuous ass. What exactly had made me think I was special to him?

I stiffened, feeling Nate's presence directly behind me.

"I hope they don't all think I'm just trying to get into their pants," he whispered.

Cringing, I turned to Nate. Not surprisingly, a huge grin was plastered across his perfect face.

"You bought donuts for everyone," I said.

"Yeah."

"And then I went on a rant assuming you just brought one for me because you're interested."

His smile broadened.

I blew out a sigh. My face felt hotter than the clay courts in July.

Nate laughed out loud, shaking his head. "Enjoy the donut, Olivia."

I watched as he began to saunter off towards the court.

I was still mortified hours later as I told the story to my roommate, Addie.

She tossed back half a glass of her sweet red wine then laughed uproariously. "Did you actually say the part about trading sex for donuts?" she asked, covering her mouth as she burped.

I winced. "I think so." I reached for the bottle of wine. I wasn't a big drinker, for an abundance of reasons. I'd seen firsthand the strong correlation between bad decisions and alcohol consumption. I didn't want to spare any calories on alcohol. And I couldn't risk a hangover or anything of that nature impacting my athletic performance at all. For the most part, I was content to wait to drink until my tennis career was over, whenever that day may come.

But that night, a little wine might actually help ease the pain of the memory of what an ass I'd made out of myself. I took a swig straight from the bottle, blinking back tears as the syrupy liquid hit my throat.

"Ick. How do you drink this? This is not real wine."

Addie giggled. "It is so. It's kosher. See?" She pointed to the label.

I cringed and handed back the bottle. "I almost made a comment about blow jobs," I admitted.

"What? No. Your blow jobs are worth way more than a donut. I've never seen a dissatisfied customer," she teased.

I rolled my eyes, certain she'd never seen any customer. We'd only lived together for a couple months, and I hadn't been involved with anyone in that amount of time. I'd dated a couple of guys my freshman year, but no one I'd liked enough to sleep with. And last year there'd been one guy, but that was long over.

I pulled the throw pillow up to my face, still feeling the heat of my embarrassment. "Why can't I just let things go? Every time I see him, it's like he draws these long-winded rants out of me. I just can't shut up."

Addie made a face. "You like him."

"I don't. He's horrible. And that cocky shit-eating grin on his face…ugh!"

"What's his last name again?" she asked, snatching my phone out of my hands.

"Aldridge," I said, curious what she was up to.

Of course she went straight to social media and pulled up his profile picture. "Oh wow. He is hot. You have good taste."

She angled the phone towards me. As much as I didn't want to look, I couldn't resist. The first photo was him playing tennis. There was another picture of him posing by his car, a few of him with some guys from the tennis team, and a close-up where his eyes sparkled so brightly that my mouth went dry. I scrolled quickly past the dozen or so tennis-related shots, then paused on the one of him wearing swim trunks, posing by the sail of some luxury yacht.

"If this doesn't capture his entire persona, I don't know what does," I said, gagging dramatically.

"Oh please, since when is it a crime to have a pretty face and a rockin' bod?" she retorted. She grabbed my phone back and clicked the button to follow him.

"Addison!" I snapped.

She simply smirked.

I gritted my teeth together until they hurt.

"You have to apologize anyway," she pointed out.

God. She was right. My drunk roommate actually made an excellent point. I had made totally unfair assumptions about Nate and, while I was still confident my overall character assessment was correct, the donut had not been a ploy to get in my pants. My mother taught me to apologize when I misspoke, and even if she hadn't, I couldn't handle another six months of practice knowing this was still hanging over our heads.

I snatched back my phone, searched my email until I found the one with the entire tennis team roster, then looked up his contact info. I contemplated email, but that seemed too formal.

"I'm sorry about the donut thing earlier," I wrote in a text, clicking "send" before I could talk myself out of it.

I watched the little dots appear, indicating he was typing a response, and then it appeared.

"Who is this?"

Shit. Duh. How would he know?

"Olivia Roberts."

He didn't respond, so I kept going.

"Anyway, I misread the entire situation and I said some things I shouldn't have. Sorry."

"Well, I wasn't planning to buy you or anyone else donuts ever again, but now that you've apologized, I can. The entire team thanks you for clearing this up." he replied.

I rolled my eyes. Of course he couldn't just accept the apology with dignity and move on.

"I am curious though," he continued. "Is that a thing—donuts for sex? I mean, should I have been offering edible gifts to my conquests thus far?"

"Goodnight, Nate," I wrote, hoping he'd take the hint and let it drop.

Luckily, he did. "Sweet dreams, Olivia," he replied.

I sighed and stood to grab a glass of water from the kitchen. When I returned, Addie was holding my phone and grinning.

"He wrote something else," she said, holding it out for me to see.

"Just so you know," he'd written, "You weren't wrong about everything. I am interested. And now I have your number. So thank you."

I bit my lip, trying to figure out why my heart had begun thumping erratically.

CHAPTER FOUR

- Nate -

*T*o say my day sucked didn't even begin to capture it. I'd overslept, missing the start of practice. Then, instead of letting me make use of the remaining practice time, Coach opted to yell for a good ten minutes before making me run laps until it was time to hit the showers. My first class was Finance, and if I hadn't already felt nauseated from the running, the bold red C- on the test my professor handed back to me would've accomplished that, even without the SEE ME scribbled beside the grade.

"Fuck," I mumbled.

Cassie, the stalker girl who sat beside me and seemed to think we were friends, leaned over and rubbed my shoulder with her bony hand.

"Oh baby, I'm sorry. Want to grab some coffee after class? I can cheer you up," she cooed.

I cringed. "Not today." *Or ever.*

I thrust my head into my hands, determined not to see the look on my buddy's face beside me. Brogan thought it was hilarious that I hadn't managed to successfully blow off Cassie by this point. As one of my best friends, he'd serve as a buffer if I really needed him to. But for the most part, when it came to Cassie, he enjoyed watching me flail, which I did often with her.

Apparently, I sucked at rejecting the girls I wasn't into. But in general, I considered myself good with women. Flirting came naturally to me, and I typically could judge which girls were interested in me. Well, and it didn't hurt that, until Olivia, I'd never had feelings for a girl who didn't reciprocate at least a little.

Whatever.

I survived class and endured the lecture from Professor Laghari. Honestly, a C- wasn't the end of the world. As long as the grade didn't drop lower, the course would still count towards graduation. It wasn't like I needed a stellar GPA since I already had a job lined up. Still, the fact that I'd actually studied for that test was annoying. If I'd just phoned it in, fine. But when a C- actually represented my best efforts, well...

I was already mentally planning what I'd pick up for lunch before my second class of the day when Professor Laghari sealed my day's fate.

"Your father had asked how the class was going, so I let him know you seem to be struggling. Maybe he could help you out with the class, go over your outline or something before the next exam," he said.

"You..." I stammered, my mouth going dry. "Why?"

"He and I go way back and there's no sense in you struggling when your father is such an expert in the field."

An expert? If I weren't about to puke, I would've laughed at the ridiculous notion. My father was an expert at money, but that didn't exactly translate over to a finance class.

I waited a moment, then nodded. "Can I go?"

My professor dismissed me, and I found Brogan had waited. We caught up for a minute before I announced that I needed to call my dad. The sooner I got that shit out of the way, the better.

Actually, it was a little surprising he hadn't already called to yell at me.

I dialed his cell directly, hoping to avoid an awkward exchange with his secretary, but a woman answered regardless. I checked the number I'd dialed to confirm I'd selected the right one. I had.

"Hi. It's Nate. Is my dad available?" I said, assuming whoever he'd hired to answer his cell phone at least knew who I was.

"Uh, sure. Let me see," she said. Her tone lacked the professionalism and confidence of his normal secretary, so I wondered if maybe she was new. Not that it mattered. Every second she took to find my father, my pulse increased. I just needed to get the lecture from him over with and then I'd be fine.

I heard the distinct sound of running water on the other end of the line. That was odd. Maybe my dad in the breakroom, though. Certainly she wouldn't look for him in the bathroom. After another pause, I heard a deep voice in the background. I assumed it was my dad, but couldn't tell what he'd said. But then the woman spoke again, and even though her voice was muffled and distant, I got the message just fine.

She giggled and said, "babe, stop. It's your son on the phone."

Then, there was a moment of silence. I was thankful I hadn't eaten yet, because hearing someone call my father "babe" definitely would've brought up any partially-digested foods.

I considered hanging up, but then my father came to the phone. His voice was crisp and clear as always. I could even picture the condescending smirk on his face as he answered.

"Nathaniel? I'm glad you called. I wanted to talk with you."

"Yeah. I figured," I said. "New secretary?"

"What?"

"The woman answering your phone. Didn't sound like mom."

"Of course it wasn't your mother. I'm at work. Remember work? It's that place I go to earn money to fund your education. The education you seem determined to throw down the drain."

"It was one test, Dad, and…"

"Do you have any idea how humiliating it is when a Professor emails to tell me my son is failing his class?"

"I'm not failing. I…"

"Jesus, Nathaniel. If you had any idea what I had to do to get you into that school, the sacrifices I've made for you."

A snort escaped my lips. My father hadn't done a damn thing. Our last name and his pocketbook was all it took to open any door in this town. But for years now he'd been dead-set on pretending he'd sold a fucking kidney or something.

"Is this funny to you? Do I amuse you, Nathaniel?" His tone had changed again, and then I realized he was serious. My dad was always angry, but when he crossed the line from angry to truly pissed, well, you didn't want to be in his way.

"No, Sir, I just…"

"You will bring that grade up and you won't humiliate me anymore. I'll not have your laziness making a mockery out of our family name."

I opened my mouth to say something else, but the line went dead. "Bye, Dad," I mumbled, rolling my eyes at the sky above.

My next class was fine, but the day was already a wash. I grabbed an early dinner and went home to study, only to be bombarded with a reminder alert from the fraternity about a "mandatory" meeting that night.

I blew out a sigh. I'd made a couple good friends at the fraternity, but it wasn't my thing. I didn't live there anymore, I didn't socialize with most of the guys, and I barely even kept up with the news. I was only in the damn thing because I was a legacy. I *had* to pledge because my father had and his father had and, Christ, my great grandad probably started that fucking frat.

I threw my racket into my car, and the second the meeting ended, I drove to the courts. I needed to study more, but first I had to clear my head. To do that, I needed to burn off some steam. Alone.

My excitement upon seeing the parking lot empty was short lived. I'd barely stepped away from my car when I heard the distinct whoosh of a racket hitting the balls. Still, with nightfall fast approaching, I'd probably be alone soon.

I unzipped my racket case and moved towards the pro shop to grab some balls, pausing when I saw it was unlocked. The entire varsity squad had keys to the storage room, which meant the other person playing solo on the darkened court was a teammate of mine. I moved closer, guessing the player was female based on what appeared to be a long, braided ponytail. I watched as she hit serve after serve. Each time, the ball slammed into the court with precision and speed, always landing in the hard-to-return spots. There was only one girl on the team who could serve like that.

"Hey!" I shouted, adding "You missed a shot," after my sudden interruption made her serve go short and snag the net.

"Thanks, smartass," she called back. She raised her arm again, aimed, and popped the ball. Her form was impeccable. I wished I could take a picture to memorialize the moment right before she tossed the ball where she was frozen, like a graceful figurine of a tennis pro.

Inching forward, I looked even closer. The fact that she was letting me watch her without some form of criticism was astounding, until I stared at her face and realized her eyes appeared to be shut.

"Are your eyes closed?" I asked, questioning what I was seeing. There was no way someone could have such impeccable aim without even looking.

She tossed the ball in the air, caught it effortlessly, then turned to me. She opened her eyes with a sigh. "They were. Why?"

"How do you hit the ball if you can't see it?"

"Because I know where it is," she said, as if it were obvious. "I'm the one who throws it."

She had a point, but I was still impressed. "Okay, but why practice with your eyes shut?"

"Have you ever had the sun in your eyes when you're serving?" she asked.

I nodded.

"If you can feel the ball, can sense where it is and where you want to hit it, you'll never be disadvantaged by the sun. Plus, it's soothing."

"Hmm." I watched as she hit a couple more balls. "That's incredible. You're pretty impressive with a racket."

"Thanks," she mumbled, eying me out of the side of her eye.

"Do you practice at night often?"

"Yeah."

"Not to sound patronizing, but has it ever occurred to you that it might not be safe to play tennis with your eyes closed on a dark court in the middle of a college campus?"

"You afraid I'll trip and fall?"

"I was thinking more along the lines of serial killers."

"Ahh. Well, I'm confident I could defend myself. I hear I'm pretty good with a racket."

That actually made me chuckle.

"Did you come here to play or just to watch me like a creepy stalker?" she asked, pausing and reaching for her water bottle.

As she bent, I let my eyes wander down to her legs. She wore short, fitted spandex shorts, like the kind she'd wear under her skirt for a match. Her tee shirt was long enough to cover the majority of her shorts when she stood upright, but as she bent forward, the shirt lifted up to offer me an excellent view of her perfectly rounded butt. I sucked in a breath and averted my eyes before my thoughts delved too far down that road.

"Neither," I finally answered. "I just wanted to be alone. I didn't realize anyone else had the same idea."

"Well, you want to play?"

"Sure. Should I turn the court lights on first?"

She gazed up. "It's more peaceful in the dark. Your eyes will adjust."

I could still see well enough to play anyway, so that was fine by me. I walked around the net to set down my racket cover. "First to twenty-one or an actual set?"

"Actual set. We are playing by the rules."

"Fine. Winner takes the loser on a date," I replied, the darkness making me bold.

She laughed, an almost childlike melodic sound. "If you win, I'll go on a date with you. If I win, you bring me a milkshake from the diner after my practice tomorrow."

Since the men's team practiced after the women's the next day, that would work perfectly. "You don't think I can beat you?" I surmised.

"I am undefeated," she said coyly.

"I'll serve first," I said, certain I'd at least stand a better chance that way. We were mostly quiet for the first game, and I actually won, albeit by the minimum two points. As expected, she killed me when she served, but then I launched into the smack talk and seemed to distract her enough so I won the next game, too. It was almost pitch black by the time we reached the final game point. We were tied, and I hit the ball to the far corner of her court and she missed. When I hit the next shot into the exact same spot, she again swung wide, losing the game.

"I thought your backhand was impeccable," I teased, legitimately surprised she'd missed the final two shots.

Then, it hit me. I felt a smile slowly creep over my face. She hadn't missed. Well, the first ball, maybe, but the second? No way. She had purposely lost the game.

The knowledge that Olivia Roberts wanted to go on a date with me actually did more for my ego than the thought that I could actually beat her at tennis.

"You're supposed to say 'good game,' asshole," she replied, grabbing her sweatshirt and tugging it over her head.

"Good game," I said. I walked to the edge of the court and sat on the ground, leaning back against the fence. Olivia followed suit, gasping as she hit the pavement.

"At least the ground is cold," she said, shimmying her sweatshirt under her butt and tucking her knees up towards her chin. "I'm over this weather. I love summer, but it's October. When is it going to act like it?"

As she tilted her head to drink her water, her ponytail bobbed near me. I tugged the tip of the braided part. She whipped back around to face me, her expression striking me as sultry despite her annoyance.

"Why do you practice so hard?" I asked her.

"I'm on scholarship. I need to be the best."

I didn't know the terms for her scholarship, but suspected she didn't literally have to be the best to maintain it. "You work too hard. When are you going to let yourself have fun?"

"I have fun."

"When?"

She thought about that for a moment. "I had fun playing just now."

"Yeah? Me too."

We were quiet for a moment. Olivia gazed at the sky, deep in thought. As beautiful as she looked straight on, her profile was even more enchanting, particularly in rare moments like this where her face wasn't all scrunched up with worry. I wanted to reach out, to place my hand over her hand where it rest atop her knees, but I didn't. I couldn't risk her tensing up.

"Can I ask you a serious question?" I said when the silence had stretched on long enough.

She didn't answer, so I took that as a yes.

"Who hurt you?"

She turned to me, frowning.

"I mean, was it one specific guy? A whole lot of guys?" I paused. "I'm serious. It's obvious you don't like guys, so…"

"I like guys," she interrupted. "I just don't trust men in general."

That didn't surprise me. "Okay, so was it one man or all men? You still didn't answer."

"All men I guess. Or maybe no man."

"I don't follow."

She took a deep breath, then blew it out. "My father was in a fraternity. He was wealthy and privileged and apparently thought he was entitled to everything he saw. He invited my mom to a party at his house, then they both got drunk. She said no, he pretended to hear yes, and I was the result. She tried to press charges and no one cared. She told him she was pregnant and he laughed."

Olivia shook her head and rubbed her palm along the back of her neck. "Since then, I've watched my mom get disappointed by one jerk after another. It's hard to have a lot of faith in men when that's all I've seen."

It took me several breaths to figure out what to say to that. I'd asked her for honesty but hadn't expected quite that much. "So you have daddy issues," I finally said, grinning so Olivia would see I wasn't altogether serious.

She swatted my arm and rolled her eyes.

"Okay, well, obviously your birth dad or whatever you want to call him was a total creep. For the record, not all frat guys are like that. Most of us like our women conscious and willing." I paused, but she didn't speak. "And for the other guys, has it ever occurred to you that your mom just has bad taste in men?"

Olivia laughed. "Yes, definitely. The problem is that she always goes for guys who are out of her league. She'll hook up with the business man in a pricey suit that flirts with her when she waits on him, even though he lives out of town and has an obvious tan line from a wedding ring. Her logic seems to be the richer the better. Except when he eventually reveals himself as a total creep, she then swings in the opposite direction and dates the guy who just got out of jail and is mooching off of her even though she's already broke. She can't ever just agree to go out with the hardworking guy who owns the diner or, God forbid, be single for a while."

"God forbid," I agreed. "So that's your plan, to show her that a successful woman is perpetually single?"

"I have no such plan. I just don't intend to repeat her mistakes. I'm not going to put myself out there to get hurt until I know I can trust a guy." She paused and turned to me again. "I'm not going to date a guy who's only interested in me so he can piss off his parents."

I wasn't about to let that dig slide by unnoticed. "My parents would love you. My mom thinks I'm lazy, so seeing me with someone who works hard all the time like you would thrill her. And as for my dad, well, you are exactly his type. Tall, blonde, blue eyes…"

"Your parents are divorced?"

"Nope. But doesn't seem to stop my father from dating younger women."

She made a face. "Sorry."

"Sorry about my dad, or sorry for making shitty assumptions about me all the time?"

"Both?" Olivia gazed up at me through dark lashes. "Although, telling me your dad is a serial philanderer doesn't exactly help restore my faith in men."

Solid point, but I was too distracted to care. *God*, she was enchanting. Even up close, even in this dim lighting, even after playing tennis… Olivia was pure perfection. She was easily the most beautiful woman I'd ever met. Olivia licked her lips casually, drawing my eyes to her mouth. I couldn't look away. I needed to know if her lips were as soft as they looked, couldn't help but wonder if she tasted as good as she smelled. But I didn't dare try.

So instead, I just stared.

Olivia stared back at me with the same intensity. I hoped maybe she would make the first move and breach the six inches between us. Instead, she spoke.

"I'd love to know what you're thinking right now," she said. "You look so serious."

My heart beat faster. "I'm trying to guess if you'd slap me if I kissed you right now."

Her perfect lips curved upwards into a grin she tried to hide. "What did you decide?"

I considered my next words, then spoke slowly. "I decided that you've had plenty of time to turn away." I leaned forward, placed my hand on her cheek, and when she still didn't move, I pressed my mouth to hers.

Before I could even panic that I'd done the wrong thing, she kissed me back. Her lips were velvety smooth against my own, and they parted willingly, welcoming my tongue into her warm mouth. She tasted sweet, like oranges and cinnamon, which, oddly, reminded me of Christmas.

Her hand brushed against my bicep, startling me at first, then egging me on as she pressed her fingers against me, practically squeezing the muscle. I reached to place my other hand around her arm, missing and inadvertently grazing the side of her breast before landing on her arm. Still, she didn't slap me.

The kiss went on and on, reminding me of makeout sessions in high school, where we never had any intention of taking it past first base. Olivia sure didn't kiss like the innocent girl she claimed to be, but I wasn't about to complain, either. Her lips fit perfectly against mine, and I was positive that the rest of our bodies would fit just as well.

All of a sudden, all the court lights flashed on, flooding us in full light. We broke apart in an instant, leaving only our fingers entangled. We both gazed down, as though neither of us had realized we were holding hands, and then we each winced from the light.

Glancing around, I didn't see anyone else on the courts.

"Must be on a timer," Olivia said. She rubbed her lips together then averted her eyes as color rushed to her cheeks. She stood slowly, tugging her shorts down over her butt before offering a hand to me.

"Thanks." I tried to think of something cool to say, but the moment had clearly passed. Olivia walked to the net and began zipping her racket into its case.

"Come on, I'll drive you home," I offered.

She glanced down at her attire. "I'm not dressed for any detours."

"Straight home then," I promised.

She was quiet during the short drive to her apartment, which was fine by me since I couldn't think of anything to say, either. I prayed that she'd invite me inside, but I wasn't surprised when she didn't. Instead, she flew out of the car.

"I'll um see you after my practice tomorrow I guess," she said, waving as though we hadn't just spent the better part of an hour making out on the tennis courts.

CHAPTER FIVE

- Olivia -

*W*hen I got home, I lingered in the shower until the water ran cold, then I tried to finish some homework. I couldn't concentrate on anything though, so I climbed under the covers and switched off my light. But in the dark, my mind continued to wander. I couldn't stop replaying the kiss—the feel of Nate's mouth on mine or of his arms beneath my palms. Physically, he was exactly my type- tall, muscular, and annoyingly handsome. And I surely could've handled that, if he hadn't also been surprisingly gifted in the kissing department.

Actually, there was nothing surprising about his skill, and that perhaps was what plagued me the most. Everything about the way Nate carried himself told me he would be a good kisser, and I was equally certain he'd be good in bed. *Too* good. Sex with Nate would be more satisfying than scoring the final two points in a previously tied game. And now that I knew how his lips felt on my mouth, I couldn't help but picture how they'd feel elsewhere on my body. I had the same problem thinking about his hands.

I groaned and pulled my pillow over my face. Why was I letting myself fall for Nate? He clearly wasn't boyfriend material, not for me anyway, and even if he were, I didn't have time for an actual relationship. A crush, fine. That, I could handle. And if I were being honest with myself, I'd had a crush on Nate since the first time I saw him. He was hot. I'd have to be blind not to notice that. But kissing him? No. That was not okay. And obsessing over it after was definitely bad.

Nate Aldridge was not the type of guy I could afford to fall for. No matter how sexy, sweet, or surprisingly kind he seemed to be, we came from different worlds. Anything that happened between us now would only serve to distract me from my studies and my tennis. I just needed to accept that I didn't have time for my stupid fantasies.

Except, an hour later, my body still hadn't gotten that memo. My lips still tingled from his touch, my heart still pounded in my chest. Even my breath continued to fall faster than it should. I was a total mess. My morning practice was sure to be a disaster.

When my alarm ripped me from my peaceful dreams, my eyes felt heavy and dry. I sluggishly dressed for practice, barely making it to the courts on time. My focus kicked in just as we began warmup volleys, but it waned the instant the men's team waltzed onto the courts. I hadn't yet decided how to act around Nate, but I hadn't expected him to offer me one solitary nod and then completely ignore me as the women's team vacated the courts to head into the weight room.

Luckily, I had a full class schedule that day and zero time to overanalyze Nate's weird behavior. It wasn't until early evening, when I was trying to slurp down my Pad Thai without dribbling peanut sauce all over my Econ textbook that I finally heard from Nate.

"You owe me a date," was all his text read.

I reached for my phone, narrowly avoiding dropping a chunk

of tofu on the screen. As I tried to think of a suitable reply, another text came in.

"Dinner Thurs? Pick u up @ 6?"

I knew without checking my calendar that I was available. I had no legitimate excuse not to go, and I wasn't sure I wanted to bail anyway. The sooner I could prove to myself that I was right, that Nate and I didn't actually have good chemistry, the sooner I could stop obsessing over that damn kiss.

"Fine," I typed, before dropping my phone like it was a hot potato.

A small thumbs up sign appeared beside my response, but I received no other acknowledgement. I sighed, already regretting my actions. We hadn't even gone on the date yet and already I was ridiculously distracted.

* * *

- Nate -

I figured I'd come on too strong with Olivia from the start, so after the kiss, I decided to play it cool for a few days. At least until our big date. Now that I knew she liked me, I didn't have to try so hard anyway.

Or so I thought.

When I reached Olivia's apartment Thursday, she seemed annoyed with me from the start. Well, *more* annoyed than usual.

"You're late," she mumbled, tucking her skirt beneath her as she climbed into my car.

I glanced at the clock on the dashboard, which read 6:07. "I thought girls were never ready on time anyway. Don't you have to try on twelve outfits before settling on the right one?"

She flipped her middle finger at me.

Right. Not exactly how I'd planned for the date to start. I cleared my throat and then tried again. "You look good," I said. It was the truth. Her hair was down, cascading across her shoulders. She wore a denim jacket over a purple dress that fell to her mid-thigh, and brown leather boots that came just past her calves.

Her eyebrow raised as though she was questioning my sincerity, but then she quietly thanked me.

I started towards the restaurant. "Aren't you supposed to return the compliment?" I meant it in a teasing way, but wasn't surprised by her sharp retort.

"I'm sure you already know just how handsome you are."

We stayed quiet the rest of the way to the restaurant. I'd chosen the nicest steak place in town, guessing Olivia didn't treat herself very often. But the face she made when I handed the keys to the valet suggested she wasn't impressed with the location. We were seated immediately, thanks to my foresight in making reservations, but again, Olivia appeared indifferent. And then when the waiter came to take our drink orders and I offered her the wine list, she scowled.

"I have practice in the morning," she said.

"Yeah. Me too." *Duh.*

"I'll take a water with lemon," she said to the waiter.

Jesus. I really needed her to have a drink if she was ever going to loosen up. "One glass of wine isn't going to affect your game."

Her expression was unreadable, and I almost thought she was going to change her order. Instead, she addressed me.

"Why is it so important to you that I drink? You think if my judgment is impaired, you might get lucky?"

I blew out the breath I'd been holding and turned to the waiter. "I'll take a Jack and Coke. Make it a double. Thanks."

He nodded politely, clearly struggling to bite back his laughter, then left us alone.

I rubbed my eyebrows, trying to recall why I thought the date would be fun. Sure, Olivia was hot, and yeah, we had a lot in common. And, we certainly had chemistry. But this was ridiculous. I had enough work on my plate between classes and tennis and my parents. I didn't need to work for sex. I knew plenty of girls who would happily come home with me without giving me a migraine.

I gazed up at Olivia slowly, locking on her bold blue eyes for a moment before panning down to her full, pale pink lips. Olivia wasn't just pretty. She was gorgeous. She was the type of woman artists painted and kings started wars over. That was why I'd decided she would be worth the trouble. Well, that and the fact that she was so intriguing. I could tell she had so much depth to her and I was desperate to break the surface.

"I'm not riding home with you if you're drunk," Olivia said, breaking the spell in an instant.

I laughed out loud, then focused on my menu.

By the time our food arrived, we'd managed to transition to pleasant enough small talk, but her voice was void of any of the warmth I'd felt that night on the court. We also seemed to be missing any hint of the connection we'd shared the last time we'd dined together. She'd been feisty then too, but in a way that felt almost fun. Now, she just seemed bitter.

One of my fraternity brothers texted while we were eating, and since Olivia and I weren't talking much anyway, I didn't see any harm in replying. He sent me some funny memes about sorority girls, and then when I told him I was on a date but wouldn't name the girl, his many guesses were downright hilarious. I chuckled aloud before setting down my phone to reach for a roll. Olivia was glaring at me.

"Sorry," I mumbled. "It was, um, my fraternity brother."

She nodded. "Am I keeping you from something?"

"No. I, uh, nevermind. So how come you never joined a sorority?"

Olivia raised her shoulders. "Seemed like a waste of time."

I thought most people considered friendship a fairly good use of time, but apparently not Olivia. "You're an only child though. You didn't think you could use some sisters?"

She actually appeared to consider that. "Maybe. I'm not the most social person though."

"You're kidding," I replied, feigning shock.

We both laughed until she finally shook her head.

"Look, I clearly suck at this whole date thing, and I tried to tell you that before, but you were really insistent." She paused, but not long enough for me to decide whether I should protest her assessment of my behavior. "It's not that I'm wholly opposed to fun or whatever, but I'm focused on my priorities. I need to keep up my grades and my tennis game, and I don't know how to do that and have a well-rounded social life at the same time. Plus, my roommate had some drama with her ex, so I was up all night trying to keep her distracted and it's possible I'm a little cranky when I don't sleep."

"You don't say," I teased. I appreciated her honesty, and I supposed she had warned me in advance. It was just, well, that kiss made me assume things would be different. The kiss showed me that *we* were different. We were good together. Or at least, we could be if she'd just loosen up.

"Look, you're a nice guy. You've got a lot going for you. You're perceptive, surprisingly funny, and not a total pig. I can admit I was wrong about you." She paused, but not long enough for my shock at her admission to wear off. "I was also wrong to kiss you. It's just that you're hot, and you were being such a good listener, and I was lonely, and…"

"You think I'm hot?" I interrupted.

She glared, then continued. "When I let myself relax and just do whatever I feel like, I tend to make mistakes. I'm too rash sometimes. And now that I've had time to think about this, I realize it's a bad idea for us to date."

I let her words wash over me for a minute. I truly couldn't picture Olivia doing anything impulsive, so that part surprised me. The rest, not so much. She wasn't denying the chemistry between us, just the logic of us dating. And maybe her resistance to that idea wasn't so bad after all. Maybe she just didn't want to date me because she didn't trust herself to get closer to me.

"So no dessert?" I concluded.

"No thanks," she replied, flashing me a sincere smile that traveled all the way to her eyes.

I motioned for the check.

As I started the engine, I switched the radio to the first station that was actually playing music, certain we'd need something to distract us from the awkward silence. It was an eighties station, as I didn't dare risk a debate on talk radio or even a controversial commercial. I pulled out of the parking space, then glanced at Olivia. To my surprise, she was bopping her head and singing along to Def Leppard.

I caught her eye and quirked an eyebrow, but Olivia simply grinned and cranked up the volume. I fought the urge to pull over and focus all of my attention on her instead of driving, but barely. She looked so carefree, so completely un-self-conscious as she rocked out. It was quite possibly the sexiest thing ever. I turned to watch her as the stoplight switched from yellow to red, feeling my own grin widen as she launched into an epic riff with her air guitar.

I laughed out loud, and she joined in, but still finished the song. When the station switched to commercial, I immediately flicked off the radio. I expected Olivia to blush, but she just smiled.

"Come on, you really don't like Def Leppard?" she asked.

"Umm, no, I do. I just didn't know anyone actually memorized every word of that song."

She scoffed. "Everyone knows Animal."

"Everyone maybe knows the chorus. Or maybe the whole song, but only if they're currently in their fifties."

Olivia bit back a grin. "My mom was a huge Def Leppard fan.

41

They were her go-to breakup music, so I heard their songs a lot growing up. We've actually seen them in concert five or six times. Those tickets were her only big splurge when I was a kid."

The car behind us blared its horn, and I managed to cruise through the intersection right before the light turned yellow again. *Oops.*

"Olivia Roberts, you are full of surprises," I said.

She licked her lips, but I couldn't help but notice the rosy color flooding her cheeks. "So far, you are too," she replied.

"So far? Ouch." I clutched my chest as though suffering some grave injury.

As I slowed to a stop in front of her apartment, she thanked me for dinner, then paused. Our eyes met, and my heart pounded in anticipation of her leaning in for a kiss.

Instead, she turned away. "Thanks for understanding on the whole just friends thing too," she added.

I clenched my stomach muscles but kept my expression void of the disappointment I felt. "I'll see you at practice," I said.

She nodded and offered me a timid wave, then climbed out of my car.

I watched to make sure she made it inside safely, then gazed down at my phone. I needed a distraction, so I texted my buddy Mason. He also played varsity tennis, so there was no risk of him keeping me out too late.

Just as I hit the main road, he texted back and agreed to meet me at the pool hall near my apartment. Relief flooded my bones. The last thing I needed was to sit around my apartment replaying Olivia's 'just friends' speech in my head while trying to decide how to best get over my crush.

CHAPTER SIX

- Olivia -

*a*ddie cringed the entire time I told her about the date. It wasn't like I'd thought it had gone well, but seeing it all through her eyes made me wonder if I'd intentionally sabotaged it.

"I actually feel sorry for the guy," Addie said.

"Don't. He's fine. His ego will recover just fine. And I never pretended to be good at this whole dating thing. He's known from the start that I'm a total bitch around guys."

Addie reached for my phone and toggled over to his Instagram account again, clicking and zooming on the photo of him in swim trunks. "You couldn't have just pretended to play nice for an hour and a half? I feel like a bad friend for not texting you a reminder of what you would've gotten at the end of the night if the date had gone better."

I rolled my eyes and snatched back my phone before Addie sent dirty DMs to Nate from my account. "I'm well aware of what I could've gotten. And I don't want that. Not from him or anyone else."

Addie winced. "That's sad. You're too young to be a nun. But I can tell when you're lying."

I gritted my teeth. She was right. I did want that, and specifically from Nate. Or rather, with Nate. But that was precisely the problem. If *not* sleeping with Nate was this distracting, I wouldn't be able to function if I actually did sleep with him. I groaned just considering the dilemma.

"Fine. I can't stop thinking about him. Ever since we made out, I can't even look at him without my pulse skyrocketing. He's so hot and the best kisser ever and he's not even remotely the pretentious asshole I assumed he'd be."

Addie's eyes widened.

"But that doesn't mean I can afford the distraction now, or that there's any potential for a long-term relationship between us," I continued.

"Maybe you just need to get him out of your system," she suggested. "You know, like when you have one last Snickers bar before going on a diet."

"That's not how it works. The more you eat sugar, the more you crave sugar. I'm pretty sure it's the same with sex."

Addie pondered that theory. "If that were true, then I would be completely oblivious to the opposite sex now since I've gone so long without getting any."

We both laughed.

"Seriously, I'd hoped things would work out with him and then I could live vicariously through you. I'm clearly never going to date again."

Guilt washed over me. I'd been so focused on my stupid date that I hadn't even asked how she was doing in the wake of all her boy drama. "Just because things didn't work out with Eric doesn't mean it'll never work out for you with anyone."

Addie rolled her eyes. "I know, I know. You told me last night. Which, by the way, thanks for that and sorry I didn't let you sleep."

"That's what friends are for," I reminded her, patting her hand.

"That's what you said two months ago when you held my hair back while I puked all night. Someday, you'll need to let me repay you for all this friend shit." She paused and narrowed her eyes. "Although, you're never going to experience an epic breakup and the most heart-wrenching devastation of your life if you never give a guy the chance to break your heart."

I had to smile at her level of drama. Her breakup had sucked. She and Eric had been high school sweethearts. Then, the past summer, he'd dumped her out of the blue, claimed he never wanted to get married. He kicked her out of their shared apartment and that was how Addie and I ended up as roommates. Later, she'd learned Eric had moved in with his chem lab partner. As if that hadn't been bad enough, he then changed his social media status to "engaged," thus the crying that kept me up the night before.

I leaned forward and hugged Addie. "You are an amazing person and any guy would be lucky to have you. You dodged a bullet with Eric and now I'm doing the same with Nate...but before all of the epic heartache crap sets in. We can just skip to the part where we're both happily single, okay?"

Addie giggled, and we both retreated to our rooms to study before bed.

The next morning, Nate and I managed to be cordial at practice, and by Saturday evening, I wasn't even thinking about him anymore.

But when I awoke Sunday morning, I was breathless, sweaty, and my heart was racing. For a moment, I assumed I'd had a nightmare, but then the dream flooded back to me and it was worse than a nightmare. Much, much worse.

I'd been dreaming about sex. With Nate. Really good sex with Nate.

I tried in vain to go back to sleep, then finally got up and finished as much homework as I could before noon. Sundays were the only day we didn't have any sort of official team practice, so it was typically my most productive day. I tidied the apartment, ran to the grocery, and prepped some meals for myself for the upcoming week.

I was feeling completely on top of my game when my mom called. She usually worked the early shift on Sundays, so I'd grown accustomed to our late afternoon calls. Typically, I even looked forward to them. From the moment she slurred my name though, I knew this call was going to be different.

"Have you been drinking?" I asked, confused. It was just after five, but still seemed early in the day to be completely trashed.

"Don't lecture me. I'm the parent here," she retorted.

I withheld my comment on that irony.

"Speaking of parenting, you want some advice?" she asked.

No.

"Men are scum. All of them. You can't trust any of them."

I counted to five as I inhaled, held my breath, then exhaled through my mouth. It had zero effect on my overall relaxation. "Did something happen?" I asked, certain she'd tell me whether or not I wanted to know.

"Well, Dan and I broke up."

"I'm sorry," I said. It was a lie, but there really was nothing else to say. I hadn't met Dan, but from everything she'd told me, he sounded like a complete loser. He had a nice butt, according to my mom, but that was the only redeeming characteristic she'd ever mentioned.

"All of the good ones are either married or just screwing you for money."

My mother had no money, so that left one option. "He was married?"

She roared with laughter. "No! A woman would have to be a fool to marry that dimwit. He had the math skills of a kindygardener. To think I actually believed he had a shot at starting his own business." My mom snorted.

I rubbed my finger along my brow line, trying to smooth the wrinkles as they appeared. "What do you mean? What business?"

"Oh he was full of ideas. Dumb ones, I guess. But I figured any investment was better than no investment. Anyway, they all went belly up, and now I find out he's not even into blondes."

I cringed. My mom was not a natural blonde, and though she occasionally became one thanks to a box of Clairol, her dark brown eyebrows and fast-growing roots never fooled anyone. But that was beside the point. "Did you loan him money?"

She fell uncharacteristically quiet.

"Mom?"

"Oh honey, it was supposed to be an investment..." she began.

My head began to swim and I tuned out the majority of her sob story. My mom didn't have any cash to spare, which meant *I* needed to figure out a way to earn more money. I could maybe squeeze in an extra lesson or two each week, but that would hardly be a cash cow.

It was well after six by the time I finally got my mom calmed down and off the phone. My stomach growled, but no food sounded good. Instead, I reached for a drink. I knew it was a terrible idea, that I should just go for a run or something instead. But between the relentless thoughts about Nate, the drama from my mom's miserable dating life, and my stress about finances, alcohol sounded really good.

I chugged my first drink, pleased to feel slightly lighter before I'd even finished mixing my second one. I didn't drink often and I realized I had a low tolerance. But when I polished off the second drink and decided to walk to the bus stop, it didn't even occur to me that I was making a bad decision.

CHAPTER SEVEN

- Nate -

$\mathcal{I}$ was flitting between my finance notes and my social media accounts when my phone buzzed. Olivia's text gave me no clue whatsoever as to what she wanted to talk about or why she was coming over, but I barely had time to panic before the doorbell rang. I did a two-minute cleanup of the living room, then glanced down at myself to ensure I didn't look horrible. That was when I noticed my shirt.

It was the softest tee shirt I owned, but I never wore it out of the apartment since it portrayed a lewd picture of two crudely drawn stick figures engaging in oral sex. It was actually funny, but in the inappropriate way I'd only ever admit to the frat brother who gifted the shirt to me.

I scanned the room quickly for a different shirt, but finding none, I went with option B—no shirt. I yanked the shirt up over my head and shoved it under a couch pillow.

I opened the door right as Olivia raised her hand to knock again. She froze in place, her lips parted, and she slowly gazed up, her eyes visibly widening.

"Holy shit," she mumbled.

"Hi," I said.

"I'm interrupting, aren't I?" she said, still openly gawking at my abs.

"Nope. I'm home alone and bored to death," I said, still flexing my entire midsection. I couldn't even pretend to mask my pleasure with how distracted she was by my shirtlessness. "Hey, my eyes are up here," I teased.

Olivia's cheeks flushed as she squeezed her eyes shut and turned her head. She opened and closed her mouth several times without speaking. I'd never actually seen Olivia so discombobulated and it was utterly thrilling.

"You want to come in?"

She stumbled forward, still averting her eyes. "Why are you half naked?"

I debated my options, then went with the truth. "I had a shirt on, but figured you'd find it offensive, so I took it off."

"Offensive...how?"

I reached under the pillow and retrieved the shirt, handing it to her.

She unfolded it, inspected the picture and caption, then laughed. "You're right. That's terrible. This is a much better look," she said, gesturing to my stomach.

"Thanks?" I still didn't know why she'd come over, but I was more than happy to flaunt my half-naked self around her until she decided. With how much time I spent in the gym and on the courts, I deserved that response from women. "Can I get you a drink? I've got soda, water, beer, vodka..."

"Yes!"

Her enthusiasm startled me. I'd actually been kidding with the last option. Well, I did have vodka, but I didn't expect her to drink that on a Sunday night, especially after she acted like I was an alcoholic for drinking at dinner on a date. I motioned for her to follow me into the kitchen.

I pulled open the fridge so Olivia could see the soda options, but when I turned around, she'd found a bottle of coconut rum on the counter.

I located a clean glass for her and offered her some orange juice to mix with it, then watched as she poured her drink. There was something unusually casual about her movements. I was about to ask if everything was ok when I realized what was different.

"You're drunk!" I said.

"I am not drunk. I had two tiny little beverages."

I snatched the rum and juice out of her hands and chugged half of it. Olivia wasn't big enough to absorb that much alcohol if she'd already gotten a head start.

She pouted but accepted the rest of the drink.

"Do I get a tour?" she asked.

I nodded and showed her around. It wasn't the biggest apartment, but it was nicer than ninety percent of the other crap on campus. The rent was insane. I ended the tour in my bedroom, which was unusually clean.

She paced around the room, still holding her drink, then finally sat on my bed.

"So..." I said, still not sure why she had come over. "Did you want to talk?"

"Ugh!" Olivia rolled her eyes, tossed back the rest of her drink, then stared pointedly. "Are you really that dense?"

"Me?" I actually turned around to see if she was talking to someone else, effectively proving that yes, I was indeed that dense. "I don't even know what...oh."

A wave of dizziness washed over me as the realization hit me. She wasn't here to talk or to practice tennis. This was a booty call.

"You want me," I said aloud.

Annoyance flashed through her eyes, but she didn't disagree. I stepped closer, appreciating the direction the evening had taken.

Olivia had returned to staring at my abs and chest, which made me feel even bolder.

"You said I was arrogant and dull," I reminded her, wincing at the memory of how awkward our date had been.

"You are sometimes."

"Uh huh. But...you seem to like what you see." I took another bold step closer.

"I can think you're annoying and cocky and still appreciate... this," she replied, licking her lips and waving her hand loosely towards my stomach.

I would've protested her adding new insults, but she'd reached out her hand and was literally stroking my abdomen. My skin tingled from the contact, and every single part of my body responded. In a flash, my brain went to all the dirty places. I still vividly remembered her skill at kissing and assumed we'd have the same chemistry in bed. I couldn't deny I was eager to see her without her clothes, and to touch her...

"Liv, come on. I'm not going to take advantage of you just because you're drunk and clearly confused."

Her hand froze in place, flush against my lower belly. "Confused?"

"Well, yeah. You said we should just be friends. You don't even like me."

"I'm not asking you to marry me or even to be my BFF. I'm talking about sex."

I wouldn't have thought it possible for me to get any harder than I already was, but I did. I shut my eyes for a moment, trying to concentrate on all the reasons we shouldn't do it. That task was difficult though, especially with Olivia on my bed, touching me, and talking about sex.

"You liked kissing me," she said. "And you're obviously interested." Her eyes darted just below my waist where my erection strained against my jeans.

"Of course I'm interested. I've been throwing myself at you

for weeks now, but you have made your feelings abundantly clear. You want nothing to do with me."

Olivia stood, bringing our bodies less than a fist width apart. She was several inches shorter than me, but when she tilted her head back, I could see directly into those piercing blue eyes. "If you don't want me, I'll go," she said.

I swallowed and the sound of it reverberated in the quiet room. Olivia turned her head as if she were about to move away and I panicked, grabbing her arm. "Stop. You know I want you. You are the most mesmerizing woman I've ever met." I paused to catch my breath. "And I haven't stopped thinking about that kiss."

As if to prove it, I leaned in, kissing her. Olivia responded instantly, her body leaning into mine in a way that felt so, so good. *Shit*. I was a goner. I reached to cup her cheeks in my palms right as her hands went for my waist. The sensation of her fingers against my bare flesh was indescribable. It was everything I'd been yearning for and more. I shifted one hand to the back of her head, letting her soft hair tickle my fingers before letting my other hand join.

The kiss deepened, and our tongues brushed together lightly before tangling around each other. At some point, Olivia's hands shifted around my waist, reaching between us to unbuckle my belt. As her fingers gripped the button on my jeans, I pulled back, causing her to freeze in place.

Her lips were already swollen and red from the kissing, and she looked even more tantalizing than before, if that was even possible. "Are you sure?" I asked.

Olivia actually had the nerve to laugh at me. "Yeah, I'm sure." She yanked down the zipper on my jeans then cocked an eyebrow, as if to say "your move."

Olivia didn't have to tell me twice. I reached for the hem of her shirt, tugged it over her head, then ran my hands up her back until I found her bra. I unfastened the clasp and nudged the straps off her shoulders, wondering if she could actually hear my heart thudding excitedly as I caught the first glance of her bare breasts. They were a creamy pale color compared to the rest of her skin, and were every bit as perky and rounded as they appeared when she bounced around the court.

I reached up, placing one palm over each breast, appreciating the way they filled my hands and then some. I squeezed lightly, then traced my thumbs across her nipples, eliciting a sharp moan from Olivia. Her head fell backwards as she arched her back slightly, thrusting her breasts further into my hands. I touched, tickled and teased her chest for a moment longer before dipping my head down and tracing my tongue along her pert nipple. Olivia moaned again, gently pressing her hand into the back of my head, so I continued, this time sucking harder before moving to the other breast.

Olivia's breathing matched my own, and as I tilted my head to kiss the side of her neck, I felt her pulse racing too. Enough with the foreplay, I decided.

I wrapped a hand around her back then nudged her onto the bed, tumbling with her but bracing myself on my extended arm. We kissed again, this time more frantically, and I gradually worked my free hand lower until I reached the waistband of her pants. She was wearing leggings, thankfully, so as she lifted her hips, I was able to tug them lower with ease. Once I got them past her thighs, I used my knee to nudge them down further.

Her hands slid inside the back band of my boxer briefs, squeezing my butt cheeks with purpose. I followed suit, slipping my fingers inside her panties, exploring until I reached the warmth at the crest of her legs. She was already wet, already ready for me, and I couldn't help but growl in appreciation.

We kissed for another moment, until I worried I'd combust if we didn't take it further. I pushed off of her, rising to my knees, then reached over to my nightstand.

I quickly located a condom and dropped it onto her chest, smiling at the sight of her gorgeous body, stretched out and nearly naked, waiting for me. Olivia ripped open the foil packet and scraped her teeth along her bottom lip.

"God, you're sexy," I murmured. I shucked my boxer briefs, feeling my smile widen in response to the delighted look she gave me. Olivia may have found me arrogant and annoying, but at least she appreciated what I had below the belt. I suspected there was some ironic joke in there somewhere, but I was too hungry for her to think straight.

I crawled over Olivia, lowering her panties down and over her foot, pleased but not altogether surprised that she had only a thin strip of hair between her thighs. I liked to think she'd done this special for me, that our tryst wasn't just a drunken urge, but I wasn't quite that naïve.

I ran my tongue along her inner thigh, bending her leg as I moved upward so that by the time I reached the apex of her legs, I could kiss and lick her there. She stiffened at the initial contact, then relaxed against me, her hands again finding my hair as she ground against me. After a moment though, she tugged me upwards and when our eyes met, she handed me the condom.

Everything moved quickly after that, in a blur of sighs and moans and shared glances. I closed my eyes as I moved above her, certain I wouldn't last long if I could actually see her beautiful face looking up at me or her hauntingly gorgeous body moving beneath me. When I did briefly open my eyes though, Olivia was gazing right back at me, her lips parted in an erotic half-smile, half-gasp.

We were completely in sync with our movements, right until the end. When Olivia clenched her fingers tightly into my hips, moaned my name through gritted teeth, then spasmed around me, I acquiesced to the release my body had been craving all night. I couldn't have held off another minute if I'd tried.

When our bodies both stilled, I opened my eyes, half afraid Olivia would be glaring back at me. Instead, she smiled drunkenly and pulled my head towards hers for a kiss.

"So there *is* something you're good at," she teased.

Everything about her statement reassured me. I was glad she'd enjoyed that as much as I had, but I was even more relieved that she still felt comfortable being her usual, snarky self with me. Somehow, through all the bickering, I'd grown to like Olivia. I didn't want sex to change that. Nor did I want it to change our charming repartee.

"I'm really good at tennis too," I said.

"Not as good as me."

"I beat you," I reminded her. "Don't you recall our date?"

"As if I could ever forget." She snickered. "But I should confess, I let you win."

"I already knew that, actually," I said, relaxing against her.

She let me cuddle her for a moment and then wriggled beneath me. "You are way too big to just keel over on top of me. I can't breathe."

I pressed up onto my elbows and faced her. "I'm too big for you, huh?"

She rolled her eyes. "See? Arrogant. Now get off me."

This time, I complied. I grabbed my boxer briefs and darted into the bathroom. I didn't waste time as I cleaned up and pulled on my boxers, certain Olivia would bolt from my room if given the opportunity. Instead, when I emerged from the bedroom, she was still sprawled out on my bed. She'd put on her own underwear along with my inappropriate tee shirt.

I laughed so hard I nearly cried. "When did you even bring that up here?"

She shrugged coyly. "I might have stuck it in my purse before you got my drink. I mean, it's really bad. I was going to take it home and dispose of it for you."

I feigned shock. "But it's my favorite shirt!"

Olivia wiggled and ran her fingers along her stomach, likely oblivious to how sexy she looked. "I see why. This is literally the softest thing that's ever touched my body."

I raised an eyebrow. "Well, if you keep doing that, you can keep it." I tumbled into the bed beside her and casually rest my arm on her stomach like we'd been together for ages. "How did you get here anyway?"

"The bus."

"What bus?"

She opened her mouth to answer and then shook her head. "Sometimes I forget how completely disconnected from reality you are."

I shrugged. "It's kind of nice. You should try it sometime."

She rolled her eyes.

"So I guess you're pretty much stuck here overnight then," I said.

"There are late night buses. Or I could über."

"Geez, I was kidding. I can drive you home whenever, but if you cut out before round two…"

Olivia snorted. "Like you could go a second round."

I tugged her hand to my groin, proving how very wrong she was.

She raised an eyebrow then sat up and swung a leg over me. Her hair was so long that it tickled my chest as she straddled me, but I brushed my hands past it to venture up under the super soft tee shirt she stole.

"Hey," she said, catching my hand in place. "Before we, um… well, I just wanted to make sure we're on the same page."

"Page," I repeated, incapable of mustering more than a single word while her powerful thighs clutched my hips.

"I mean, we aren't like an item now. I'm not your girlfriend. You're not my boyfriend. This is just sex. And neither of us are telling anyone about this." She paused, sounding infinitely more sober now than she had an hour before. "Right?"

"Oh, yeah. Right. Definitely."

"There will be no public kissing, okay? Actually, no public

displays of affection whatsoever. Tomorrow morning, we will go back to our usual witty banter and insult-sharing relationship."

I shook my head. "You say this now, Liv, but by tomorrow morning, you're going to be singing my name opera-style all over campus."

She reached for a pillow and smashed it against my face for a moment before laughing and yanking the shirt up over her head.

I wasn't completely sure what would happen with us in the morning, but for the moment, I couldn't be happier. I reached around Olivia's back to lift myself up enough to capture her breast between my lips. She shrieked, and we both happily moved towards round two.

CHAPTER EIGHT

- Olivia -

I awoke to the creak of a floorboard. I was disoriented for only a moment before I saw Nate, frozen in the corner of the room, a coffee mug in his hand.

"Sorry, tried not to wake you," he said.

I rubbed my eyes and stifled a yawn. Then I panicked, realizing it was a weekday. "Shit! What time is it? I have—"

"Practice?" he supplied. "Yeah, I know. Me too, remember? It's six-fifteen. I didn't know how long you take to get ready."

"Not long usually, but I don't have my clothes here." I snatched the coffee mug from his hands.

"You could wear that," Nate said, gesturing to the offensive tee shirt that had somehow found its way back onto my body.

"Lord," I mumbled, rolling my eyes. I took a long sip of the coffee, wincing at the overwhelming sweetness. "Too much sugar."

"That was for me, actually."

I shot him a look, but he merely shrugged.

"I'll get you another cup and then I can drive you home to get ready and then I will drive you to practice."

"I can't arrive at practice with you."

He rolled his eyes at me. "I've given you a ride before. No one would ever guess that you lowered yourself to my level for a whole night."

I thrust the coffee mug out to him. "No sugar. Just a splash of milk, assuming it's not expired."

Nate shook his head but headed out.

I paused a moment to take stock of everything that had happened in the last twelve hours, then rolled out of Nate's bed and dressed in my clothes from the previous night. I spent a few minutes in the bathroom, working Nate's comb through my hair before twisting the strands into a loose bun on top of my head. I swished around some mouthwash for a minute, washed my face, then located a men's facial moisturizer in the cabinet. I snickered at the realization that Nate maintained a skin-care regimen, then dabbed a bit of the lotion on my cheeks, using the pads of my fingers to smooth it onto my skin.

I scurried downstairs, nearly smacking into Nate as he offered me a large, steaming travel mug. I thanked him, then stumbled to the car. He drove through a fast food place on the way to my apartment, but I limited my response to eye rolls and dramatic sighs rather than verbal criticism. By the time we hit my apartment, I still had ten minutes to change before we'd need to leave to avoid being late. That was more than enough time.

"You really don't eat food before practice?" Nate asked as I tossed my duffel bag and tennis racket in the back seat of his car. When I'd gone into my apartment to change, he'd waited for me in the car, consuming a yogurt and the two giant breakfast sandwiches he'd bought.

"Nope. Just coffee before practice. I'll have an egg white omelet and some oatmeal after."

Nate made a face but didn't say anything else about it. After the late night, it was too early for conversation anyway. We were both fine with driving in silence.

Usually, at morning practices, the men's team would use the weight room and the women's team would take the courts, then we'd switch. This morning though, the outdoor courts were damp from an overnight rain and the coaches wanted to mop them first to get rid of the puddles. So, both teams hit the weight room together.

I started on the treadmill, accustomed to the group jog to wake up my body. I slipped in headphones, selected the most upbeat, distracting tunes I could find, then took off. The first half mile or so went great, but then I glanced to my right.

A large mirror on the wall adjacent to me reflected a crisp, clear image of a shirtless Nate, dangling upside down from a pullup bar. A bored teammate gripped one hand over Nate's feet. I was about to look away when Nate then tightened his abs into a sit up. All my breath whooshed out. As he stretched back for his next rep, I couldn't take my eyes off those deep ridges along his abdomen.

I remembered exactly how it felt to run my palms across every inch of Nate's chiseled core. My skin still tingled at the memory of his smooth flesh against my own. I could still taste him on my tongue.

I didn't need him half naked dangling behind me, too.

I tore my eyes away and stared at the display on the treadmill. I'd warmed up long enough. It was time to throw in some sprints. If I had energy to gawk at a boy, I certainly had energy for a real run. I cranked up the pace, keeping my eyes squarely focused on the bright red numbers displaying my speed, time, and wildly inaccurate caloric burn. I poured all of my effort into the repetition, the evenness of my footsteps as they pounded the rubber belt faster and faster.

I made it almost to the end of my first sprint when I heard a thud behind me. I glanced up—not to check him out again so much as to make sure he hadn't fallen and cracked his stupid head open. But Nate was fine, still hanging there, still crunching.

Geez. He had to be on like his fortieth rep by now. Why was he spending so long on abs, anyway? Yeah, it was a critical muscle group for a sport that involved lots of twists and turns, but come on. No one needed *that* strong of a core for tennis. Nate was clearly going a tad overboard.

I licked my lips, practically feeling the tip of my tongue drag along his skin. Just then, Nate gazed over. Our eyes met and he smiled.

Jerk.

In an instant, my feet were all tangled up. I lurched forward and smacked my forehead into the display console of the treadmill before the evil machine flung me to the side. I bounced off of the armrests of the treadmill next to me, then landed on my butt between the two machines.

In an instant, four of my teammates were at my side. I didn't have to look up to know that Nate had also rushed over to mock me.

"Alright, alright, give her space," a deep voice said. I glanced up as the head coach for the men's team stepped over the treadmill and crouched in front of me. "Are you okay?" he asked.

I nodded.

"What hurts?"

I avoided the temptation of saying *my pride.* "Nothing."

"You hit your head, so the team doc needs to take a look."

"I'm really fine."

"Your ankles feel okay?" he asked.

When I nodded, he breathed a soft "thank God." "Can't have our star player sidelined," he added, louder.

His large hands gripped under my arms and effortlessly lifted me to my feet. Mortified, I let him walk me back behind the treadmills. I kept my eyes on the ground, determined not to look at Nate's gleeful smirk.

"Aldridge," the coach said. "Can you get her to the doc down on the second floor?"

"Not necessary. I'll walk myself," I said, jerking free.

"No prob, Coach," Nate's chipper voice replied.

* * *

- Nate -

*A*s soon as Coach turned the corner, Olivia shook free of my grip.

"I can walk fine," she snarled.

I didn't protest. As we neared the athletic department physician office though, I couldn't resist the urge to comment on her ordeal.

"If you come over tonight, I can do some shirtless sit-ups for you then," I said, unable to contain my smug grin.

She flipped me the bird.

"Seriously, Olivia. You nearly killed yourself checking me out. I'm offering a safe environment for you to get your fix."

She stopped walking for a moment and turned to me, her bright eyes filled with anger. For a brief moment, I actually thought she might hit me. Instead, she just glared a little longer and then went into the clinic.

Coach had clearly called ahead, so the nurse showed us right into the exam room.

"Okay, you got me here safely. You can go back to practice now," she said.

"Actually, the athletic department regulations say we need someone else present when we do the checkup," the doctor said, coming up behind me.

Olivia made her scary face again.

I plopped into a chair in the corner and selected a magazine. The doctor looked at her ankle, asked her a lot of questions to rule out a concussion, then did a cursory exam before saying she could return to practice. He listed some symptoms to watch for that might suggest a head injury, then sent us on our way.

Once we were alone in the hallway, I resumed my taunting. "We could probably sneak into one of the empty offices for a quickie before we return to practice," I offered.

Olivia turned to me, rolled her eyes, then continued down the hall, sighing.

"Okay, I get your point. You aren't the quickie type of girl. You like when I take my time. I can do that. Eight o'clock good for you? My place?"

"Are you even being serious?"

"Too early? Too late? What? I can be flexible."

"No! We had a bad date, good sex, and now it's done."

I smiled. "It was good, wasn't it?"

Olivia blushed, making me think that particular compliment had inadvertently slipped out.

"My point was, it's out of my system now," she clarified.

"Out of your system? Geesh, you make it sound like I'm a stomach virus."

She shrugged.

I jogged ahead of her then turned to face her, walking backwards. "Wow, okay, well, unfortunately for you, now that I've gotten a taste of you...and I think you know I mean 'taste' in the most literal sense of the word..." I paused to wiggle my eyebrows. "I want more. And I can be quite persistent when motivated."

Olivia sped up and walked around me. I jogged to catch up, but then she stopped abruptly and I nearly slammed into her chest as she swiveled to face me.

"I don't get it. Last night, you couldn't have been less interested. You tried repeatedly to turn me away. And now you're threatening to stalk me?"

I hadn't expected that. "Not interested? I am the picture of interested when it comes to you. You just caught me off guard last night. I'm used to this—to you hating me. So when you suddenly seemed to be coming on to me, I just wanted to make sure it was for real and that you weren't being forced to seduce me by some brilliant terrorist. Despite what you think about all of us guys, consent still matters to most of us."

Her eyebrows furrowed together in an adorable expression as she tried to piece together everything I'd just said. "I don't hate you."

"You've literally told me you hate me at least a dozen times."

She rolled her eyes. "Well, I don't. You're annoying and arrogant and entitled and demanding and self-absorbed and—"

"Olivia," I interrupted. "You started to tell me that you don't hate me, but all of these words suggest otherwise."

That earned me a half smile.

"You frustrate me. But I think I could see us being friends. Except..."

"Except you want to jump my bones every time you see me?"

Now she scowled. "I really don't get it, though. I mean, that date was bad."

"Awful," I agreed.

"We are obviously not meant to be anything other than frenemies."

"Frenemies," I repeated with a laugh. "The problem with your theory is that while the date was bad, the sex was...in your words, good. You can't deny we had good chemistry in bed."

She gazed up at me. The fact that she didn't argue with my assessment clearly meant she agreed. I leaned forward and kissed her, walking her backwards a few steps until she reached the wall. I planted an arm beside her head and deepened the kiss. She definitely kissed me back. I thought I actually heard her moan a little, too.

But then her hand reached up between us and shoved me. Hard.

"You can't just kiss me in a hallway!" she shouted. "That's what I'm trying to tell you. I don't want to go out with you. We are not compatible and I don't want a boyfriend."

I considered her words and tried to read her body language. She'd pushed me away, but she hadn't moved. Her cheeks were flushed, she was breathing hard, and she was trying really hard not to stare at my chest. There was not a doubt in my mind that Olivia wanted me. And I was not too cocky to admit I wanted her, too.

"Okay, so you don't want to date me. You just want to argue publicly then screw like bunnies when we're alone," I concluded, struggling not to smile at the way her bold eyes widened and filled with fury. "I can live with that. So back to the initial question, eight o'clock at my place okay for you?"

"Ugh!" she groaned, shaking her hands towards the heavens. She pushed off the wall and resumed the walk back towards the gym in silence. When we were nearing our destination, Olivia slowed her pace and turned to me.

"I'm busy tonight. So, eight o'clock tomorrow. And I'm not sleeping over. You're driving me home after." She said the last part so seriously that I actually wondered if she thought I'd protest. *Crazy.* If the sex was half as good as it had been the last night, I'd give her my damn car if she asked.

"Deal," I said.

With that, she strode back into the gym and promptly ignored me the rest of the day.

CHAPTER NINE

- Nate -

*T*he next night, I showered to relieve some tension, then spent half of an hour doing sit-ups and pushups to ensure my torso looked just the way Olivia liked. I'd put on jeans and a tee shirt, determined to look casual even if I had spent a fair chunk of time choosing the most flattering shirt and jeans I owned. Still, I half expected her to ditch me, so a mixture of nervous surprise fluttered through me when she actually showed up at precisely eight p.m.

Olivia pulled off the casual look better than I did. Her hair was loosely braided so the shorter layers of her hair hung free around her face. She wore yoga pants, a tank top, and a zip up hoodie. The sight of her ass in those pants made my mouth water, but I was certain she'd dropped by in the outfit she'd already been wearing. The magic of Olivia was that she looked *that* good without putting an ounce of effort into it.

I offered her a drink, and she chose a flavored electrolyte-infused water over alcohol.

"You don't drink very often, do you?"

Olivia shook her head.

"Because alcohol makes you do crazy things?" I guessed.

A soft laugh escaped her lips. She lifted the bottle to her mouth and unscrewed the cap, sipping slowly without breaking eye contact. I had so many more questions for Olivia, but they could all wait. I tugged her by the hand upstairs.

I'd barely shut the bedroom door when Olivia pounced, unfastening my jeans and nudging them to the floor with impressive dexterity. I reached for her clothes, but she ducked my hand and dropped to her knees. She gazed up at me, the sweet innocent look in her sparkling eyes a stark contrast to her actions as she wrapped her full pink lips around my cock.

I groaned at the intensity and let my head fall backwards, smacking into the door. It didn't hurt, but I probably could've withstood a full limb amputation without pain as long as Olivia kept her mouth on my cock. She giggled at my clumsiness, and her laughter vibrated around my shaft. I reached my hand to her head, careful not to force her to take more of me than she wanted. The urge to take control, to completely dominate her sweet little mouth, was overwhelming, but I was even more eager to get inside her. I wanted to feel her body spasm around my own as her release washed over her.

I nudged Olivia backwards, ignoring the sexy pout she offered. I squeezed her firm buttocks through those perfect pants she wore, then set about ripping all of her clothes off of her. We kissed, but only for a moment, and then my thoughts again flitted to her beautiful ass. I guided her onto the bed, then motioned for her to roll over. Olivia complied without question, shockingly, but she sprawled on her stomach as if anticipating a gentle massage. I had something entirely different in mind.

I gripped her hips and lifted them into the air, eliciting a sharp squeal as I slapped her butt cheek then dropped down to trace my tongue along her slit. My tongue struggled to reach her clit from that angle, so I used my finger. I licked and sucked her delicious flesh for only a minute before deciding we were ready. I grabbed the condom, pausing to admire the beautiful woman poised on all fours on my bed, eagerly awaiting my next move.

Olivia turned her head and her gaze met mine. "Are you going to fuck me or stand there and stare?"

All my breath whooshed out as if I'd been punched. I fumbled with the condom like a teenager, thwarted by my own trembling hands as Olivia wiggled her ass in the air. I grabbed her hips, then fully sheathed myself in her warmth. Olivia moaned and dropped her head, and as I pulled out, she shifted her hips back to meet me. I didn't dare comment on her eagerness, but I also wasn't about to disappoint her.

I bit back my own moan, using my grip on her hips to steer my movements as she arched against me. Once we fell into a delicious pattern, I worked my hands along her torso, palming her dangling breasts. Olivia's breathing grew faster and louder as my fingers lightly caressed her nipples. When I sensed she was close, I tightened my grip, lifting her arms off the bed until she was upright. With her back nearly touching my torso, I could kiss and suck the side of her neck. Olivia writhed against my hands, rubbing her own breasts against my palms.

I shifted one hand to her neck in hopes of steadying her now that her movements had become more frenzied. The moment I did so, Olivia's body clenched around my cock and she moaned a stream of expletives. Then, she chomped down on the finger I hadn't even realized had drifted to her mouth. The sudden pain zinged through me and added to the exquisite pressure already building inside me. Olivia dropped her torso to the bed and I blanketed her body with my own, lasting only a few more thrusts before my own orgasm swept through me with an explosive ferocity.

I pulled out of her and slid to my knees on the floor, resting my head on Olivia's ass. I couldn't have moved further if I'd wanted to. My legs were shaking, my heart was racing, and the room was spinning as if I'd overindulged in booze. But really, it was just her, the intoxicating power of Olivia.

When I finally garnered enough energy to stand, I ducked into the bathroom to dispose of the condom. I returned a moment later to find Olivia lounged out on my bed, clicking through emails on her phone. She'd pulled on her tank top and panties, but no bra or pants. I would've enjoyed the sight of her without any top more, but the whole braless look was pretty hot on her too, especially since the cool temperature of my room was causing her nipples to protrude fairly prominently.

"What's with the shirt?" I asked, flopping onto the bed beside her.

"It's cold in here."

"But no bra?"

She eyed me over her phone. "Are you complaining?"

I shook my head quickly.

"Bras aren't really that comfortable," she said, typing something else on her phone before dropping it onto the nightstand.

I tried to think of something to say, but nothing came to mind. After sex, my brain was useless for at least an hour. I did think it was a good sign that Olivia still clearly enjoyed hooking up with me even when she was sober, but it didn't seem appropriate to comment on that.

"Did you see the schedule for the tournament at the end of this month?" she asked.

I turned away, hiding my wince. I was painfully familiar with every detail of that tournament, but I wasn't about to admit that. And I was even less likely to admit *why* I knew so much about that tournament. "Yeah. You don't like your matches? Is the great Olivia Roberts actually nervous?"

She snorted. "No, I'm fine with it. I was just making conversation. I'm just not really sure how this is supposed to go." Olivia gestured between us.

It took a moment before I realized what she meant. "Oh, you mean you don't know proper protocol for when you're using a guy for sex?"

Olivia stuck out her tongue.

"You're doing just fine. A little cuddling, some conversation, that's all perfectly appropriate. When you get bored, I'll drive you home and then you can text me in a day or two when you need your next fix."

I smiled peacefully at her scowl. "Since we've established you don't drink often," I began, leading into what I was really curious about. "I'm curious what made you decide to get drunk Sunday."

Her smile faded as her gaze turned to the ceiling. "I was just stressed," she finally admitted.

"About...me?"

"It will never cease to amaze me how arrogant you are," Olivia said with a groan. "And no, not about you. About my mom, mostly."

"Oh. Is she okay?"

"She'll be fine. She just has crappy taste in men."

Olivia had mentioned that before, so I wasn't surprised.

"Some loser she was dating broke up with her and she was all upset over it. Nothing too shocking, until she mentioned she had loaned him a bunch of money. Actually, she called it an investment, but it's all gone."

I winced. Once, years ago, my father had chucked a crystal vase across the room and then told my mom he'd lost seven hundred thousand dollars on some investment that day. At the time, I had no sense how much money that was, but I'd known from his behavior that it must have been huge. So, I'd been surprised when, a couple weeks later, we added the tennis courts off the back of the house and renovated the pool house. Eventually, I began to realize the way my parents worked... my dad apologized for losing money by letting my mom spend money the way she wanted. Clearly, that model only worked for the super rich.

"Sorry," I finally mumbled, certain my own family's financial drama wouldn't reassure her in the least. "It must suck to have to worry about money for practical things."

I didn't even realize how ridiculous that sounded until I caught the way she was staring at me. Fortunately, she didn't seem offended.

"You have a yacht," she said instead.

I raised a brow at the seemingly out of the blue comment.

"My roommate is obsessed with your Instagram account," Olivia continued. "You look like a total douche, posing by a bunch of boats, by the way. It's like you're trying to fulfill every single rich, white-boy stereotype in one single social media account."

"Umm thank you?"

We both laughed.

"It's not *my* yacht," I clarified. "But if this is your not-so-subtle way of asking if my family is loaded, the answer is yes."

Her lips curved upwards. "That must suck, being filthy rich."

I knew she was teasing me and that I should just keep my mouth shut, but that was never my strong suit. "It really does sometimes."

She rolled her eyes.

"I'm serious. Look, my grandfather built this whole empire and then my dad grew it more. Our family business has reached its peak and there's nowhere for it to go but down. Nothing I do my whole life will ever impress either of them and I'm never going to live up to their standards. You, on the other hand, have been exceeding everyone's expectations for over a decade now, I bet. You could just give up now and already be a success."

Olivia didn't answer for a minute, so I thought maybe I'd made my point.

"Boo hoo. Poor little rich kid," she teased, continuing the fake crying until I tackled her, tickling until her taunting turned into laughter.

"You should take me home now," she said when we both stilled.

I was tempted to push my luck and protest, but instead I just drove her home.

CHAPTER TEN

- Olivia -

Somehow, Nate and I fell into a comfortable pattern of sleeping together two or three nights a week while continuing our routine of flirt, argue, and ignore when in public. The sex was predictably good every time, but I was surprised to find we were getting equally good at talking. Aside from Mia and Addie, I didn't really talk to a lot of people, and already I'd gotten to the point where I felt as comfortable talking with Nate as either of them.

I hadn't expected Nate to be a good listener, but he was. And even though I still struggled to not be overly judgmental of him, he never seemed to judge me. We didn't just talk after sex, either. We'd begun texting each other several times a day and even shared a few late-night phone calls. I begrudgingly admitted I considered Nate Aldridge to be a good friend. Of course that, when combined with the sex, complicated things. We hadn't attempted another official date, nor had either of us even brought up the prospect. But, then again, we had grabbed a quick bite to eat after practice a couple of times.

As I packed my bag for the tournament, it hit me that I might actually, albeit unintentionally, be dating Nate.

I dismissed the idea as quickly as it had come to me, reasoning that the mere combination of eating, screwing, and talking did not a relationship make. Dating would require one of us to actually ask the other out, or say the words aloud. Besides, for all I knew, Nate was still dating a dozen different girls.

Our tournament was in a super wealthy Connecticut suburb, a couple of hours from campus. Both teams rode the same bus up Friday evening, and even though Nate said he was saving a seat for me, I ducked into a separate row with Mia. Nate made a face, but quickly recovered.

I felt bad, but surely he understood. It was one thing for everyone on the team to think we were friends. It would be another issue altogether if people thought we were dating. And since I myself was confused on the line between friendship and relationship, it was too risky that others would make the same mistake.

All it would take was one stray touch or a glance that lingered a little too long and everyone would know. There weren't any official rules against dating other players, but the Coaches left no questions about their stance on the matter. Besides, it was a complication I didn't have time for.

I settled into the seat, wedging my water bottle between my hip and the arm rest, before realizing Mia was eying me warily.

"What's up?" I asked.

She shrugged and dropped her gaze to her book. "I figured you'd sit by Nate."

My body tensed so abruptly that I nearly pulled a muscle. "Why would you think that?" I asked, keeping my voice eerily calm as I rubbed the side of my now sore neck.

Luckily, Mia didn't seem suspicious. "I don't know, just seems like you guys have been talking lately. Bonding over your boring business classes?"

"Pretty much," I replied with a soft laugh. Mia was an English major. When she wasn't playing tennis, she immersed herself in carefully crafted fictional worlds and had zero understanding of why some of us spent our days dealing with facts and numbers. Sometimes, I questioned the logic of my choices too.

As Mia flipped the pages of her novel, my phone buzzed.

"Feeling #rejected," was all Nate wrote.

"Sorry. Didn't want to raise suspicion."

"Right. Forgot u can't keep ur hands off me."

I giggled, then peered forward on the bus to confirm the seat beside him was still vacant. "Perv," I texted back. Then I turned to Mia. "Actually Nate has an Econ question, so I'm heading up there for a few. I'll be back."

She lifted her eyebrows in acknowledgment of my words, but clearly didn't care. Her novel must be truly engrossing. I darted to Nate's row before the driver could yell at me, practically falling onto Nate as I slumped into the seat. I was pleased to see he actually had a notepad and pen in front of him, rendering my excuse even more plausible.

"Hey stranger," I greeted him, smiling widely. "How's it going?"

"Better now," he said, his voice soft. He sat up and motioned towards the window. "Switch seats with me."

I did, and for once, I didn't even question why. "I told Mia we were discussing Economics," I said.

He quirked an eyebrow and peered around the bus. No one seemed remotely interested in what we were or weren't discussing, and Mia couldn't even see us from her row.

"Fine, point taken," I conceded, even though Nate hadn't uttered a word. I wracked my brain for a different, equally safe topic. "Have you been to the town we're competing in before?"

He nodded slowly.

"Are you very familiar with it?"

Nate cringed but nodded again.

"Anything I should be sure to see or do while we're there?"

Nate looked confused.

"We're going to have some downtime," I reminded him. Typically, we arrived shortly before the first match and left immediately after the final match. This tournament was spread out over an entire weekend, which seemed odd. But, if it was a chance for a mini-vacation, I didn't want to waste the opportunity.

"There's nothing worth seeing near the tournament," Nate said finally. "Just a bunch of entitled rich people."

His sassy expression made me smile.

"Ahh friends of yours?" I teased.

Nate chuckled. "Actually, yes. I grew up near there."

"Really? That is fascinating."

"No, it truly isn't," he replied. He arranged his oversized sweatshirt over our laps. "Let's talk about something else."

"Like what?" I asked. I was about to nudge the sweatshirt away since I wasn't cold, but just then, Nate's hand slipped under the thick material, landing squarely on my crotch. My breath hitched.

"We could discuss why you should have worn a skirt," he said, fumbling with the waist band of my leggings.

"I could've worn high waisted compression leggings," I pointed out.

"You'd only be punishing yourself," he replied, right as his fingers reached their target.

I focused on appearing calm and relaxed, even while certain parts of my body were rapidly tensing. "I'm not sure what your goal is here, but there is no way I'll ever actually…you know, in a bus."

"Really? Because I was thinking maybe I'd make you come twice, just in case there's not an opportunity at the hotel."

Between the growing dizziness and my efforts to ensure I didn't look hot and bothered, I couldn't formulate a reply.

"The only real challenge is going to be seeing if you can stay quiet."

"Of course I could stay quiet," I said. My voice already sounded breathy.

"Mmm hmm," he replied. "Remember that time when I was doing that thing with my tongue? You about knocked me unconscious with your pussy, but the noises you made? Deafening. People down the street probably heard you come."

"Oh my God. Can you stop?"

His finger stilled. *Shit.*

"No, not that. Stop saying things like 'pussy.' We're on a bus."

His laughter came out like a low rumble that reminded me of the sexy way he growled whenever I was sassy in bed.

"So I can touch it but I can't say it?" he asked.

I didn't answer. I was panting like I'd just run a few laps and I was dying to let my eyes drift shut so I could picture all of the finely sculpted muscles of Nate's torso rippling as he hovered over me when we made love.

"This is going to be better than the time you let me win that tennis game," he continued.

I wanted to argue with him, to insist he wasn't about to win this bet by bringing me to climax on a stupid bus, but my body didn't seem to care that we were surrounded by people.

"Close your eyes," he said. "No one can see you over by the window, so just relax. Quietly," he added.

I would've giggled if I hadn't been so tightly wound. Instead, I shifted in my seat, increasing the friction against his fingers. I let my eyes drift shut, and instantly felt every move even more intensely.

"So, back to my tongue. I know you enjoy it when I'm eating you out and fuck you with my fingers at the same time, but I almost think you prefer when it's just my tongue on your pussy. You like the challenge. You like making me work for it," he said, his voice barely a whisper.

I opened my mouth to argue, even though technically, he might've been right, but it was too difficult to speak while concentrating fully on not panting. I'd have to lecture Nate later about the impropriety of using such dirty words in public.

"You can bite either your lip or your finger, Olivia, but try not to draw blood. I'm going to make you come now and you have to stay quiet. Do you understand?"

I could've laughed at his arrogance, but part of me did wish it worked like that, that I could orgasm simply because he commanded it.

Two of Nate's fingers curved further inside my body, pressing roughly against the sensitive bundle of nerves tucked right against the internal wall. The heaviness in my core intensified, and my breasts tingled. Then his thumb rubbed back and forth against my clit. Suddenly, bright light flooded my eyelids and a jolt of pleasure zapped through me like an electrical current.

My hand flew to my lip and I dug my teeth into the side of my thumb, struggling against the moans so desperate to escape. As the sensation passed, I inched my hand away from my mouth and I felt Nate's hand wriggle out of my pants.

Feeling equally sheepish and exhilarated, I dared a glance at Nate. His smug grin was predictably cocky.

"I love being right, but I think you like it too," he whispered.

And then, he licked each of his fingers, one at a time.

What a cocky bastard.

CHAPTER ELEVEN

- Nate -

I played in the first game the next morning, which was fine by me. I was desperate to get it over with. The only thing more intimidating than my parents watching me play was knowing their friends and business associates were also spectators. Our family business was the corporate sponsor of the stupid tournament, but luckily, no one on the team seemed to realize that. The tournament was also located in my home town, minutes from my house, so there was zero chance of escaping without excessive interaction with my parents.

I'd defeated my opponent just in time to catch Olivia's singles match. I'd hoped to sit with the team, but Coach had encouraged me to join my parents in the stands. Despite my victory, they'd still have plenty to criticize, so I braced myself for a painfully awkward discussion. But to my surprise, my parents both loved watching Olivia so much that they forgot to critique my every move. I'd never heard them so complimentary about anything or anyone, so when they said they'd love to meet the team's top player, I agreed to ask her.

After the match, which Olivia won in two quick sets, I went to look for her. I bumped into Coach Katelyn near the locker room. She seemed excited when I told her my parents wanted to meet her star player. Coach Katelyn said Olivia was dressed and alone in the locker room, but I knocked on the door anyway. When Olivia didn't answer, I walked in, covering my eyes.

"Liv?" I called.

I heard her laughing, so I opened my eyes.

"What are you doing in the girls' locker room, pervert?"

"Coach K said I could come in. She also said you were alone." I wiggled my eyebrows suggestively at that last part.

"For the moment, I am alone. But I'll be out in a few minutes anyway. I need to hydrate before the next match."

I checked my watch. "You have a while."

"Yeah."

"My parents are here," I blurted out. "And they want to meet you."

Olivia blinked several times. "Why?"

"Why are they here? Well, um, you know the sponsor, Jameson Enterprises? That's my dad. I mean, his company."

"No, I meant why do they want to meet me," she said. "Wait, what? Your family business is the sponsor?"

I nodded sheepishly.

"I thought you were named after your father. So isn't his name Nathaniel Aldridge? You said you were the third."

"His name is Jameson Nathaniel Aldridge. So's his father's, and mine. I just go by the middle name."

Olivia stared at me, slowly shaking her head. "I had no idea. So your actual first name is James?"

"Jameson," I said with a shrug. I didn't make a point of telling many people my full name anyway.

"You told your parents we're—"

"No, I didn't tell them anything. They just want to meet you because you're a badass on the courts. Since they know we go to the same school, they asked if I knew you. I couldn't exactly say no."

"So they want to meet me as a tennis player and not because they think you and I are involved?"

"Correct. Unless you want me to tell them…"

"Nope." She stood and began re-braiding her ponytail. "I can chat with them in a few minutes if you want. I got time before the game."

"You don't think it'll mess with your head?"

Olivia shrugged. "I don't get distracted easily."

That didn't surprise me about her. For as neurotic as she was about most things, Liv was calm and focused when she played. There could be an explosion on the court beside Olivia, and she'd still return the ball just fine.

I let my eyes wander up then down her body appreciatively as she finished her hair. For having just played a full tennis match, she sure didn't look too shabby. "If I forget to tell you later, your ass looks fabulous in that little getup."

Olivia raised an eyebrow. "Why thank you." She looked at herself in the full-length mirror, lifting her skirt slightly to reveal bright red scrapes along her left hip. "Does the skirt cover this?"

"Jesus! Is that from when you dove for the shot?" I leaned closer to inspect the damage. Her skin looked angry and red, but there wasn't a hint of green from the court, so she'd at least washed it off.

"Yep. Feels like my fabulous ass is on fire."

I gently kissed her hip right beside the road rash. "You should get some antibiotic ointment or something."

"Yeah," she agreed, swatting me away. "Alright. Let's go schmooze some rich people."

I couldn't help but laugh at that, but then I realized we were completely alone, in a locker room. What were the chances that opportunity would present itself again? I turned to Olivia and reached for her hand.

"Absolutely not," she said, correctly interpreting the look in my eyes. "But you can give me a kiss for good luck."

"You think you need good luck for this next match?" I asked, pulling her close.

"No, I meant for meeting your parents," she replied, closing the gap between us and planting her lips on mine.

* * *

- Olivia -

*N*ate led me to a small tented area off to the side of the main courts. A table with a fancy spread of appetizers was in one corner along with a makeshift bar. There was a handful of people inside the tent, but it was easy to spot which ones were Nate's parents.

They were both attractive, which shouldn't have surprised me given that he did have their genetics, after all. They also both looked exceptionally young. I wondered how much plastic surgery was involved to achieve that look.

"Mom, Dad!" Nate called. The couple turned. "This is Olivia Roberts. Olivia, these are my parents, Jameson and Jackie Aldridge."

Mrs. Aldridge turned and grabbed a younger woman standing beside her. "Honey, come meet Olivia. She won that last match," she said.

The younger woman smiled stiffly. "Pleasure. I'm Leighton McAllister. My husband Charles is around here somewhere."

"Leighton is my sister," Nate added.

I smiled and politely shook hands with everyone while they gushed over my last set. Nate's mom asked who I'd trained with before college, clearly assuming I'd worked with some famous coach and not just the random public high school coaches. She also asked my plans after college and if I planned to go pro.

"I'm only a Junior," I said. "I'm studying business, so the plan is to find a good job after college. Playing tennis professionally would be amazing, but that's not the most practical. We'll see though," I said.

I thought my response sounded pretty good, but both of Nate's parents immediately turned to him, frowning.

"See? Some people have a work ethic," his mom said.

"This girl has options and she's actually choosing business," Mr. Aldridge chimed in.

I caught Nate's eye and flashed an apologetic smile.

"Can I get you a drink?" Mr. Aldridge offered.

"Dad! She's got another match in a little while."

"Yeah, thank you, but I really should get back so I can talk with my coach. It was so nice to meet you both, and um, thanks for all your support for this tournament."

Mrs. Aldridge pressed her hand to her husband's arm. "James, she should join us for dinner. Don't you think that would be lovely? The other guests would adore talking with a real tennis star."

Nate flung his hands in the air at the snub. I bit my lip to keep from laughing.

"That's a very kind offer, but I'm not sure if we have plans as a team tonight or what," I said.

"Okay, well, if you can make it happen, we'd be honored to have you join us."

Nate and I walked off. He shoved his hands in his pocket, presumably to resist the urge to touch me. "You should come to dinner. It'll be catered. You like good food."

"I'm sure it'll be amazing, but it's definitely not my style of gathering."

"I'll be there," he said. "You could see the house I grew up in, probably find some baby pictures of me to mock. You might even meet some rich people that don't fit your preconceived notions."

"Doubtful. What would I even wear?"

"You could borrow something from my sister."

I wrinkled my nose. "I don't think she likes me."

"Not Leighton. Ansley. You'll like her."

"I'll think about it," I promised. Then I wished him good luck on his next match before heading off to prep for my own.

* * *

*N*ate -

Olivia and I both won our second matches of the day, which seemed like a good omen. During the game, my mom apparently accosted Coach Katelyn and asked if Olivia could come to our party and stay the night at my family's house. Surely the fact that my family singlehandedly funded the recent repaving of the outdoor courts and purchased all new cardio equipment for the workout room had nothing to do with the fact that Coach quickly agreed.

Olivia also agreed to the plan, clearly still high from her win. Before long, she was back at my family's estate with me.

"Holy shit," Olivia said, stopping dead in her tracks as she stepped out of the car.

I blew out a sigh, having expected that reaction. There was nothing original about the display of wealth at my family home, but it still tended to catch visitors off guard if they were unaccustomed to the same degree of opulence. Following the solid stone and wrought-iron gate, a tree-lined paved drive led up to a roundabout in front of the main entrance. A fountain with a ridiculous clichéd statue of a naked baby took up the center portion of the roundabout.

The façade of the house was beige and featured a series of oversized white-trimmed archways. I nodded for Olivia to follow me up the steps leading to the solid wood door, but she paused, glancing back to the car.

"Brian will bring your bag," I promised. I tried to remember why I'd encouraged her to come to my house. Clearly, I'd been focused on the opportunities we'd have in the night, staying in the same house as opposed to separate hotel rooms. But part of me wondered if Olivia would ever even speak to me again after seeing the way I'd grown up.

Her lips parted to protest, then she seemed to think better of it and followed me inside.

I didn't dare give her the full tour yet. Still, standing inside the massive foyer, which my mom had taken great pains to ensure revealed exactly how much money we'd spent on the house, was enough to give her a fair taste for the property. The dining room was off to one side, a formal living room to the other. Just beyond that was my father's office and a music room. The back side of the main floor housed the kitchen, a couple more sitting rooms with various pretentious sounding names, and a sunroom with another dining table.

I led Olivia straight up the wide, curved staircase to the second floor. She paused at the large landing at the top of the staircase, her eyes still wide.

"My parents' room is that way," I said, nodding the opposite direction of where we were headed. Now that Leighton had moved out, there were three guest rooms on the floor. I, of course, selected the one closest to my room for Olivia. Ansley's room was across the hall from mine.

"I can't believe you grew up here," Olivia mumbled, making her way to the loft at the end of the hall. My sisters and I had spent hours in there as kids, playing board games and avoiding our parents.

I cringed, certain I'd have to give her the rest of the tour eventually. She'd hate me even more after seeing the rest of the house. Even the basement was over the top, holding the gym, a billiards room, a theater room, and a massive bar and seating area. Sliding doors from the basement led directly to the stone patio surrounding the pool and offered a decent view of the gazebo and pool house. From the deck one floor above, you could see the tennis courts and firepit off in the distance.

I turned to the sound of footsteps, expecting to see Brian with Olivia's bag, but instead it was Ansley.

"Hey, loser!" she shrieked, scampering close for a hug. "Sorry I missed your match earlier, but I'm sure you were awesome."

"Always am," I replied, stepping back so she could see Olivia behind me.

"Ansley, this is Olivia Roberts. She's on the team at my school and mom dragged her back here for the party so she could brag to her friends about knowing the Number One ranked player in the division."

"Wow, Number One, huh? That's impressive," she said, extending her hand to Olivia.

Olivia blushed but smiled politely.

"So do you have to spend a lot of time with my brother if you're on the women's team?"

"Not really, no. They're completely separate teams. Our practices sometimes overlap, but that's about it," Olivia said casually.

Ansley looked disappointed. "I'd hoped you could tell me some embarrassing stories about my big brother."

"Sorry." Olivia shrugged.

I cleared my throat. "So, Ansley, since mom essentially just kidnapped Olivia, I don't think she has anything with her to wear to the party tonight. If there is anything you could loan her…"

At the mention of fashion, my sister's eyes widened. She grabbed Olivia by the hand and dragged her into her bedroom. I chuckled, but took the opportunity to retreat into my own room. Ansley would probably keep Olivia occupied for at least an hour, giving me plenty of time to shower and change.

CHAPTER TWELVE

- Olivia -

*N*ate's sister, Ansley, was as friendly as his older sister was cold. I suspected she was the type to happily lounge by the pool and dish gossip with me all weekend. By the time we were alone in her room though, the enormity of the house had fully shaken my nerves. I didn't just crave solitude; I needed it to survive.

Ansley offered me six dresses to try on, complete with matching shoes and coordinating accessories for each. I thanked her and escaped into my room. I closed the door and sunk onto the bed, catching my breath as I gazed around. My coat had been hung on the back of the door and my bag was resting on a dresser adjacent to the bed. Standing, I poked my head around the corner, surprised to see the sizeable bathroom, complete with a walk-in shower and separate jetted bathtub. Another door off the bathroom led to a walk-in closet.

As I peered out the window, taking in the gorgeous view of the manicured back lawn and what appeared to be private tennis courts, it hit me. This hadn't always been a guest room. This was Leighton's former bedroom. I retreated to the bed, trying to imagine what it would have been like to grow up in such a place. The bedroom suite alone was over half the size of the apartment where I'd grown up. Adding in the rest of the house, and it was a tad nauseating. If children played hide and seek here, they could legitimately remain hidden for days.

I shuddered right as I heard a noise from next door. It sounded like a shower shutting off, so my mind flitted to images of Nate fresh out of the shower. I smiled at the thought, then realized that might mean I had limited time to get ready. I popped to my feet and began shimmying into the first of Ansley's dresses. I'd assumed I'd wear the black one, provided it fit, but she'd really encouraged me to go with the blue. As I slipped into it, I could tell why. The vivid color really brought out my eyes and reminded me of a swimming pool on a hot summer day.

I changed back into my own clothes right as a knock came at my door. I poked my head out, relieved to see that it was Nate. I opened the door wider and he came in, his gaze immediately falling to the dresses I'd spread out on the bed.

"Care to model them for me?" he asked.

"I think I've already decided."

"Good. I want to be surprised anyway," he replied with a wink.

I nodded and took a measured breath.

"You okay?"

I wasn't sure how to answer that. It seemed silly to admit, but I was regretting not heading back to Olive Garden and then the hotel with the rest of the team. "This place is a little overwhelming. This was your sister's room, wasn't it?"

"Yeah. But Leighton is not coming tonight, and I wanted you in the room closest to mine."

"Why?"

"Less of a walk for you to join me in the night," Nate replied with a cocky grin.

I didn't even try to hide my relief. "Good. I don't want to sleep in here alone. I might get lost."

Nate pulled my chin towards his face and kissed me firmly on the lips. "I don't want to stress you out more, but my mom will want us downstairs in about an hour. There should be shower stuff, a hair dryer, really anything you need already in there, but just text me if there's something else you want."

I locked the door after he left and carried the blue dress into the bathroom. I figured I'd be dressed and ready to go with a half hour to spare, but somehow I'd lost track of time, luxuriating in the waterfall shower. I only had ten minutes remaining by the time I was slipping my feet into the shoes. A knock shook the door, and I went to open it, ready to lecture Nate about being early.

But it wasn't Nate. It was Ansley.

Her jaw dropped when she saw me. "Oh my God, Olivia. You look amazing. Like, wow. OMG." She brushed past me into the room. "You might as well keep that dress because I could never wear it again, knowing you look that much better than me in it."

"Um, thanks. You look gorgeous," I said, certain I'd never keep the dress but desperate to shift the attention from myself. Ansley really did look beautiful though. She wore a deep purple dress that was sophisticated yet sassy and mirrored her personality perfectly.

Ansley waved a hand dismissively then opened the box she held in her other hand. It was a longer necklace with alternating diamonds and pearls. Inside it was a matching bracelet. "I do need these back after tonight because, well, they're expensive, but they match your dress better anyway. Ooh! I forgot the earrings."

She scampered across the hall before I could tell her I didn't need the earrings. I gazed at the necklace, afraid to touch it, and didn't notice Nate walking in until the loud wolf whistle snapped me back to attention.

"Holy crap, you clean up well," he said.

I rolled my eyes at him right as Ansley returned.

"You've really never seen her dressed up?" she asked her brother.

He shook his head. "A sweaty tennis skirt is about the dressiest thing she's ever worn near me," he replied. Then he stepped closer and reached for the necklace.

I recoiled and shook my head when it became apparent he intended to fasten it for me. "I can't wear that," I said. "I'll feel out of place."

"You haven't seen the guests. Trust me, you'll fit in better with this," Ansley said.

"I'm really not comfortable. I lose things all the time..."

Nate stepped closer, wrapped his arms around me, and fixed the clasp in place. "Don't stress it. If you lose it, I'll buy my sister a new one." Everything about his proximity felt too intimate for his sister to see, but she didn't seem suspicious in the slightest.

Ansley handed me the bracelet, still beaming.

Somehow as we made our way downstairs a few minutes later, I was even wearing the earrings, oversized teardrops containing both a diamond and a pearl. I felt like the prostitute accompanying the billionaire business man to an important meeting, but having Nate at my side did reassure me a little. It was astounding to see the rest of the house, especially as it had now been filled with uniformed waiters carrying trays over-flowing with drinks and hors d'oeuvres.

Nate and his sister both helped themselves to a drink, but I declined. I never drank the night before a match, and especially not when I needed to keep my wits about me. Nate's father came over to greet me, his eyes roaming up and down my body a little too slowly for comfort.

"Is that Ansley's dress?" he asked.

I nodded, relaxing as I realized his prolonged stare was due to the familiarity of the dress and nothing less savory.

"Olivia didn't exactly know she'd need to pack formalwear," Nate chimed in.

Mr. Aldridge continued to make polite small talk with me until the guests began to arrive. Nate was pulled to the side into a discussion with some older man I didn't recognize, and Nate's mother latched on to my elbow, dragging me to one guest to another, showing me off like a new pet.

My feet had begun to ache by the time Nate found me and motioned for me to follow him. He walked out a sliding door off the side of the kitchen and led me outside, where a crowded tray of appetizers was sitting on a side table adjacent to the fire pit.

"Figured you might be hungry," he said, laughing.

I bit back a smile, already shivering.

Nate shrugged out of his suit jacket and draped it over my shoulders, then flipped a switch to turn on the firepit.

"Wow, that's a cool party trick," I said, sitting at a chair adjacent to him. I was starving, so I launched into the various appetizers, as did he.

"I can't believe you grew up like this," I said, gazing around, still in shock. "Just to be clear, when I was giving you a hard time and calling you a privileged rich kid, I had no idea you were *this* privileged or *this* rich. I was thinking millionaire, not billionaire. It's a wonder you're not a complete sociopath."

Nate grinned, confirming my guess about his family finances by not correcting my assumption.

I wiped my mouth on a napkin and took a bite of the second appetizer, chewing quickly. "It's also a miracle you're not obese. Does rich people food always taste this good? I mean, these crab cakes are orgasmic. No, they're better than an orgasm."

"Ouch," he replied. "I'm both moderately offended and seriously turned on by that comment. And, yeah, pretty much. It's great now, but lobster bisque and filet mignon aren't exactly kid-friendly foods. I would've killed for a chicken nugget or a hot dog a decade ago."

I could see that.

"You really do look gorgeous tonight, in case I forget to tell you later," he said. Before I could reply, Nate was standing and turning to the side. He greeted another guy who appeared about our age, then introduced me. And just like that, I felt like I was on duty again.

Around ten o'clock, Nate encouraged me to tell his mom I needed to rest up for the match. He promised to join me shortly. I slipped out of the borrowed shoes and crept back up the stairs to the guest room, a little creeped out by the size of the house. Someone had shut all of the doors upstairs, so it took me a moment to even remember which door led to my temporary abode.

I changed into my pajamas, washed my face, and carefully returned Ansley's jewelry to the box. Just as I was debating what to do with it, there was a knock on the door.

"You decent?" Nate called.

I opened the door in reply. His smile quickly faded.

"I was looking forward to taking that dress off of you," he said, pouting.

"Sorry. I figured I should return it to your sister."

He took the dresses and the jewelry across the hall for me, returning after a minute. "You need anything else from in there?" he asked, gesturing to the guest room.

I considered the question, then shook my head. Nate peered out the door then motioned for me to follow. I did, then watched with amusement as he locked the door from the outside using a bent paperclip. Then, we tiptoed furtively into the room next door.

I hadn't seen Nate's room before, so I appreciated the opportunity now. Structurally, it was similar to his sister's, but there was an extra seating area near the window which I assumed had been converted into a larger closet in hers. There weren't a lot of personal effects or décor that struck me as things Nate would have chosen for himself, but I supposed that wasn't too surprising. He had his own apartment on campus after all, so he probably kept his belongings there.

"I promised your coach I'd make sure you got to bed by eleven," he said.

I frowned, certain that implied we were together.

"Relax, she was just concerned my parents would keep you out too late. I promised her I wouldn't let them. She doesn't think you like me at all. No one does."

I turned to face him, licking my lips as he began unbuttoning his shirt. I still felt stress—from the two matches that day, from the weird party, from the astounding realization that Nate was not just rich but insanely rich. No part of my brain was focused on sex, and I suspected my body wouldn't shift gears so easily either. I was about to tell Nate that maybe we should just sleep, but then he slipped my shirt up over my head and ran his palms up my torso.

And just like that, I realized sex with Nate was the only thing that would release the tension that had been building all day.

A breathy moan escaped my lips as his palms kneaded my breasts, his mouth trailing from my collar bone up the side of my neck, licking and sucking the flesh along its path. I pressed my fingers against his abdomen, stroking the firm ridges of his muscles as goosebumps began to dot his skin.

"Did you lock the door?" I whispered, our eyes meeting for a fleeting moment before he gazed past me to the door and then nodded. I lowered myself to my knees, working his belt buckle then tugging his pants to the ground. Nate groaned the moment my tongue reached his bare skin, and I relished the praise as I licked him several times.

When I finally wrapped my lips around the tip of his hardened length, his hands tightened against my head. His arms tensed as he struggled to restrain himself, to not fully lose himself to the pleasurable sensations. Nothing made me feel more powerful, more desired, than the way he was completely under my spell when we were like this. Before Nate, I'd never believed the women who claimed to love giving oral sex, but now I understood the full eroticism of turning a powerful man into a trembling, incoherent puppet with a few strokes of my tongue.

I would've happily taken him to completion, but after another minute, just as his breathing grew even more ragged, Nate released my head. It broke the spell and I gazed up at him, smiling to see his eyes glossed over and his face more relaxed than ever.

"Enough," he whispered, his voice barely audible over our breathing. He stumbled backwards one step then reached for me, pulling me to my feet. He pressed a sloppy kiss to my lips then tossed me onto his bed, stepping fully out of his own clothes before yanking my shorts down my thighs. He climbed over me, kissing my stomach, then my thighs before finally moving to the spot that was aching for his touch.

Nate teased me with his tongue and his fingers until it wasn't enough, and I shifted my hips to force him to climb back up my body. He did, releasing a deep guttural growl as he licked his way up my chest before positioning himself over me. He held himself just inches above me as though performing a pushup, then lowered down to one elbow to kiss me. I squeezed his muscular thigh, pulling his hips towards me until he acquiesced, relaxing his full torso against my own. He reached his arm around us, scooting my thigh to the side to make room for him. Then, he stopped abruptly.

"Shit," he breathed. "I don't have any condoms in here."

I took a moment to collect my breathing, reminding myself we could very easily finished what we'd both started with our lips. But then Nate pushed away, hopping to his feet in one svelte, athletic movement.

"Wallet!" he declared, his grin causing me to bite back a smile. He located his wallet, thumbed through it, then held up one precious foil-wrapped gem. He tore open the wrapper, then dropped it on my chest, letting me slide it onto him. "Let's just hope you don't want me more than once," he teased.

"You better last long enough to satisfy me the first time then," I replied.

Nate laughed, both of us knowing that had never before been an issue for us. On my next breath, we were joined together. Nate was kneeling in front of me, his hands gripping my bent thighs both to balance himself and steer his movements. My hands felt useless, with no part of him close enough to grip or squeeze, but my body was already primed and ready to explode.

As his movements sped up, a warmth began to spread through me, centered at the connection between our two bodies and radiating all the way to my fingers and toes. Nate released my legs, licked his thumbs then rubbed them roughly across my nipples, ratcheting up the intensity of the pleasure thrumming throughout my body.

"Come for me baby," he panted.

As he rolled my nipples between his fingers, his hips still slapping against me with a dizzying rhythm, I had no choice but to obey the command. My eyes flitted shut as my body exploded into wave after wave of toe-curling pleasure. A moment later, his hands tightened against my chest and his movements became less controlled, so I knew he was close to his release, too.

When he pulled out and collapsed on the bed beside me, I felt warm and cozy. He lay there for a minute, then ducked into the bathroom. I toyed with redressing, but only found my shirt and was too tired to look for my pajama shorts. My legs were always too hot when I slept anyway.

"You look comfy," Nate said, tugging the covers to slide in behind me.

"Mmm," I groaned, suddenly too sleepy to formulate real words.

"I set the alarm," he whispered, pressing a kiss to the back of my head before draping an arm around me and settling against me.

I was asleep before I could even ask what time.

CHAPTER THIRTEEN

- Nate -

*O*livia passed out moments after our vigorous lovemaking, leaving me replaying the full event in my mind. I'd officially lost track of how many times we'd hooked up, which astounded me. I'd never dreamed I'd get to fool around with a woman as hot as Olivia once, let alone countless times. And the realization that we'd just shared one of our hottest encounters together in my childhood bedroom, with my parents and their stuck-up friends right below, well, that brought an even bigger smile to my face.

But I was also intrigued by the rest of the day. My parents adored Olivia. And despite all her talk about how she didn't fit in with rich people, Olivia had held her own just fine. I sensed her discomfort with all of the attention, but she hid it well, and I doubted anyone else would've guessed that she wasn't accustomed to this type of wealth. Over time, surely she would feel more at ease in my world.

Olivia pretended there was no future for us, but the last twelve hours had shown me she was wrong.

I just hoped she'd reached the same conclusion.

I slept soundly with Olivia's warm body pressed against me, waking with a jolt when the alarm rang.

Olivia groaned and plucked my hand off of her abdomen like it was a dead bug. "Where are my shorts?"

I sat slowly, rubbing my eyes, then crawled out of bed to retrieve them. I grabbed a pair of sweatpants for myself, then stretched.

"I need you to unlock the door," she reminded me, already waiting by my bedroom door. I nodded, opening the door a crack and peering into the quiet, silent hall before deeming it safe. I scurried across the hall, unlocked the door to my sister's former room, and let Olivia enter first.

"What time do you play today?" she asked.

Not wanting to risk waking Ansley, I followed her into the room. We talked about our final individual matches, both slated for eleven am, which meant we wouldn't get to watch each other play. Olivia brushed her teeth and fixed her hair, then turned to me with a mischievous grin.

"Last night was fun," she said.

Her words surprised me. She'd looked like a caged rat during the party.

"Not the party. The kinky shit after."

That made more sense. "If you think that was kinky," I began.

Olivia giggled and pushed me to the door. I leaned in to kiss her, loving the soft warmth of her lips first thing in the morning. Then I inched the door shut, careful to latch it quietly. I exhaled once I was alone in the hallway.

"What are you doing?"

I froze like a deer in headlights, slowly turning to face my younger sister. In retrospect, I probably could've told I was making sure Olivia was awake or something equally lame and she would've bought it. But as it was, I was still too groggy to come up with a plausible excuse.

I also didn't want Olivia—or my parents—hearing our discussion, so I motioned for Ansley to follow me back to my room.

Once we were alone, I shut the door. I was still struggling with my explanation when my sister's eyes widened. She went over to my bed and grimaced as her gaze landed on the torn condom wrapper on the floor. I lunged to pick it up and crammed it into the bottom of my waste basket.

"You dog! Did you seriously just seduce our poor guest?" she laughed as though it were a ridiculous notion.

"I didn't—" I began.

"Oh my God. You so did. Jesus. Do you sleep with everyone on the tennis team? Or all of our houseguests?"

Clearly, Ansley was a little over the top on all of her assumptions.

"Oh shut up. I don't sleep with all our houseguests. And Liv is the only person on the tennis team I'm sleeping with."

"Liv?" she repeated with a smug smile. "Well, she certainly didn't put up much of a fight. Was the big fancy dinner last night foreplay?"

I flipped Ansley the middle finger, even though she was mostly kidding. "It's not like that. We've been..." I paused, searching for the right words to describe my relationship with Olivia. I certainly wasn't about to tell my sister the truth, that we'd been fucking like rabbits and that the sex was great but Olivia barely tolerated me the rest of the time. Ansley and I were close, but the condom wrapper was probably traumatic enough for her for the day. I needed to keep my explanation G-rated.

"We've been together for months now," I finally said.

Ansley's jaw dropped and she sat on the end of my bed. I gave her a moment to absorb that bit of information before remembering the other key tidbit.

"Olivia doesn't want people to know we're involved, so keep your big mouth shut."

Ansley frowned. "*She* doesn't want anyone to know? That's ironic."

"How so?"

"Mom did some research on her. Apparently Olivia is dirt poor. She got into school on scholarship and she's up to her ears in student loans. She also has a single mom who breezes through rich guys like it's her job."

"I already know all of that. What's your point?"

Ansley shrugged. "Mom and dad would never approve of you dating her."

"They love her! They practically kidnapped her last night. She's like the perfect son they never had."

"They only love her because they don't know you're dating her. If they knew that, well, Dad would probably threaten your trust fund if you didn't end it and Mom would tell you to use a condom even if she says she's on the pill."

Even though my sister didn't personally share those opinions, I suspected she was right about my parents saying that. But it didn't matter. "Olivia isn't like that, and I actually don't care what mom and dad think. If Olivia wanted people to know, I'd tell the world."

"You're not worried that everyone would assume she's only with you for your money?"

I winced. I got the impression Olivia firmly believed everyone would jump to that conclusion if they knew we were together, but I liked to think others might actually assume I said some redeeming qualities outside my wallet. And regardless of what people thought, *I* knew that wasn't why Olivia was with me. If anything, she was with me *despite* my wealth.

"People who'd make assumptions like that are dicks. I don't care what they think. And even if they do jump to stupid, wildly inaccurate conclusions about our involvement, Olivia is worth whatever hassle that creates. She's..." I paused and shook my head. Words always failed me when it came to Olivia. I wanted to tell Ansley that Olivia was amazing in every possible way, but then she'd mock me. As it turned out, she'd mock me regardless.

Ansley smiled. "Aww, that's so sweet. Does she know that you're a total douche?"

I flipped her off again.

"You can't tell anyone," I said.

"Don't worry. I won't tell the 'rents. It's actually fun having secrets from them."

"You can't tell Leighton either. She'd rat me out in a heartbeat."

"True. God, she's become such a bitch lately. Do you think it's Charles's doing? Or am I just imagining that she's gotten worse lately?"

"I don't know." Leighton had seemed more uptight than usual the past couple of years, but she'd never been as laid back as me and Ansley anyway, so it was hard to say.

There was a soft knock on the door. I quickly opened it to let Olivia enter. She was already dressed in her warmup with her hair pulled back. I tugged her in the room, shutting the door behind her.

"Oh, I didn't mean to interrupt," she stammered, eying my sister uncertainly.

"She saw me sneaking out of your room," I said. "She knows."

"Knows…?"

"I know that you're doing dirty things with my brother and I absolutely do not want any details about that," Ansley said, still chipper. "I am curious how you put up with him though, because losers ask me out all the time and I just can't tolerate the boring conversation, and…"

I glared at my sister until she shut up.

"Sorry," I said to Olivia. "She won't tell anyone else, though."

"I think you're way out of his league, for what it's worth," Ansley said.

Olivia smiled nervously.

"What did you need?" I asked her.

"I was just seeing if you were ready to go downstairs for breakfast. I need caffeine."

I glanced down at my pajama pants. "Not quite."

"I'll take her!" Ansley volunteered.

Olivia stiffened at the prospect.

"We'll meet you downstairs in a few," I said to my sister, watching Olivia relax the moment she realized she wouldn't have to face my family alone.

Ansley made a face but scampered out of the room.

I locked the door then shucked my pants, dressing as quickly as I could. I half expected Olivia to ask what Ansley and I had discussed, but she didn't. I shouldn't have been surprised. Olivia didn't concern herself with what the rest of the world thought nearly as much as I always worried she would.

Still, I had to say something. "Ansley loves you," I told her.

Olivia smiled sweetly. "She's nice. She seems a lot more… relaxed than the rest of your family."

I chuckled at her way of putting it. "Yeah, she and I missed out on the uptight genes."

"My parents like you a lot, too," I added, despite my better judgment.

She quirked an eyebrow and tilted her head to the side. "Everyone loves the story of the star tennis player who worked her way up from nothing."

"They do. And it isn't a story, Liv. That is you. You are this amazing person who worked your butt off and earned your success."

"I'm sure your parents would be thrilled to hear I'm sleeping with their son, the heir to their precious empire," she continued.

My lips parted, but I had nothing to say. We just stared at each other until finally, Olivia broke the silence.

"It's fine, Nate. I don't need their approval and if you do, we can stop hooking up."

"I don't," I replied as fast as humanly possible.

"Okay, well, I need coffee. Can we go downstairs now?"

I nodded and reached for her hand, needing to touch her soft skin one more time before walking her back into the lion's den.

I'd hoped to avoid my parents, but wasn't surprised to find them in the kitchen. Luckily, Olivia and I had kept our distance as we rounded the corner into the room, so they had no reason to suspect anything. I showed Olivia to the coffee bar near the large picture window. We had one of those fancy machines that made cappuccinos, but there were also large carafes of coffee, along with any syrups, creams, or other additions someone would want to make. I started to pour Olivia a cup of coffee, but my dad squeezed in between us.

"I could make you a latte if you'd like," he offered, leaning close like he'd just promised her some secret treasure map.

"Oh, I'm fine with just basic coffee," she mumbled, dropping her eyes to the floor.

My father hesitated, then started to refill his own mug. His hand brushed against Olivia's arm in what she hopefully interpreted as an inadvertent, casual touch, but I could've sworn it was intentional. Then, a beverage napkin fluttered to the floor and when Olivia bent to retrieve it, my dad's gaze landed directly on her ass.

I scowled pointedly at him when he turned back to me, but my perverted and arrogant father simply smirked and offered me a shrug.

"Ella could make you an omelet if you like," my dad said to Olivia.

"Olivia isn't a breakfast person," I replied before she could ask who Ella was. It was definitely too early to admit we had full time staff at the house.

Olivia shot me a desperate look just as I'd realized my mistake. Luckily, neither of my parents seemed too suspicious about my familiarity with Olivia's breakfast habits.

"Let's head to the sunroom," I said to Olivia, eager to help her escape my father's leering, ideally before she noticed it.

* * *

- Olivia -

*A*fter surviving an awkward breakfast with Nate's parents, I won my final match of the tournament. That afternoon, I even made it through an interview without forgetting how to speak. All in all, I considered the weekend a success.

The local media's sudden interest in my talent was unnerving though. Since I'd been winning my games for years without reporters or journalists caring, I assumed the Aldridge family had something to do with the new coverage. The local paper printed an article about my tennis career, and a reporter had interviewed me right alongside the coaches when we'd returned to campus. It was...weird. I clipped a copy of the article to send my mom, but other than that, I wasn't really sure what to do with the newfound attention.

I'd never particularly enjoyed being in the spotlight, and I wasn't eager for more attention now. It felt premature, drawing attention to my successes when I wasn't yet even in my final year at the university. If more people started watching and rooting for me, maybe I'd develop a nervous tic or stop playing so well. I consoled myself with the theory that few people paid much attention to news stories about college tennis players anyway. Maybe no one had actually heard the news.

As I left practice the next week, I learned I was wrong.

Nate and I had planned to grab some food and study together. I hoped that would lead to amazing sex and keep my mind off the embarrassing slew of media attention. I adjusted the strap of my racket across my shoulder and turned to Nate while we walked. He shielded his phone with his hand, angling it to the side and wincing to see through the glare. I wondered what was so important that he couldn't wait until he reached the shade of his car.

"Worried you missed a call from your girlfriend?" I teased.

Before Nate could answer, a man stepped onto the sidewalk, blocking our path. I would've just walked around him, but there was something oddly familiar about the guy. He looked to be in his early forties, with sandy blond hair and sunglasses that likely cost more than my rent. He was tall and his khaki shorts and polo shirt displayed just enough of his athletic build to make me wonder if he was a former tennis pro.

"Olivia? Olivia Roberts?" he said.

I stopped in my tracks, thoroughly confused. "Yes?"

The guy gawked at me a moment longer, then lifted his sunglasses off his nose and shifted them to his head.

A part of me must have realized who he was the instant I saw those cerulean blue eyes. I'd always wondered if that would happen—if I'd instinctively know the moment I first saw him.

I stepped forward only to stop abruptly as Nate's hand nudged me back with a soft touch.

"Can we help you with something?" he asked.

The man's mouth fell open. "I…" He staggered forward slowly, as though pulled towards me rather than choosing the movement. Not once did his eyes leave my face. "I thought she had an abortion," he finally said.

"Excuse me?" Nate said. He gripped my elbow and tugged me in the opposite direction.

I shook free and turned back to the man. "How do you know my name?"

He cleared his throat and blinked, breaking the trance. "It was on the news, the tournament that you won. You have her last name. And then I saw your picture—"

"Whose last name?"

"Your mother's."

"Liv," Nate said, his brows tightly furrowed. "Do you know this guy?"

I was certain I didn't, and yet at the same time…

"I'm her father," the man said.

Nothing about his words surprised me, yet hearing them aloud caused the bile to churn its way up my throat.

Nausea washed over me. "I don't have a father."

"Did she tell you I was dead?" he asked.

I opened my mouth to answer but quickly snapped my lips together. I owed this man nothing. He didn't get to waltz onto campus and accost me on my tennis courts demanding explanations.

He waited in vain for another moment and then reached into his pocket. He stepped closer and handed me a business card, but I couldn't tear my gaze away from his face long enough to even read his name. Aside from the eyes, the resemblance was negligible. But still, I sensed he wasn't lying about our connection.

"I honestly had no clue you even existed until Tuesday. I'm sorry. I, um, well, my number is on the card. If you call sometime, we could get coffee or something. I don't know. Or maybe hit some balls around."

"You play tennis?"

He shrugged. "Used to. Had a killer backhand," he added with a cheeky grin, as though that quality was genetic.

We stared at each other for another minute, and then he turned and left.

I watched as he walked off and climbed into a tiny red sports car that screamed "midlife crisis." Once he was gone, I gazed down at the business card.

Peter Wilkerson, Consultant.

I now knew five things about this unexpected man. His name was Peter, he worked in business, he was rich, and he played tennis. Also, he was apparently my father.

I snapped out of my thoughts and turned to Nate, who simply stared back, wide-eyed and slack-jawed.

Typical guy.

I glanced at my phone, realizing I had at least another hour before my mom was off work. "Shit."

Nate placed his hand on my back rubbing in small circles like I did when my roommate was sick from drinking too much. "Do you think he's telling the truth?"

I blew out the breath I'd been holding. "Yeah, I do."

He nodded, seemingly relieved by this response. I wanted to know why he was so quick to believe the man too, but I couldn't focus on anything other than the list of questions for my mother.

"Are you going to call him?"

"I don't know. I need to speak with my mom."

"Do you want to talk about it?"

"I need to call my mom," I repeated. "Rain check on the study date?"

I barely thanked Nate for the ride when he dropped me at my apartment, too eager to get to my computer. I spent the next hour using every internet tracking skill I possessed to learn everything I could about Peter Wilkerson. Mostly, I just stumbled across details about his professional life. I found nothing that either collaborated or disproved my mother's story, but I had a growing suspicion that this man wasn't exactly the evil rapist she'd painted him to be.

I called my mom four times before she finally answered.

"Hi baby," she greeted me. "How was your day? Are you just getting home from practice?"

I relished the comfort and ease with which she spoke, certain I was about to make the conversation tense.

"No, I'm home, doing homework." I heard the familiar clank of dishes in the background. "Are you still working?"

"No, but I just had a bite here at the diner. I told Kelly I'd wait around 'till she's off and we can go get a drink somewhere decent."

I didn't want to have this discussion with her in public, but I couldn't wait any longer. "Peter Wilkerson came to see me today. He said he's my father." I paused. "I have his eyes."

My mom swore under her breath. "Baby I can't talk about this here. Why don't we table this until tomorrow?"

"I've waited twenty-one years, Mom. I'm not okay with another hour, let alone another day. I want answers."

My mom didn't answer, but I could tell she was moving. After a moment, the background noise had disappeared. She must have gone outside.

"I need a cigarette," she mumbled.

I'd never smoked, but I had to agree this seemed like the occasion for one.

"What do you want to know?" she finally asked.

"Is he my father?"

"Yes."

I held my breath. Mom hadn't paused, hadn't wavered in the slightest. "You knew all along who he was and didn't tell me."

"It was easier that way."

"For who?"

"Everyone! He didn't want anything to do with you. I didn't want you asking a bunch of questions and trying to make him out to be some knight in shining armor in your mind."

"He said he didn't know about me, that you told him you got an abortion."

Now she paused. "He wouldn't have been involved anyway. They made that perfectly clear."

They? "Who did?"

"Peter. And his family. They hated me, treated me like trash."

I squeezed my eyes shut and focused on my breathing while she trailed off into her rant. I knew this part already. My mom didn't like rich guys. Guys like my father, apparently.

Guys like Nate. They were all the same and they were all trouble.

"Did he rape you?" I braced myself for her response the instant the words left my mouth.

"Do you think I'd make that up?"

I didn't answer. She'd just admitted to fabricating much of her story about my conception, so of course I was questioning her honesty. I wanted to think that my mom's story had at least a shred of truth to it, that she *was* the woman I'd believed her to be my entire life, but I also wanted it to be a lie. I'd only seen the briefest glimpse of this man and already I wanted him to be a good person. I needed him to not be a rapist at least.

"Honey, it's complicated."

"It's really not. Either he forced himself on you or he didn't."

My mom blew out a sigh and I wondered if she actually had bummed a cigarette off someone. It would figure if this was what started her up smoking again, after years without so much as a hint of nicotine.

"We had a thing, Peter and I. We weren't exactly dating...he had some preppy girlfriend at a different school, anyway. But we hooked up from time to time. We were both drinking, and we argued, and then I woke up pregnant. I'm sure I either said no or I was too drunk to consent anyway."

I rolled my eyes at my ceiling.

"The rest of the story is true. He wouldn't even talk to me after that, acted like he didn't know who I was. He would've been a terrible father."

My mother kept talking, rambling on about how terrible he was, how lucky I'd been not to have him in my life, but I couldn't even hear her words. A buzzing filled my ears and grew louder and louder.

"Okay, Mom," I interrupted. "I have to go. Tell Kelly I said hi."

I hung up before she could say anything else. I shook my head, trying to shake off the buzzing, but to no avail. I wanted to scream. No, I needed to scream. I needed to run. And I needed to hit something. Hard.

"Want to hit some balls?" I texted Nate.

"It's 9:30," came his quick response.

I supposed that was a no.

I tossed my phone onto my bed and stripped off my jeans. I changed into joggers and a sports bra and zipped a thin hoodie over that before lacing up my sneakers.

I grabbed my phone and my racket, then took off.

It was darker than I'd anticipated, but that was okay. I could turn the lights on at the courts if necessary. The roads were relatively empty, which wasn't surprising for a weeknight.

I jogged the rest of the way to the courts, enjoying the way my legs felt as I picked up the pace. But I needed more. When I arrived, I got the lights on, then dumped my racket and phone on the bottom row of bleachers and began jogging up and down the center aisle. I went as fast as I could go without falling, embracing the burn as my lungs struggled to pull in enough oxygen.

When I was tired enough that I started to worry about tripping, I stopped, sinking to the cold metal seat.

"You're insane, you know?"

I flew off the seat at the sudden noise, then quickly relaxed as I saw Nate approaching.

I took a few breaths then sat back down. "Yeah. I'm aware."

He joined me on the bleachers, sitting so close that our thighs touched. "Good. Just so you know."

I noticed Nate had brought his racket, but he was clearly not dressed for tennis. And now that I'd sprinted, I no longer felt compelled to hit balls until my arms were weak.

"Didn't go well with your mom?" he asked.

I shrugged. I couldn't envision any path that discussion could've taken as being good.

"She confirmed he's my father. And that she knew it all along but chose to tell me that she didn't know his name."

Nate placed his hand on my thigh but took his time answering. "Well, that's understandable, given what happened."

"Except that's not what happened."

His eyebrow rose.

"He didn't rape her. She said they'd been together before. It sounded like it was all totally consensual but then he was a jerk and she got her feelings hurt or whatever."

Silence fell everywhere. It was still too early in spring for the bugs to be overly active, and the campus had apparently all gone to bed for the evening. My own breath was the only sound filling the air between us.

"Sorry," Nate finally said.

I leaned my head on his shoulder, nestling against him as he wrapped his arm around me. Nate had no fault in this whole ordeal, yet *he* was sorry. My mom—the person who basically orchestrated this whole ridiculous scenario—couldn't even muster the briefest of apologies. *Figured.*

"Are you going to call your father?"

"Eventually. I'd like to hear his side of the story."

"Do you think your mom was lying about him, maybe he's not actually a jerk?"

I considered that. "No, he probably is. I mean, how would he not know that she was pregnant? She couldn't have hidden a baby forever."

"Maybe he didn't see her again. Maybe he graduated?"

"Maybe." I blew out a sigh. From everything my mother had said —both that evening and over the years in her made up tales of the wild nameless frat boys—I got the impression my father was a lot like Nate. Well, or a lot like Nate seemed to be, before I got to know him. He was rich, his parents were probably judgmental snobs, and he liked sleeping with girls way down the social ladder from him.

Hopefully history didn't repeat itself in the rest of the story.

"I'm here, you know. If you want to talk about it sometime," Nate said, his voice soft.

"Thanks." As close as I felt to Addie and Mia, I couldn't imagine ever talking to them about this stuff. Even though my mom had, apparently, lied to me my entire life, it felt like a betrayal to even consider telling someone else.

Except Nate.

For some reason, I trusted him to listen without judgment and to keep my terrible family secrets to himself. But I still didn't know what to say or even how to feel about it all. I'd spent my entire life thinking my own dad was a monster. Actually, I'd grown up thinking *all* men were monsters. My entire world view was based on a lie.

So what did that mean for me?

"Your legs are like ice," Nate said. "Can we please go home?"

I nodded and let him pull me to my feet. "Okay, but I'm not sleeping over. I don't have anything to wear to practice tomorrow."

"Wear what you have on."

I glanced down. It was, actually, what I'd probably wear in the morning to practice.

"Well, I don't have any pajamas."

"You won't need pajamas for what I have planned."

I thwacked his shoulder.

"What? You need a distraction. I'm going to provide that. Over and over and over…"

I swatted him harder until he shut up and we both laughed.

CHAPTER FOURTEEN

- Nate -

*T*he day after Olivia's father randomly appeared in her life, my mom called to tell me she'd arranged a date for me with the daughter of one of her friends. It wasn't the first time my mother had pulled such a stunt, but it was the only time I could legitimately claim I was already seeing someone else.

Except I couldn't actually tell her that.

I was spending most of my free time with Olivia, including multiple overnights each week, but she still didn't want my family to know we were anything but friends. I'd never before been *that* guy, pressuring a girl to accept us as a real couple rather than just something casual, but with Olivia, I had no choice. I could easily see her enduring our current arrangement until the end of time whereas I, for once, wanted more.

I wanted to hold Olivia's hand in public, wanted to talk with Mason and Brogan about the hilarious things Olivia said. I wanted to have a reason to make other guys stop hitting on her. I wanted the whole world to know that the girl who could choose any man secretly spent her nights in my bed.

Ever since the night she'd stayed with me back home, I'd been planning to talk with Olivia… not so much to issue an ultimatum as to make sure she saw the benefits of no longer hiding our involvement. I didn't anticipate she'd be easy to sway, but I was persuasive and, in this instance, I was right. Olivia would eventually see it my way. Sure she was stubborn, but ultimately, she was reasonable. There was no reason for us to not be a normal couple.

Well, except that my timing sucked. I couldn't in good conscience pressure Olivia into anything at the moment, not when she was already processing something hugely life changing like this shit with her dad.

So I lied and told my mom I'd been dating a girl from my finance class and didn't want to jinx it so early in the relationship. My mom had been surprisingly accepting of that explanation and passed the phone over to my father. He proceeded to lecture me about my many failings the past week until, thankfully, his other phone rang with an incoming call from someone infinitely more important than his son.

* * *

- Olivia -

*W*hen I finally called Peter Wilkerson, we made plans to meet at a diner Sunday evening. Specifically, the same diner Nate had taken me months ago. I figured it wasn't Peter's type of place, and I wanted someplace that felt more comfortable to me than to him.

I hadn't intended to guilt Nate into coming along. But when he offered, I couldn't deny that the promise of his presence made me infinitely more at ease with the dinner. Nate and I arrived early at the diner and sat together, Nate eagerly distracting me with a collection of offensive memes on his phone. But as soon as the bell above the dingy glass door chimed signaling Peter's entrance, Nate moved to a barstool at the counter.

Peter greeted me awkwardly and thanked me for agreeing to meet him. Then, we sat, both of us suddenly feigning interest in the sticky menus.

I peered over the top of my menu at the man. My father. Dad. Peter. Or was it Pete?

That was weird. I should know what to call the person who contributed fifty percent of my DNA.

He looked fairly similar to how I'd pictured him over the years. Actually, he looked a bit like a Ken doll.

"Is your wife's name Barbie?" I blurted out, eying his thick gold wedding band.

He frowned, clearly confused. I pointed to his ring.

"Oh. No."

He turned back to his menu, practically hiding behind the plastic-sheathed pages. Since my mother was a brunette with hazel eyes, I'd always assumed my father would look more like me. Peter fit the bill perfectly. His sandy blond hair was a smidge darker than mine, but his bold blue eyes were eerily reminiscent of the ones that stared back at me in the mirror each morning. He did, however, look much younger than I'd pictured.

"How old are you?"

"Just turned forty-one."

So that made him a little over a year older than my mom.

"What's your birthday?" he asked.

I told him, trying not to dwell on how depressing it was that my father didn't know such basic information. He nodded in response, probably trying to do the mental math and figure out how old he would've been when I was born.

"Mom was eighteen when I was born," I offered.

Peter nodded again just as the waitress arrived. He gestured for me to order first, and I did. Then, he ordered a burger and fries. As the waitress left with the menus, I glanced over at Nate.

He was seated at the counter, sipping his milkshake with his back to us, but his legs were angled to the side, so I could tell he'd been turning to check on us frequently.

"Does your boyfriend want to join us?"

"Not my boyfriend."

"Bodyguard?" he asked with an awkward smile.

I laughed at that. "He's fine over there."

Yet another uncomfortable silence ensued.

"You don't actually think I'd hurt you, right?" Peter asked suddenly.

I shook my head. "Nate is a friend. He's on the men's tennis team. And he can be a tad overprotective." I paused. "Although, my mom did tell me that you raped her, so…"

"I did not!"

His voice was loud enough that Nate turned quickly. I offered him a sweet wave before turning back to Peter.

"I figured. She has a lot of anger stored up about how things went down between you two. After you showed up after my tennis practice, I talked to her about it and she explained a little more. But, that is the story she'd told me my entire childhood."

"That I was a rapist?"

I shrugged. "She said that she was drinking at a fraternity party and several of the rich frat boys took advantage of her and she didn't even know who my father was."

He winced.

"Now her story seems to be that she knew it was you, but you were an irresponsible, self-absorbed asshole and you wanted nothing to do with me, so she thought it would be easier to tell me the rape story and let it serve as a cautionary tale."

"I never knew you existed."

I raised an eyebrow at his dubious tale.

"She told me she was pregnant. We weren't even together really. We had just…well, you know, a couple times. She told me she was on birth control."

I rolled my eyes dramatically. Of course in his mind, birth control was always the woman's responsibility.

"I was in college. I didn't have time for a baby," he paused, and his cheeks flushed. "And I had a girlfriend."

"Pig," I mumbled, reaching for my soda.

"I went to my parents and my mom said she'd talk to her."

"So you're also a momma's boy," I deduced.

He gritted his teeth. "My mom came back and said that your mom wanted an abortion. I called your mom to make sure that was true, that my mom hadn't pressured her or anything. She said it was and that she never wanted anything to do with me again."

"So you just disappeared, lived your stress-free life, and left my mom to raise me all alone without a college degree or any viable source of income," I concluded, knowing how that part of the story went at least.

"My mother gave her fifteen thousand dollars to stay out of my life," he said.

My stomach tightened. My mom, not surprisingly, hadn't mentioned that detail. But the more I thought about it, it changed nothing. "Is that supposed to make this better? Do you have any idea how child support laws even work? With your income, you probably owed her twice that for every year of my life."

"I didn't know you existed," he repeated, swallowing. "And if you need money, I can—"

"I don't." I interrupted, shaking my head. I blew out a sigh. I had waited my whole life to meet this man, and now I was just picking fights.

He narrowed his eyes until frown lines appeared at the edges, aging him a few years.

"Do you go by Peter or Pete?" I asked.

"Peter."

"And you're a consultant," I said, remembering his business card said that. "What's your work like?"

He told me about it for a few minutes, and then our food arrived. We spent an inordinate amount of time fiddling with the condiments to mask the fact that we'd both lost our appetites.

"How long have you been married?"

"Two years."

"What's her name?"

"Stella."

"Do you have any kids?" I asked.

He nodded slowly. "Two sons. Logan is eleven and Noah is nine."

So I had two brothers. Well, half-brothers. I'd always wanted a sister, and hadn't really pictured my life with a little brother, but I supposed it was a nice surprise. "You waited until they were seven and nine to get married?"

"Carol, my ex-wife, she's their mom. We divorced three years ago. She has custody of the boys. I see them on weekends, some holidays, and for a couple weeks in the summer."

"When did you and Carol get married?"

"Right out of college." Peter paused, clearly uncertain if he should continue. "She was my girlfriend in college."

"Ahh, the one you cheated on with my mother?"

He nodded sheepishly.

"She never knew about my mom? Or me?"

Peter shook his head. He reached for his burger and took a bite before continuing. "Carol was a family friend. I mean, our parents were friends. It was almost like an arranged marriage. We were never really in love, I guess."

"Did you love my mother?"

Peter hesitated again. "No."

At least he was honest. I dipped another French fry in ketchup before biting off the tip.

"Your mom was...a force to be reckoned with. She was care-free and fun and wild. I'd never met anyone like her." Peter smiled. "But we had nothing in common and never would've had a chance at a real relationship. My mother would've had a heart attack if I brought your mom home for dinner."

I stared pointedly, hoping he'd realize how offensive his words were.

He didn't.

Not surprising.

"So you married the girl your mom liked, popped out some babies, and then lived happily ever after until you fell for your secretary?"

He froze mid-bite and gazed up at me.

"I was kidding. Seriously? Your secretary?"

"Stella was an intern at the time, not a secretary."

I rubbed my temples. I wished I had some Hollywood connections so I could sell this depressing story to a soap opera or something. "Could you be more of a cliché?"

He shrugged. "I loved Stella."

"Right. So you abandoned your family for her and now you're living happily ever after."

"I didn't abandon anyone. Carol divorced me when she found out about the affair."

"Again, not exactly her fault. You cheated. Your behavior ended that marriage, not hers."

His chest rose and fell as he gazed back at me as though trying to figure me out. Finally, he spoke again. "Well, Stella and I have now separated, so I guess that one's probably my fault, too."

"I'm sorry," I said. And I meant it. He did look sad when he talked about her, and the fact that he left his ring on seemed to mean something.

He nodded appreciatively. "Tell me about yourself. You're obviously good at tennis and smart. Feisty, too."

I chuckled at that part, assuming Nate would agree with his assessment.

"I'm here on a tennis scholarship. Mom's been a waitress my whole life, so I've known for years that tennis was my only hope at college. I mean, my grades were good, but not that good. And then I'm using school loans to cover my living expenses."

"I'm sorry," he said. "If I'd know, I…"

I shrugged. "I probably wouldn't be so good at tennis if I'd had any other way to pay for college, so it's fine. I'd never say I had an easy childhood, but it made me who I am today. And I'm strong."

"I can tell," he said, nodding. He glanced over at Nate, who was staring at us again. "So your…friend…he plays tennis too?"

"Yeah. He graduates this year. His father is on Wall Street so he's going to work with him."

"He seems to like you."

"He does. But if his parents knew he liked me, they'd probably react the same as when your parents found out about my mom."

Peter frowned. "I doubt that. You're…you're a nationally ranked player. I read that scouts have been trying to get you to go pro."

"I grew up in a shitty apartment along the railroad tracks. I have a single mom who waits tables and bounces from man to man like they're dinner specials. Sometimes I walk to class because I'll be short on rent if I take the bus too much. I'm not the kind of girl a boy like him brings home."

I paused, feeling vindicated that that, at least, seemed to raise guilt in Peter. Then, I added, "I might someday be his Stella, but I'm no Carol."

Peter made a face and nudged his barely-touched burger to the side. "I have money," he said. "I can pay for your apartment, or the bus, or…hell I could buy you a car." He reached for his wallet as though he were going to find enough cash in there for a car.

"I don't want your money," I said.

He stared at me, then frowned.

"This is all really strange for me right now. I spent my whole life hating you, thinking you were this monster, and now it's just going to take some time for me to adjust to the real story."

"You don't think I'm a monster now?" he asked.

I shook my head. "No. A fuckup maybe, but..." I shrugged. "And I know you feel guilty for everything—as you should—but paying me off isn't going to help anything."

He stared, then slowly nodded. "Okay."

The waitress handed Peter the bill. He slipped cash inside and returned it.

"Do you think you'll ever mention me to Carol? Or your boys?"

He considered that for a moment. "Would you like to meet them? The boys, I mean."

"I think so. I've never had siblings."

"Sure. Yeah. I might as well. Carol already hates me."

I stood slowly, then nodded to Nate. He rushed over.

Peter extended his hand to Nate and introduced himself. "I'm not sure we formally met the last time we saw each other."

"Nathaniel Aldridge," Nate said, returning the handshake.

"Any relation to Jameson Aldridge?"

Nate nodded uncomfortably. I cleared my throat, eager to leave.

Luckily, Peter took the hint. "Well, thanks for bringing Olivia here. And babysitting to make sure she wasn't in any danger."

Nate laughed."Oh, I was here for your safety, not hers. Liv can handle herself. It was you I was worried about."

Peter offered me a sheepish smile, then stepped out of the diner.

CHAPTER FIFTEEN

- Nate -

I wasn't surprised when Olivia wanted to hit balls right after meeting her dad. She invited me along, but I declined. I had homework, a fraternity meeting, and some papers from my dad that I was supposed to have already reviewed. I offered to wait at her apartment while she changed clothes so I could drive her to the courts, but she insisted on running there instead. Clearly, the reason Olivia was so successful was because this was the way she handled stress—running and hitting balls on her only day off of practice.

By the time I reached my apartment, I had less than an hour until I needed to leave for the frat house. That wasn't enough time for any meaningful progress on my homework, so instead, I broke the seal on the manila envelope a courier had delivered days before. My dad had asked me to review the contents of the envelope and fax signed versions back to him the day I received it, but I hadn't. I already knew what was in the envelope, and I wasn't particularly eager to finalize it.

I pulled out the thin stack of papers, skimming the cover

letter. It was a form letter, informing me that Jameson Enterprises was extending an internship to me upon my graduation. I chuckled at the ridiculousness of it all, certain I was reading an exact copy of the letter sent to real applicants—the ones who had worked hard to qualify for the position, applied for the job, and even interviewed. My letter might as well have been signed the day I was born, since that was all I'd done to merit the job offer.

I flipped through the remaining pages, detailing such trivial facts as starting dates, job expectations, and salary. The position was contingent in enrollment in an approved MBA program, which I knew my father had already handled on my behalf, and the assumption was that I'd be promoted to associate upon graduation from that program.

I went back and read the pages more carefully, my stomach churning as I paused on each pertinent detail. The salary—which didn't even include the full tuition repayment promised for my graduate education—was comically high for an intern. I tried to recall the precise amount of the monthly trust fund payments I'd begin receiving upon my graduation, suspecting my gross earnings right out of school were about to surpass that of most hardworking adults at the peak of their careers.

As I poised my pen above the first blank, I couldn't shake the feeling that I was signing away my soul. I hesitated a moment longer, then scrawled my initials in each of the first several blanks before signing and dating the last page. I wasn't kidding anyone by pretending I had a choice in the matter. My fate had been sealed decades ago.

* * *

- Olivia -

*T*he next week flew by, with tennis occupying way more of my time than usual as the weather heated up. I hadn't realized how spoiled I'd become in the off-season. Had I been involved with a guy outside the tennis world, he might not have understood, but Nate was well-versed in the sleep-tennis-class-tennis-sleep way of life. He was every bit as busy as me, if not more, since he also had graduation-type activities to contend with.

I'd made plans to stop by Peter's house and meet his kids after my next match in that area. To my surprise, he'd actually brought the boys—my half siblings, to my game. After, I rode back to Peter's house with him and the boys, stopping for ice cream on the way, and then enduring a painfully awkward tour of their house.

Much to my relief, it was just a house, not a full-on estate like Nate had grown up in. Granted, it was a nice house, especially considering it was just Peter living there the majority of the time. The two-story brick home contained four bedrooms, an over-sized, modern kitchen, and a large, private yard, surrounded by mature trees and well-manicured flowers. I was a tad envious of the boys, having the chance to grow up in such a place.

Logan and Noah were both shy, and seemed about as uncertain about what to make of me as I was of them. I didn't get to meet Carol or Stella, but that did not surprise me. As it neared dinner time, Peter offered to drive me back to the hotel where the rest of the team was staying. It was obvious he didn't really want to leave the house though, and besides, there was no reason for the boys to come back out again. I could've called Nate for a ride, but instead, I took a cab, accepting the hundred-dollar bill Peter handed me to pay for the ride. It was more money than the ride would cost, even with tip, and we both knew it. But I was too tired to refuse the extra, although I did wonder how much of his guilt this tiny sum would actually assuage.

When I got back to the hotel, Nate and the rest of the team were already there. Mason had snuck off to some girl's room, leaving Nate and I free to enjoy the privacy of their shared hotel room. Nate tried to make conversation about Peter, but I wasn't interested. The day had been exhausting enough without now un-piling all of the details and analyzing it to death.

So instead, I stripped. I invited Nate to join me in the shower. He did, and by the time we made it back to the bed, neither of us had energy left for serious discussion.

We sprawled out across the stiff bed and after a few minutes, Nate grew so still that I thought he might have fallen asleep. That would've been okay, except neither of us had set an alarm so I didn't dare fall asleep. And I was so comfortable, tucked against the side of his body with my head propped on his firm chest, that the risk of me dozing off was a very real risk.

But then, Nate spoke.

"We can't keep doing this," he said, his voice gravely with sleep.

"Set your phone alarm," I said with a yawn, letting my eyes drift shut.

"What? No, I mean *this*." He swept my hair out of my face and I felt his chest muscles flex as he raised his head to look at me. "The sneaking around."

"Relax. We're not doing anything wrong."

"I agree. So why does it have to be a secret?"

I sighed. There would definitely be no napping now, and if we were going to discuss serious shit, I needed my own space. I felt too vulnerable pressed against his bare skin.

"I'm not your girlfriend, Nate. There's no point in telling people, not now especially."

"What does that even mean, not now?"

"It means we have an expiration date. You're graduating, moving, starting your life. I'll still be here." I glanced around the hotel room. "Okay, well, not *here* per se, but you know what I mean. You're moving on and I'm not. It may feel like we're in the same place now, but we really aren't. And in a couple months it'll be blatantly obvious that we are worlds apart."

"So you're just going to keep sleeping with me until I graduate and then we'll just wave goodbye and go on our merry ways?"

The unfamiliar bitterness to his voice unsettled me. I hadn't meant to upset him, not when I'd just been feeling so happy and relaxed with him. I wanted to lighten the mood. "No, I'll keep sleeping with you long after you graduate, whenever our paths cross. We're good at this part."

"The arguing?"

That hadn't been what I'd meant, but he was right. "Don't be like that, Aldridge. You know how I feel about you. I don't want to lose you. I'm just being realistic."

"No, you're being stubborn," he retorted, pushing up to his elbows. The position made his biceps bulge and he looked like a cover model for a men's fitness magazine. "Have you ever even considered that you're wrong about us? That if we stop hiding everything and have a real relationship, that we could actually keep dating after I graduate? I'm not moving that far away. It won't even count as a long distance relationship."

I let my gaze drift over him for a moment, then forced myself to look away. "What do you want from me? You really just want to tell the team? Is that what this is about? You need the guys to all know about your conquest?"

Nate snorted. "They all know. The way you look at me? We're not fooling anyone."

I agreed with his conclusion. They all knew, even the coaches. But it certainly wasn't *my* fault. "I don't look at you any certain way," I insisted, glancing over at him to prove it. But damn if he didn't look ridiculously sexy, his skin still flushed and his hair still mussed from our recent activities.

Nate's response was laughter from deep in his chest. "You're literally doing it now. I can't tell if you want to eat me or…"

I swatted his side to shut him up. "Then put on a shirt if you want me to take you seriously."

Unfortunately, he did just that. *Damn.*

"If not the team, who are you so worried about finding out? Your mom?"

I cringed. My mom would love Nate. She'd probably hit on him and then she'd praise me for finding someone like him who could take care of me. In other words, she'd assume exactly what everyone else would assume. Despite that, *my* mother hadn't been my primary reservation. "More like *your* mother."

"I'm not scared of my parents."

"Can you honestly tell me they won't assume I'm some gold digger?"

He sighed. "It doesn't matter what they think. I know you aren't."

"Right. And you know how I feel about you. So it doesn't matter if they think we're friends or something else. It's not their business."

He was visibly annoyed at how I'd turned his words around on him, so I continued.

"Look, we are so good together. Let's enjoy what we have while it lasts. I don't want to waste time with you arguing about what your parents might think when they'll never need to know."

Frown lines appeared between his brow. "I'm not your dad, Liv. I don't have some Carol waiting on the sidelines."

I sighed. "Maybe you should."

Nate ruffled his hand through his hair. "This is stupid. We're both tired, you've had a stressful day, let's just go to sleep. Okay?"

Finally, something we agreed upon.

CHAPTER SIXTEEN

- Nate -

Olivia flew out of bed in the morning when the alarm went off, claiming she needed to get back to her room in case her coach checked on them. I kissed her goodbye and said nothing, certain she already knew that I realized her words were a lie. Olivia just wanted to get away from me before I forced her to talk about our future anymore. I wondered if she'd even tell Mia where she'd spent the night. I groaned into a pillow, then convinced myself to think about something else.

If I pushed Olivia too hard, I'd never win. She was the most emotionally closed-off woman I'd ever dated, plus between her mom's made-up stories about men and her father's actual track record, Olivia had very good reason to resist a normal relationship. She'd literally never seen a relationship work out in the real world. To be honest, I wasn't sure I had, either. My parents were still married and still happy, on the surface anyway. But, my dad had been unfaithful at least a handful of times, if not more. And if I knew, surely my mom did, too.

I pushed all the serious thoughts out of my mind and worked

on homework until Mason returned. Then, we met up with the rest of the team in the hotel lobby for the continental breakfast. Olivia was there with Mia, chugging coffee like it was air she needed to breathe. She smiled politely at me and asked how my morning was, like I hadn't just been inside her hours before. Olivia was equally friendly with Mason, then left to chat with Coach Katelyn.

My games were at different times and different courts from Olivia's match, so I didn't see her the rest of the day. When a text came in that night, my first thought was that it was her, checking in on me, saying hi, or maybe even inviting herself over.

I cringed at the sight on the caller ID. It was Cassie, my stalker.

"A little birdie told me you don't have a date for your fraternity formal yet," was all she'd written, but the implication was clear enough.

Not living at the house anymore, it was easy for me to forget about most of the fraternity's social activities. Not that I minded them—on the contrary, most of them were fun. But between my classes, the grad school applications, tennis, and now Liv, there just wasn't time for much else. My senior year formal though, *that* I'd planned to attend. Especially since it fell on a Saturday evening following a home game, with no tennis whatsoever on the calendar for the next day. I quickly checked the women's schedule to confirm Olivia was free, then brainstormed excuses for Cassie.

If not for Olivia, I probably would've invited Cassie. She wasn't a person I'd choose to spend an eternity with on a deserted island, but I didn't doubt she'd be a blast at a party. More importantly, *she* wouldn't be embarrassed to show up with me. I didn't want to hurt her feelings by rejecting her, but telling her I was already going with someone else was a legit enough excuse. I decided to wait until the next day to reply to her text so that it was actually the truth.

* * *

- Olivia -

I wasn't avoiding Nate per se, but as he approached me after practice, it did occur to me that we hadn't actually spoken in private since our disagreement over the weekend.

I smiled, determined to move past that. "Hey there, Aldridge. How'd you play today?"

"Not bad. Listen, do you have a minute?"

If I were being responsible, I'd say no. I was behind on all of my classwork, thanks to tennis. But I'd never before been responsible when it came to Nate, so there was no reason to start now. "Of course. But literally just a minute. I've got to finish a paper tonight."

He nodded. "I need a date."

I felt my eyebrows dip. "And you're telling me? What, do you want, like, recommendations?"

Nate's eyes widened and then he deadpanned. "No, Liv. I'd like you to be my date."

"Oh." That made more sense. "No."

"You can't just say no. I—"

"I just did, and I already told you I'm busy."

He gripped my hand to stop me from walking away. "It's for my fraternity formal. It's my last one. I want to go. And I'd really like you to go with me."

At the mere thought of walking into his fraternity function with Nathanial Aldridge, my heart thudded so loudly I worried he could actually hear it. God, his frat brothers would have a field day with that one. I'd probably graduate before we lived it down. And the chances of Nate keeping that date from his family were close to zero.

"No thanks," I replied.

He scowled. "Liv, come on. Don't make me beg. Please?"

I glanced around us, relieved to see the other players had left. Still, I didn't want to make a scene. I shook my hand free. "That isn't what we do, Nate. You and I both know you can get a different date. Invite someone your frat brothers will like, someone who can get along with all of their dates."

"I don't want a different date. I want you. Why can't you just admit you'd have fun with me?" He flung his hands up dramatically. "We had one bad date, right? But that was ages ago. If we had a redo now, it would be a blast. You can't seriously pretend all I'm good for is sex."

I actually laughed out loud at that line. "I'm not even sort of pretending that's all you're good for, and this has nothing to do with that one horrifically bad date. It's just not a good idea. I'm not comfortable going, okay?"

Nate's gaze dropped to the sidewalk. He shuffled his foot against a pile of gravel near the curb, shaking his head.

"I promise I'll understand if you take someone else," I reiterated.

He blew out a sigh, then after a painfully long minute, raised his eyes back to me. "You seriously won't just do one little thing for me? It's one night, Olivia. Like three hours of your life. It doesn't interfere with tennis and you don't even have practice or a game the next day. I'll even buy you a dress."

"Right, because of course it's about the money," I rolled my eyes, wishing I'd followed my instincts and left for the library right after practice. "You don't get it, Nate. I can't just jump into your world. You and I are not alike and we never will be. Why is it so important to you that I go to this? You just want to get me all dressed up before you humiliate me? Ask. Someone. Else."

I was panting by the time I finished my spiel. His expression was unreadable, but I assumed I'd made my point. I half expected Nate to apologize, to realize he was being ridiculous. But that isn't what happened at all.

He stared at me for a full minute, almost as though he

expected me to say something else. Then he licked his lips and bobbed his head, first up and down and then side to side, almost like he was having some argument in his inner monologue. Finally, he spoke.

"You know what? This is bullshit. I'm done. Before you got to know me, when you made these assumptions that I was just using you or mocking you or whatever evil, rich, frat-boy plot you thought I had going on, that was one thing. But now, you know me. If you seriously still think I'm the type of guy that would hurt you like that, then that's offensive. And this isn't going to work."

His deep brown eyes locked on mine just long enough for the full effect of his words to wash over me. Nate was the most confident person I'd ever met, and it was obvious now that he was crushed. I'd hurt him, badly, and I hadn't meant to at all. He'd taken my words, and completely twisted it all.

He turned abruptly and started towards his car.

"Nate, wait!" I called.

He spun around, shaking his head. "I can't, Liv. I just can't."

I stood there holding my racket like a fool until he was in his car, and long out of the parking lot.

CHAPTER SEVENTEEN

- Nate -

I was still in a shitty mood hours later. I should've just gone to bed, or at least taken Brogan up on his offer to grab a beer together, but what was I supposed to say to him? Some girl that I'd been seeing for months now just admitted she thought I was a complete douchebag? No thanks.

I was staring at my phone, debating how to respond to another text from Cassie, when my doorbell rang. I swung open the door, gasping at the person standing before me. She was drenched, with her matted hair covering a sizeable portion of her face. Her arms wrapped protectively around herself and she was huddled over, shivering. Her eyes were red and damp but I couldn't be sure if that was from crying or the rain.

"Olivia? Jesus, how long have you been out there?" I reached for her and tugged her into the apartment, kicking the door shut behind her to stop the torrent of sideways rain from following her in.

Olivia shook her head dismissively. "Just a minute. I came to talk to you, but then I changed my mind..." Her teeth chattered louder than her voice.

"Hang on," I said. I jogged to the bathroom, grabbed two bath towels and came back, wrapping both around her.

She accepted them, and didn't shrug my arms off when I lingered on her body, securing the towels in place. Olivia was still shaking violently, but I didn't know how to stop her while she still wore the soaking wet clothes. I gazed down and noticed the water pooling at her feet.

"Come here," I said, crouching down. "Let's get these wet shoes off."

"Oh God, I'm sorry. I'm soaking your floor. I didn't mean... I'll go."

I gripped her ankle firmly, holding her in place. "Liv, stop. I don't care about the floor, but if you get pneumonia and can't compete, your coach will kill me. We need to get you out of these wet clothes."

She let me help her out of her shoes, but then I wasn't sure what to do. The best thing for her would be a hot shower followed by dry clothes, but I wasn't about to strip her naked and force her into my bathroom.

"Did you walk here?" I asked.

She shook her head, "Bus."

I couldn't believe she'd gotten that wet in the short walk here from the bus stop. I let my eyes linger on her for a long moment. Sopping wet, her hair looked much darker than usual, but her face appeared paler in contrast. Maybe it was the way she was holding herself, curled up for warmth, but she looked so small, so fragile.

Instantly, I felt horrible for yelling at her earlier.

Moments ago, I'd still been pissed. I'd been nice to Olivia, treated her well, and still she acted like I was a class A jerk. I didn't deserve that, and I was stupid to let a girl treat me like that, even if she was the hottest girl I'd ever see. But now, guilt replaced my anger. Maybe I hadn't been as good to her as I'd thought. I was crude at times, not the most PC. Maybe she was right to question me.

I opened my mouth to apologize, but that isn't what came out. "Why are you here?" I asked instead.

Her teeth chattered loudly as she peered up at me through thick, damp eyelashes. "To talk. What you said earlier...I..." she shook her head. "You were wrong."

I suppressed an eye roll. "I wasn't wrong. I said how I felt. You don't get to tell me how to feel."

She sighed, rubbing her hands up and down her arms but still shaking.

It was pathetic to watch, so I took over for her, running my own hands over her body while she tightly clutched the towels in place.

"No, you made assumptions about how *I* feel and those were wrong."

Olivia's shaking intensified while I tried to piece together her words.

"This isn't working," I said.

"Let me finish."

"No, I mean warming you. I can't even concentrate on what you're saying with you shivering like that. Can you just go take a hot shower and then we'll talk?"

She made a face. "I don't want to get my hair wet."

I reached for her hair and squeezed a clump of it. Several ounces of water poured out.

"Oh," she mumbled. "Well, okay?"

I motioned for her to follow me back to the bathroom. "If you throw your clothes out to me, I can toss them in the dryer while you're showering."

"You can't dry jeans and a sweater," she insisted.

I blew out a sigh. Only Olivia would argue with me while freezing to death. "Fine, you can borrow some of my clothes."

As we reached the bathroom, I helped her out of the wet towels and her coat, started the shower, then ducked out to give her privacy. I was in my bedroom, trying to find any pants that wouldn't fall right off her when I heard her soft voice calling.

I dropped the stack of clothes I'd been holding and returned to the bathroom. Olivia had cracked the door open, her head and arm the only thing I could see.

"I think you're out of towels," she said sheepishly.

Duh. I had taken the bath towels out to dry her off. "There should be another somewhere," I said. "Can I come in?"

She hesitated, then reached for her shirt and backed up to allow me to open the door fully. The way she held her shirt, it covered a fair portion of the front of her body, but I suspected she didn't realize that the mirror behind her offered me the perfect view of her bare butt. I couldn't resist the tiniest glance before turning to search for a towel in the cabinet.

Breaking up with Olivia had been hard enough when she was fully clothed, but I didn't think I actually had the willpower to end things with a beautiful woman when she was naked. Why had I let my pride get in the way anyhow? So what if she thought I was a spoiled asshole? She made me laugh and the sex was good. Not just good—it was amazing. And Olivia was the most fascinating person I'd ever met. I could talk to her for hours.

Luckily, there was a towel in the back of the cabinet, under a stack of several bars of soap. I stood and handed it to her, disappointed to see that the steam of the shower had now fogged up the mirror enough to blur her reflection.

"You know, I've seen it all before," I said, my eyes gesturing to where she still clutched her shirt.

"Yeah, but you didn't hate me then."

As if I could hate her now. "I can see your ass in the mirror," I added instead.

Olivia glanced behind her then rolled her eyes. She stepped behind the shower curtain, tossing the shirt out at the last minute. I figured I should leave, but I didn't. If Olivia wanted me to go, she'd say so. Besides, if she already thought I was a pervert, what was the point?

She didn't say anything for a moment, so I wondered if she thought I'd left. But then she spoke.

"It wasn't raining when I left. My plan was just to come over and apologize and explain everything and then go. I wasn't even going to come inside," she said. "And now I've soaked your entire apartment and used up all your hot water."

"The apartment will dry and the water will regenerate," I said. "Wait, apologize?"

I thought I heard her sigh, but the sound of the water muffled it.

She took her time answering. "I didn't mean to make you feel bad. Honestly, I didn't even realize your ego was capable of being bruised."

I leaned back against the sink, having no response to that. Judging from the changes in the sound of the water hitting the shower floor, she was actually washing her hair and not just huddled under the water for warmth.

"I don't think you're a jerk," she finally continued. "Or a pervert or an entitled rich boy." She paused, adding, "Well, you are rich, but you can't help that."

I supposed it was good to hear her say, but it changed nothing. "Thanks for clarifying, but that hardly fixes our problem. I thought by this point, you'd know who I really am and accept that. I can't keep spending all my time trying to convince you I'm worthy of your affections."

The rings attaching the shower curtain to the rod screeched as she tugged it open a few inches. "You think *you're* not worthy?" she asked, confusion filling her beautiful face.

"I think that's what you think," I replied, my eyes dropping to the pool of water collecting on the bathroom floor from the gap in the curtain.

She followed my gaze and quickly tugged the curtain shut, mumbling an apology.

Olivia was silent for a moment, then continued. "I don't think that at all, Nate. I think... I think you are perfect. You're funny and sweet and thoughtful. You're generous, and you really listen. You really care about people, and while you're good at putting on a show and pretending to be this cocky jerk, you're actually one of the least stuck-up people I know."

I swallowed as a lump began to form in my throat. She sounded sincere, but none of that made sense. If she thought any of those things about me, then why—?

"You are so far out of my league, but you never treated me like some broke girl here on a tennis scholarship. You've always acted like I deserve to be here just as much as you do."

"You do," I said. If anything, she deserved it more. I got in based on my last name. Olivia actually worked to earn the grades and the tennis scholarship.

"You make me feel like I matter, like someone could actually see the real me. And I can never thank you enough for that. But that still doesn't mean we're a good fit for each other romantically."

Olivia wasn't making any sense, and it hit me that the only way I could really understand what she was trying to say was if I could see her face and read her expression. I shucked off my jeans and shirt, but stopped short of taking off my boxer briefs. The last thing I wanted was for Olivia to stop talking to me because she thought I was trying to seduce her.

"You deserve so much more than me, Nate. You deserve a woman you can take home to your family and who can fit into your world. You should have a woman you're proud of, and somebody who..."

Her voice trailed off as I opened the shower curtain and

stepped in to the other end of the shower. My breath caught in my throat as I saw her, standing directly under the spray of water, completely naked and vulnerable, devastatingly gorgeous despite the black smudges of makeup residue around her eyes.

"I *am* proud of you, Liv. You are literally the most amazing person I know," I said.

Her hand rose to her face, sliding her wet hair out of her eyes. And then her lips curled into a shy smile.

"You're still wearing clothes," she said, her eyes twinkling in a way that brought a smile to my face.

I opened my mouth to either explain or make some pervy offer to take them off, but nothing came out. Instead, I just stepped closer, cupping my hand around her jaw as water beaded off her face.

"You work harder than anyone I know. You're focused and determined and..." I shook my head. "How do you not see that?"

Olivia broke our gaze. "I'm good at tennis. That doesn't make me a good person."

I took another step closer. "Not being born into money doesn't automatically make you a bad one, either."

Her eyes flitted back up. "I know that. But it's not just the money. I'm not like you, Nate. I can't just accept things for how they are. I don't trust people, I always jump to conclusions, and I always assume the worst. I'm snarky and judgmental. You don't need that negativity in your life."

"But I need you," I said, the words rushing out of me with my next exhale.

"You deserve happiness, not someone who's going to complicate everything and drag you down with her grumpiness."

I stroked her cheek, searching her expression until those gorgeous eyes flitted open enough for me to really see her. "I don't know how to make you see yourself the way I see you and I hate that, but... Olivia, you're beautiful, inside and out."

I had something else to say, but all coherent thoughts left my brain when Olivia's eyes locked on mine. I slid my hand around her head, pulling her close as my lips slammed into hers. She hesitated, but the moment her lips parted for my tongue, I tugged her to me with my free hand, clutching her hip and then pressing her back against the wall of the shower.

The hot spray of the water only hit my back and shoulders, but my entire torso felt the heat. Olivia's fingers crushed my hair, holding me to her with a desperation that made my heart race. Her kiss was needy, as was mine, and the sensations consumed me. I could've stayed there for hours simply kissing her, but suddenly, her hands were gone from my body. I barely had time to register their absence before I felt her lower, struggling to drag my drenched boxer briefs off of me.

I laughed, but the sound was absorbed by our still-connected mouths. As she finally succeeded in her goal, I stepped out of the final, soaked article of clothing between us, and her hand reached for me. I let her stroke me twice before gripping her wrist and settling her hand above her head. As much as I relished her touch, I didn't need any more foreplay. My body had been primed and ready since the moment she'd showed up at my apartment, sad and wet. My need to cheer her up, to heal her inner pain, had kicked into over drive, consuming me.

I dipped my head down, drawing her nipple between my lips, releasing her hand from mine only to stoke her other breast. Her moans were muffled by the spray of the shower, but her fingers dug into my neck with the familiar desperation. My free hand roamed down her side, stroking the curve of her hip, her firm butt and the top of her muscular thigh. Olivia was perfect in every way possible. How did she not see that?

I could have stayed like that till the water ran cold, licking and sucking and nipping at her breasts, but Olivia nudged me away. I was painfully aware of my racing heart for the beat where I considered that maybe she was putting on the breaks. But then she gazed at me, with those sparkling sapphire eyes, her lips parted as if waiting for me to fill the space between them.

I felt my lips tug upward, unable to resist smiling at this exquisite woman, standing breathless in my shower, waiting for me, reaching for me. She kissed me as her hands gripped my biceps. My hand went for her thigh, lifting it slowly so as not to knock her off balance. She wrapped her leg around my waist as I found her entrance.

We made love slowly, our eyes locked on each other until we couldn't control it any longer. When I finally released her, gradually loosening my grip as if scared she'd melt to the shower floor, the water was ice cold, but my skin stung when the spray hit the backs of my arms. I glanced down, realizing Olivia's nails had pressed into my shoulders and arms, leaving little red marks.

"Ow," I mumbled, smiling despite the sentiment.

Olivia dragged her bottom lip in to her mouth, blushing. "Sorry?" she finally said, smoothing her hand over the marks.

She said it like a question, so I wondered if she already knew I didn't mind, that I'd happily let her claw my entire body if it meant being with her again. Especially like that. Something about our shared desperation made the entire experience feel even more intimate. If that was par for the course after a day apart, maybe there was something to be said for makeup sex after all.

Olivia shivered as I switched off the faucet. I yanked open the shower curtain only to remember that we had only one dry towel remaining. I grabbed it, wrapping it around her. She accepted, laughing, then pulled me into her embrace.

"You should invest in a robe," she said.

I didn't disagree. I stepped out of the shower, used a hand towel to dry off the rest of the way, then dashed to my room and grabbed a pair of thin sweats. By the time I returned to the bathroom, she was out of the shower, but her teeth had begun loudly chattering again.

"We're back to square one," I mumbled. "Come on."

She followed me to the bedroom. I tossed her some pajama pants and a tee shirt then pointed to the bed.

"Get under the covers and warm up. I'll go make some hot tea."

CHAPTER EIGHTEEN

- Olivia -

*F*or some reason, I didn't mind being bossed around by Nate this time. I pulled on the clothes he'd offered me then crawled under the covers, using a hair tie to wrap my hair on top of my head before leaning back against the headboard.

I couldn't help but smile when Nate returned. He always looked hot without a shirt, but something about the way his sweats hung loosely around his hips really accented the ridge between the muscles along his sides. He handed me a coffee mug, his expression sheepish.

I thanked him, peered into the cup, then laughed.

"It turns out I don't actually have tea," he explained.

"So you brought me a cup of hot water?"

Nate shrugged.

I supposed that was sweet. I took a sip, only to appease him, then set the mug on the nightstand and scooted over to make room for him beside me.

He stretched out along the edge of the bed, scooting one arm beneath me and angling me onto his chest. I sighed happily, settling into my happiest place in the world. Neither of us spoke for several minutes, but I could tell Nate was thinking about something by the way he mindlessly traced circles and swirls on my arm with his finger.

I was the first one to break the silence.

"That wasn't my intention when I came over here," I said.

"Do I look like I'm complaining?"

"You were right to end things with me. I'm a mess, and if you give me the chance, I'll only drag you down with me." I paused, but not long enough for him to jump in. "I just came here to apologize. I never even considered you'd think there was something wrong with you. That's just...crazy. I only wanted to set the record straight."

He loosened his grip on me, tilting his head until our faces met. "What record is that?"

I took my time answering. "That it's me, not you. *I'm* the reason this isn't working."

His brows dipped in unison. "The only reason it wasn't working was because I didn't know how you felt. Now I do, so everything is fixed."

"I'm sorry," I said, glad he agreed I was to blame.

I felt his lips press against my forehead, and they lingered there while he spoke.

"No, I'm sorry. If you don't see how special you are, that's on me. This is all my fault for letting you think there's something wrong with you."

"You didn't *let* me do anything," I said. "It's not your job to make me happy. You can't fix everything that's broken."

"I can try." He rolled to his side, nudging me off of him then pinning me beneath his arm. Normally, that was one of my favorite positions, trapped beneath him, my view limited to his perfectly carved facial features and firm rippling biceps. But now, it felt restricting. Vulnerable, even. I could close my eyes to avoid his inquisitive stare, but he'd still be able to see me and all my flaws.

"I get why you don't trust people, Liv. I wouldn't either if I were you. But I honestly don't understand how you could even question how incredible you are."

I turned my face to the side. "I don't. I'm basically like a superhero."

"Come on Liv. I'm being serious. You're the most beautiful woman I've ever seen. You're funny and smart and so intense that it scares me. You've worked hard for every single thing in your life and yet you're still generous with others."

I groaned. "I already put out, you know, so you don't have to flatter me."

"I'm not. Why do you constantly undervalue yourself? You are amazing and you deserve the world."

I kissed him, realizing that was the only thing that would shut him up. I knew Nate was being sincere, that for some unknown reason he actually believed I was some wonderful, fundamentally good person. And I loved that. I did, really. But seeing the way he looked at me, it was just too much, too intense.

I wouldn't have minded a second round of lovemaking, but it was late. After an extended kissing session, Nate reached over and switched off the light.

"We have practice early," he reminded me. "And you need sleep."

"I didn't brush my teeth."

"You rinsed with hot water. That's just as good," he teased, settling against me.

It wasn't, but I was too comfortable to protest. Nate stilled almost immediately, his breathing falling into a relaxed, even pattern that signaled he was asleep. I lightly stroked his hair, enjoying its softness and the unusual gift of being able to observe him without his knowledge. He really was a handsome man, although he looked almost boyish in his sleep.

I felt so safe when I was with him, and while I loved that security, it also scared me. The more attached I grew, the more it would hurt when this ended. I'd never before dreamed I'd let a man take care of me, but that was exactly what happened when I was with Nate. And sure, for now, it was innocent enough things —keeping me warm, fed, and well rested.

But I also knew Nate was the type of guy who would happily put his life on hold to take care of me for real and that, I didn't want. I didn't need a sugar daddy any more than I needed someone to fight off my inner demons. But right now, it sure felt good to have him in my corner.

I smiled, focused on the soothing soft hiss of his breath. I didn't have to figure out my entire future now. It was okay to just relax and enjoy this moment, to let myself be happy, with him.

"I love you," I whispered, feeling my grin widen at the slight sound of my words, even though no one else was awake to hear them.

* * *

- Nate -

I awoke with a jolt to the buzzing of my alarm. I blindly groped for my phone, only to discover the sound didn't stop when I tapped the screen. I struggled to sit with Olivia still sprawled across my chest.

"I'm trying to hit snooze," I said.

"It's not your alarm" she replied, her warm breath tickling my bare chest.

She was right. The horrible racket was coming from her

phone, which was across the room. We both eyed it with similar lack of interest in moving.

Olivia hopped up before I could. I rubbed my eyes, trying to figure out why I was so tired since we hadn't stayed up that late. But then, I remembered what had happened after we went to bed. It had felt like a dream at the time, and I'd been seconds away from sleep when it happened. But I wasn't asleep. And she wasn't, either.

Olivia Roberts had told me she loved me and it wasn't a dream.

Except, it was obvious she'd thought I was asleep at the time. I'd had to stay remarkably still for a half hour after Olivia spoke the words, desperate not to let on that I'd heard her. Then, when I was certain she was asleep and it was safe for me to follow suit, I'd spent a good chunk of time silently reveling in her admission. It wasn't just that I wanted to hear those words more than anything from her, but also that I'd honestly assumed she'd never love me, or at least that she wouldn't admit it. I'd started the prior day depressed and angry, and finished it the happiest I'd been in ages.

But once the initial ecstasy wore off, I was left pondering the rest. Why did Olivia say it when she thought I was asleep? What did that mean? Should I tell her I heard? Should I say it back to her at the first chance?

I gazed up at her now. Somehow, while I'd been daydreaming, she'd shucked the pajama pants and shirt I'd loaned her and pulled on a pair of my boxer briefs instead. My heart thudded uncontrollably.

I could tell her right then that I loved her, and it would be the truth. But Olivia looked so hot at that moment, that really any man would say the same to her and she'd probably dismiss it.

She gathered her hair behind her head and turned to face me while pulling the elastic band around the ponytail. I brought my hand to my jaw to keep it from dropping. It was ridiculous, really.

I mean, I'd seen breasts before. Hell, I'd seen her breasts before. But right then, I was pretty sure I could've died a happy man at that sight.

Olivia laughed and shook her head. She came back to the bed and climbed over me. "I don't have any of my tennis gear here, so you better hurry up and get out of bed. We'll have to swing by my place on the way to practice."

"I have zero motivation to move," I admitted. It was the truth. She made a face.

"You're wearing my underwear," I said.

She shrugged and climbed off the bed, much to my chagrin. "Yeah, I'd like an undershirt too. Not white."

"Third drawer," I said, wondering why she rejected the white one she'd worn all night.

She disappeared into the hall and returned, her black bra now covering her chest. She slipped a black undershirt over and then glanced at me. "All my other stuff is still wet. Probably shouldn't have left it in a pile on the bathroom floor."

I winced. That *had* been bad form. "I'll stick your jeans in the dryer," I said, crawling out of bed.

"You can't dry jeans."

"I dry mine all the time."

"You're a guy. Yours fit differently. Mine won't fit over my ass if they spend too long in the dryer."

I reached over and squeezed the ass in question. "Unless you have a better idea, I think that'll have to do. A few minutes won't hurt them."

She relented, and somehow, we even arrived at practice a few minutes early. Olivia stayed in the car, checking her texts or something on her phone, so I walked around to her side and opened the door for her.

"What a gentleman," she remarked, accepting my hand and climbing out. As she bent to grab her racquet, I couldn't help but glance under her skirt.

"Hey, you took off my underwear," I protested.

She slapped my hand. "Of course I did, perv."

Even as she called me names, I couldn't help but smile. The gorgeous, feisty woman in front of me loved me. How awesome was that?

Olivia raised an eyebrow. "Are you okay?"

I nodded. "Yeah. I had a good night. I like waking up with you."

She stared at me for a moment before her lips parted in a shy smile. "Yeah?" she asked.

I laughed at the ridiculousness of the question. Anyone who didn't like starting the day with her was insane. I reached for her hand, barely touching her fingertips. "Yeah," I said.

She wound her fingers between mine as she leaned back against the side of the car. "I don't know. I thought this morning was a little...boring. Maybe next time we should set the alarm ten minutes earlier."

I stepped closer, relieved to see her flirty side again so soon. "I can't accomplish much in ten minutes."

"Mmm, I think you could. When properly motivated, you can be very efficient."

Her fingers left mine to stroke the hem of my shirt then rest softly against my lower abdomen.

I angled my head down so our foreheads almost touched. "If you want to climb back into the car, we could see just how efficient I can be."

She opened her mouth to reply, but a voice called out behind us and jolted us both apart.

"Hey Aldridge!"

I dropped Olivia's hand and swiveled around to see Mason approaching. His steps slowed and his expression changed as his eyes honed in on Olivia.

I cast a furtive glance at her, trying to gauge her expression, but Olivia actually didn't seem too bothered.

"It's fine," she said. "He's your friend. You could just tell him. It's not like he's the coach."

I hesitated, wanting to ask what, precisely, I should be telling him. We hadn't exactly hammered out the parameters of our relationship, at least not while both of us knew the other was conscious.

"I need to go practice," she said, interrupting my internal quandary.

I backed up enough to let her slide out from between me and the car.

"Hi Mason," she called with a wave before jogging off to the far courts where the women's team was gathering.

I grabbed my things from the back of my car then turned to face the music.

"Uh what was that?" Mason asked.

"What?" I shrugged and acted as casual as possible.

"Don't even act like I didn't just interrupt something. That was…intense. Are you guys, um…?"

"Wait a minute. If you saw I was talking to someone, why'd you interrupt?" I asked, hopeful the abrupt subject change would help distract him.

"I didn't see her at first and it definitely didn't occur to me that Olivia Roberts was the person you were making out with at seven a.m."

"No one was making out."

"You rode here together?"

"She doesn't have a car. I've driven her to practice lots of times."

He nodded. "So she didn't sleep over at your place last night?"

I opened my mouth to answer, then just laughed. Mason was my best friend on the team. I couldn't just lie to him. And he knew exactly what my silence meant.

"Right," he continued. "And I suppose last night was the first night you two…"

I shook my head.

He blew out a sigh. "We're getting a drink and you're filling in some details here later."

We grabbed our rackets and headed onto the court to start warming up. We both stood by the net to stretch first.

"I don't see why this is all so surprising to you," I said. "We were both single, business majors, and tennis players, so it makes sense." I held my breath, hoping he wouldn't make a comment along the same lines as Olivia had, about how we were worlds apart in every other aspect.

"Yeah, I guess. But honestly I thought she hated you. Whenever I see you guys, you're arguing."

I cocked my head to the side. "Okay, that's fair."

"So you somehow stopped arguing and now you're...what are you exactly? Friends with benefits? Lovers?" He said the last word with a ridiculous accent that made me cringe.

"Eww, no. We're not...any of that. I don't know. I like her. A lot."

"And she likes you?"

I bit back a smile and the urge to clarify that no, she loved me. Instead I just nodded. "We still argue though. It's part of the fun."

"Like foreplay," he said, unzipping his racquet case.

I shook my head, laughing.

"How do you think your parents will like her?"

"They love her."

His eyebrow rose, but he didn't look too shocked by that statement. "They already met her?"

"Yeah, back at that competition Jameson Enterprises sponsored."

"Wait, you guys have been together since fall?"

"Uh huh. Although actually, I guess my parents didn't know that. She stayed at the house as a friend, in the guest room. My sister busted me sneaking out of her room in the morning but didn't tell my parents."

Mason shook his head in slow motion.

"What?"

"I just can't believe you've kept this from me for so long."

I grinned. Telling someone felt so good. Like finally, it was real.

CHAPTER NINETEEN

- Olivia -

I was grateful for the distraction tennis offered, but it would've been nice if we'd gone for a jog or something out of the line of sight of the men's team. Instead we just launched right into basic drills on the court.

We stopped for a water break after we finished drills. I took the opportunity to stretch again.

"So, don't look now, but Mason King is, like, totally staring."

I chuckled, switching to stretch my other hamstring. Mia had spent the better part of the season in denial about her crush on one of the other players, Shawn, but it wouldn't surprise me at all to hear she'd now added Mason to her list of hot guys.

"Well, he's cute. Go talk to him after practice."

"I'm not the one he's staring at," she said, glaring at me.

I turned and looked. Mason wasn't staring, but he was talking with Nate, who glanced up just in time to lock eyes with me. I couldn't help but smile when he did, especially when I spotted that ridiculously adorable dimple of his even from two courts away. Nate pressed his fingers to his lips as though kissing them then raised his eyebrows. I wasn't exactly sure what the gesture meant, but that didn't stop my pulse from racing.

"I said not to look!" Mia scolded, drawing my attention back to her.

I shrugged. "Mason is not interested in me. Promise. You should talk to him."

"Well, he's looking this way again. So's Nate. They're definitely talking about us."

"Ooh, do you think they're talking about us talking about them talking about us?" I teased in my best Valley Girl impression.

"Ha ha." She set down her water bottle and tightened her pony tail. "Shawn asked one of my sorority sisters to his spring formal, so I really could use a distraction."

I turned to offer a sympathetic smile. "I'm sorry. I don't get why he's so clueless." I also didn't get how she had time for tennis and a sorority, but that was a whole different topic. "You really should give Mason a chance sometime."

She peered over my shoulder. "Liv, I know you're all anti-guys and whatever, but he is definitely looking at you, not me."

"I'm not anti-guys!" I glanced behind me and confirmed Mason was, in fact, looking, but now I knew why. "Okay, maybe he is looking at me, but not for the reason you think. I swear to you he isn't into me."

"Uh huh."

I blew out a sigh. The whole team would know my personal business within an hour thanks to Mason's big mouth anyway, so I might as well tell her. Maybe she'd be less annoyed hearing it from me.

"Look, the truth is, Mason sort of saw Nate and me this morning by Nate's car. So I think they're talking about that."

"You and Nate carpool all the time. Why is that newsworthy?"

I braced myself for her overly dramatic response. "Because he also saw us holding hands and...I don't know...touching. And maybe from his perspective it looked like we were about to kiss."

Mia's expression remained so calm that I almost thought she hadn't heard me.

"Mia?"

She continued staring. Apparently, that was an effective interrogation technique because I now felt compelled to share everything.

"Okay, so Nate and I have kind of been seeing each other for a while now and we didn't want to tell anyone on the team because it's against the rules and we didn't want to make anything awkward or complicated at practice."

"Seeing each other?"

I shrugged. "Yeah. Like dating."

"You are dating Nathanial Aldridge."

"Yes."

"Like just sleeping with him or actually in a relationship?"

I felt my face contort. I wasn't sure how to answer that one.

She sighed, annoyed. "Are you guys exclusive or are either of you seeing other people?"

"Ladies!" Coach yelled. "Get back on the court. This isn't a coffee break."

Mia raised a finger showing we needed one more minute. Now, I was really scared of her. No one had the balls to make Coach wait.

"No, I guess we're exclusive."

Mia bent and grabbed her racquet. "Since when?"

"Well, I really haven't dated since last year. I don't know if Nate went out with anyone else after we first got together, but..." I paused. "I mean, we first hooked up in the fall. Is that what you're asking?"

She shook her head and started back onto the court. "I don't even believe this."

"It's true," I said, following her lead but heading to the opposite side of the net.

"No, I mean I believe you. I just can't believe you've been sleeping with Nate Aldridge for several months now and I haven't heard a single juicy detail. I thought we were friends."

"We are."

"Friends don't keep friends in the dark about torrid love affairs, especially when said friend is in the worst romantic dry spell of her life. Friends let each other live vicariously through their sexual escapades."

I opened my mouth to respond, but only laughter came out. After I composed myself, I headed back towards the left corner, ready to work my forehand.

CHAPTER TWENTY

- Nate -

*J*invited Olivia out to lunch after practice, and much to my surprise, she agreed. She warned me that she couldn't linger after lunch though, instead insisting she had to get some homework done between her classes. I let her pick the restaurant, and she picked a food court in the middle of campus. She asked me to make a detour by the drug store on the way, but told me to wait in the car and was in and out in under five minutes.

"So, either you're no longer embarrassed to be seen with me or you're punishing me by forcing me to eat shitty food," I teased as we both filled our trays at the food court.

Olivia rolled her eyes and ordered her usual egg white omelet, turkey sausage, and fruit. I grabbed several slices of pizza.

"How did Mason take the news?" she asked once we were seated.

"He was surprised we'd hidden it for so long, but otherwise just happy for me."

"Mia reacted the same," she said.

I paused, mid-bite, at her admission that she'd voluntarily told someone on the tennis team about us. That definitely was a good sign.

"So when is this formal dance thing, and how formal is it?" she asked.

"You don't have to go if you're that uncomfortable."

"Did you already ask someone else?"

I chuckled. "No." I'd actually finally replied to Cassie and told her that I appreciated her offer but was kind of seeing someone already. Shockingly, she'd backed off.

"Well, text me the details and I can probably make it. But don't expect me to make out with you in front of everyone or anything. Officially our story is that we are going as friends."

I was still grinning so widely that it was hard to chew. "How will we explain it to people when you can't keep your hands off of me then?"

She rolled her eyes.

We chewed in silence for a few minutes and then I noticed Olivia had tensed.

"Everything okay?" I asked.

Her grimace contradicted her nod. "I um, well, I just wanted you to know I grabbed the morning after pill. So you don't have to worry about…you know, from last night, in the shower…"

My heart skipped a beat as I pieced together her words, but the terror was soon replaced with a feeling that I was a complete asshole. "I wasn't worried," I said. "I mean, I didn't even think about it."

She opened her mouth to reply, but I cut her off. I wasn't about to give Olivia the chance to second guess my intentions.

"It shouldn't be all your responsibility. You could've made me run into the drug store. I'll pay for it though," I said, pulling out my wallet.

Olivia glared. I shoved my wallet back into my pocket.

"Okay, I won't pay anything. I just, it didn't even occur to me last night. Or this morning." The more I spoke, the dumber I felt, but I just kept going. "And I appreciate you being the responsible one, since I clearly dropped the ball. But I want you to know I'm not worried. I mean, I trust you aren't trying to get knocked up or anything." I paused again, realize that sounded even worse. "But if you do, I'll obviously support you, like, whatever you decide."

Olivia cringed, her nose wrinkling like she'd just realized how foul the school food smelled. "Are you done?"

I suspected I shouldn't be, but I nodded anyway.

"Jesus, Nate. That was painfully awkward to listen to. I appreciate that you don't think I'm trying to trap you into fathering the babies that would absolutely decimate my tennis career as well as any other hope of a future. But for the record, I never thought you did think that. I just wanted you to know that I'm aware we skipped the protection last night and I'm taking care of it."

"Thank you?" I said.

She laughed at my tone.

"I should get to class. Thanks for lunch."

"Anytime." I watched as she started to stand, but had to add one more thing. "Olivia?"

She paused and gazed at me, eyebrow raised.

"Not trying to bail on all responsibility in this department, but if you were on the pill, we could enjoy a lot more showers. And baths."

Olivia's expression was adorable but completely unreadable. "I'll see you later," she said, leaving me watching as she sauntered off.

CHAPTER TWENTY-ONE

- Olivia -

*T*he next several days were a blur of tennis and exams, so when Saturday finally rolled around, Nate and I went straight back to his place after practice. He forced me to eat before I dragged him upstairs to his bedroom. A half hour later, we were both relaxed on his bed.

I was so comfortable stretched out on my side, Nate pressed against my back. I could've fallen asleep had we not just split a full pot of coffee. Nate stroked my arm absentmindedly, and I shivered at the ticklish sensation as he began tracing the letters of my tattoo.

"Breathe," he said. "I don't get it."

I rolled my eyes even though I was facing a pillow. I'd heard the jokes before. *Do you actually forget to breathe? You know it's a reflex, right?* I wasn't in the mood. I tried to tug my arm free but he held tight, then kissed right along the scripted T.

"This font is beautiful. Did you choose it?"

That was unexpected. "Yep."

"When you serve, you see this, right?"

"If my eyes are open, yeah," I teased. With the tattoo's placement on the inside of my left forearm, running towards my wrist, it was squarely in my line of sight whenever I held my left arm up.

"But you don't need to breathe when you serve."

I stayed quiet, unsure where he was headed with that.

"You are the calmest, coolest tennis player I know. You have nerves of steel. Zombies could be attacking and you'd still land that serve."

I giggled at the image.

"Did you used to get anxious when you were playing?"

I considered that. "No. Tennis has always calmed me. Even if I'm getting my ass handed to me, I still feel better on the court than off."

He was quiet for a moment, and I thought we'd switched topics. But then he spoke again. "This tattoo has nothing to do with tennis, does it?"

"No."

"So why get it there, where you'll see it during play?"

"Coincidence."

He dropped my wrist, wrapping his arm tighter around me. "Bullshit. You are the most intentional person I've met. There's a reason you got that word tattooed in that spot."

"Didn't say there wasn't," I began, impressed that he actually knew me that well. "Just that it was a coincidence that it was where I could see it during tennis."

Nate waited, but when it became apparent I wasn't going to offer more details, he groaned. "You're really making me work for this, aren't you?"

"I've never told anyone the story behind the tattoo," I admitted, not bothering to add that no one else had asked before. Most people assumed the obvious.

"Well, then this is an excellent opportunity for you to show me that you actually trust me. And for me to prove that I've earned that trust by not sharing your secret."

"I'm not afraid you'll tell people. I don't care what most people think."

"Okay, spill."

I shook my head, making my hair flop over my eyes. Nate immediately brushed it off my face. "I *do* care what *you* think," I added. "And it'll make you look at me differently."

He groaned again. "Just tell me already."

I took a breath. "I used to cut myself when I was upset. In middle school and high school."

Nate was quiet for a moment. I waited for him to scoot away from me and make up an excuse to leave.

"I don't understand," he finally said.

I didn't think I had it in me to repeat what I'd said, but then he pressed up onto his elbow.

"Wait, like you slit your wrist?" he asked.

"No!" I turned further into the pillow, not wanting him to see my face. "I didn't try to kill myself. It was just…little cuts."

"O-kaaaaaaaaay," he said, drawing out the word. "Not trying to be insensitive here, but I'm not a girl so I don't really get these sorts of things."

"What sorts of things? It's not a girl thing."

"Well what's the point of making little cuts on your arm?"

I sighed. It probably would be easier to explain to him how to use a tampon or some actual "girl" thing. "There's no point. It wasn't a logical thing. I told you, I'm messed up."

He didn't say anything, but he also didn't move, which I interpreted as a good sign.

I decided to try to help him understand. "Let's say your finger hurts. But then you stub your toe. So now you're focused on your toe and you don't notice the pain from your finger anymore."

Nate took his time responding. "So you had some other injury you were distracting yourself from?"

"No. Well, yes. I mean, mental stuff." I sighed. "Okay, that was a bad example. The thing is, it was just hard in middle school. I was always playing tennis or with the tennis team, so I didn't really have time for other friends. But I had nothing in common with the other tennis people. They were all, well, like you."

"Delightfully charming and sexy as hell?"

"They were all rich," I clarified. "And they all had dads. I mean, some were divorced, but they all at least knew who their dad was. I didn't. That, coupled with the fact that my mom thought my dad was a complete monster, well, that always made me question how she really felt about me. Did she think of the worst night of her life every time she looked at me? Was I destined to become a total asshole like my father?"

"Okay, so you had daddy issues, no friends, and a less than ideal relationship with your mom," he summarized.

"Right. Anyway, I was lonely and depressed and sometimes the pain of working my way through all that shit was just too much to handle. And then one day at practice, I dove for a ball and ended up skidding a few feet along my forearm."

"Hence the scar," he chimed in, lifting my arm again and tapping the slightly discolored, smooth patch near my elbow.

"Yeah. I probably should've gotten stitches, but my mom was working the night shift that night and I figured we couldn't have afforded an ER visit anyway. The point is, it hurt. But that night when I was trying to fall asleep, I was distracted by the stinging in my arm. I didn't even think about how my mom probably hated me or how I had no friends or how I was genetically predisposed to be a monster. I just thought about my arm."

"Because it hurt."

"Uh huh. But then it stopped hurting and I started thinking about all that other shit again, and after a while, I realized that physical pain could distract me. I started small, pressing my fingernails into my skin really hard until it made a mark. Then one day, I drew blood. And then it was like I could actually see my pain. It was real, and not just some shit inside my head."

I paused, tempted to end the story there. But since I'd started telling it, I might as well finish. I already felt some sort of cathartic relief, finally sharing my dark secret with someone.

"It progressed from there, and eventually I was using a razor blade to make tiny nicks whenever I felt anxious or out of control. I know it sounds insane, but it worked. I could actually control the pain. I could choose when and what hurt me."

"That's not how life works."

I sighed. He was right, of course. But I hadn't felt that way at the time.

"No one noticed all these cuts on your arms?"

I shook my head. "I switched to my legs, then my stomach during tennis season. And no one really paid attention to me, so..."

"I'm sorry," he interrupted.

I smiled despite the circumstances.

About a year ago, I'd gotten the courage to tell my mom that I felt like no one had paid attention to me growing up, and she'd immediately launched into a self-defense monologue. It wasn't her fault, she'd tried her best, blah blah blah. All I'd wanted was an apology, or some acknowledgement that what I'd felt was okay. And here Nate was, completely blameless in it all, apologizing for what I'd dealt with.

"Thanks." I paused. "I always wondered if my coach noticed. She started asking if I was okay a lot, telling me she was available if I needed to talk. So that was nice, but honestly as long as I kept winning, no one seemed too concerned."

"What made you stop?" he asked. Then, I felt him stiffen behind me. "You did stop, right?"

"I haven't cut myself since junior year of high school. I don't know why, really. It was like something just clicked and I realized how fucked up it was. I started pouring all my pain into tennis. If

I was stressed or depressed, I'd run a few miles. Or hit balls. Whatever was bothering me, I left it all on the court. By the time I'd get home, I was so exhausted I'd pass out the second I hit the bed."

"I guess that's how you got so good."

"Probably." I chuckled. "If I were mentally stable, I bet I'd have a really shitty backhand."

"Definitely."

"Anyway, when I turned eighteen, I got the tattoo and I picked that spot because that's where I started with the cutting. And I chose that word because I used to feel like I needed the pain to breathe, but I eventually got to the point where I could make the choice to breathe on my own, without cutting."

Nate didn't say anything.

"Now that you know I'm completely fucked up and overdue for like a decade of therapy, I should probably head home. I need to study anyway," I said, sparing him the awkwardness of booting me from his bed.

His arm tightened around me. "Veto."

"You don't get veto power. I get to decide when I leave your bed."

"You're not running away from me," he said. He swung a leg over mine and rolled me onto my back. I squeezed my eyes shut, already feeling too vulnerable without forced eye contact, but Nate didn't even try to look at me. He just pinned me to his bed, then flopped his head against my chest.

"I'm sorry you had a shitty childhood. And teen years. And I don't think you're as weird as you seem to think you are." He began. "We all did stupid shit in high school. We were all messed up, and most of us weren't dealing with the shit you were."

I swallowed the lump quickly growing in my throat.

"I'm amazed you were able to stop on your own, but now that you've told me all of that, it makes more sense."

"What does?"

"You. Why you are the way you are. How you got to be so good." He paused. "You're the strongest person I know. Mentally, I mean. I could still out bench press you any day," he added, lightening the mood. "You're focused and determined and on the surface you seem like you have it totally together."

"Well, I don't. I'm a mess."

"Thank God for that. We'd have nothing in common if you were as perfect inside as you look on the outside."

I suspected he meant that as a compliment. And somehow, I no longer felt compelled to sprint out of his room. But I did have a different type of crushing sensation. "Nate, I can't breathe," I said, wiggling beneath him.

He laughed. "Sure you can. Just choose to breathe," he teased, grabbing my tattooed arm again.

"Jerk," I mumbled.

Nate pressed up to his elbows so that his chest barely skimmed mine. "Better?"

I nodded.

He smiled. "You're a beautiful mess, you know that?"

But before I could answer, he kissed me.

CHAPTER TWENTY-TWO

- Nate -

I watched Olivia play a local match the next day. Several people from the team were there, simply because she was so impressive to watch. I couldn't focus on anything the other players were saying though. I just kept thinking about what she'd told me the day before. It was huge, for her to open up that much to me, but I wasn't sure what to do with the information.

It explained so much, about how Olivia worked so hard to protect herself and why she never let herself lose focus. In her mind, the second she lost control, she was in danger of never regaining it. As she slammed ball after ball in the corner of the court, I thought about everything else she was dealing with, and I was just as impressed as always.

Olivia hadn't quite forgiven her mom for the lie about her dad, but she also wasn't telling her mom how upset she was. It didn't seem right that the victim—the child—should be the one sacrificing to protect the parent, and yet Olivia didn't think twice about it.

I told Olivia I'd like to meet her mom someday, and she hadn't been completely repulsed by the idea. That had to be a good sign —her willingness to accept that I might still be in her life once she eventually forgave her mother. But it was pretty much the only sign I had that Olivia was considering me as anything but a fling. She hadn't brought up the birth control again, which was fine. I would've preferred to be with her without any barrier between us, but it wasn't just that or the hassle-factor. For Olivia to start birth control would signal that she was invested in us, that she could acknowledge a future with me.

I didn't expect her to be picturing our wedding or anything, but some hint that she'd still talk to me after graduation would be nice. I'd never admit it to her, but I could already envision it all. I saw myself cheering her on at games next year, texting her from my cubicle at the firm, introducing her to my classmates at business school. I could picture vacations with Olivia, moving in together, and navigating holidays with both of our families. If I let myself dwell on it long enough, I could almost see the babies we could have together.

Geez. I didn't even know if Olivia ever planned to have children with anyone, let alone with me. She didn't exactly have the best example of a healthy upbringing to model from. I wouldn't be surprised if her childhood convinced her never to reproduce. Although, she'd clearly turned out just fine. And she was making big strides with her dad.

Olivia hadn't really opened up to the guy yet, but she'd met his kids and seen his house and claimed they were exchanging emails on occasion. He'd invited her to some lunch with his parents—her grandparents, but Olivia had claimed she was busy. I got that. I wouldn't want to meet some new grandparents who paid off my mom, either.

But Olivia also said her dad had offered to help with tuition or loans and that she'd turned him down. That was the part I didn't understand. So much of her stress was related to money, or the lack thereof. If she'd just let someone help...

The spectator behind me yelled something towards the court and jolted me out of my daydream just in time to see Olivia serve the game point.

* * *

- Olivia -

J was a nervous mess the night of Nate's stupid formal. I'd ended up buying a new dress, which was completely irresponsible even though I used the money from a belated birthday check Peter wrote to me. It was a simple black gown, with a slit up the side and a keyhole design that showed off the shoulders Nate complimented so often. I told myself I could wear it again to some other event.

Nate picked me up early, and we drove to meet some of his fraternity brothers and their dates at a restaurant. He introduced me as a friend, and no one questioned it. Pretending we were just friends proved easier than I'd expected since, as it turned out, we'd been doing that for months at practice. The food was delicious, Nate's friends were entertaining, and he made me take a few sips of his wine so I was a little more chill by the time we reached the dance.

In the dimly lit ballroom where everyone divided up by couples and danced arm in arm, it was a little harder to maintain the ruse.

"We don't have to dance if you're not comfortable," Nate said, biting back a smile.

"Nope, it's fine. I can dance. Just don't grab my ass or anything."

He laughed and tugged me onto the floor. We danced and giggled through the first two songs and then a slow song came on. Nate gazed at me as if daring me, so of course I couldn't refuse. But snugly positioned in his arms, where I could smell his delicious cologne and feel the hint of his muscles beneath his suit, I struggled to remember why I wanted to pretend we were friends.

"It is really hard not to kiss you now," I admitted, gazing up at him.

A soft, low growl escaped his throat. "I'm not stopping you," he finally said.

I giggled. "I can restrain myself for a few minutes."

When the song ended, he motioned for me to follow him off the dance floor. I assumed we were heading for snacks, but instead, we walked right outside. There were a few other couples directly in front of the building, but Nate led me around to the side where we were completely alone.

"Better?" he asked.

I pressed my hands against his face, pulling him close as I kissed him. He reciprocated, and things progressed until I remembered we were still outside. I nudged him away, shaking my head.

He grinned as I wiped the last traces of my lipstick off of his smoothly shaved chin.

"We should go back inside before I molest you further," I joked.

He nodded, but made no attempt to walk away. Instead, he reached for my hand and squeezed it. "I love you," he said.

My heart actually skipped a beat. Flustered, I reached for my purse, fumbling around until I retrieved my lipstick. I began to reapply it, hoping he'd get distracted. But when I finally looked up, Nate was still staring at me.

Shit. The look in his eyes was...everything. It was the sort of look that could melt icebergs. If Nate were a puppy, I'd adopt him based on that look alone.

"You have no response to that?" he said, his voice soft.

I shook my head. "Umm thank you? I mean, I... Nate, you know how I feel about you. I just can't...say..."

"But you already did," he replied.

I felt my lips part. Instantly, I knew exactly when he was referring to. "You weren't supposed to hear that. I thought you were asleep."

He stepped closer, pressing the softest of kisses onto my forehead. "Well, I did hear it and I thought I was dreaming, but…" he shrugged.

"I know it doesn't make any sense, but if I say it out loud, it's just going to make it real."

"This isn't real enough?"

Nate was close enough now that I suspected he could feel my heart beat.

I continued without answering him. "I'm going to get hurt, and the more I put myself out there, the more—"

"*You're* going to get hurt? I'm the one who keeps putting my heart on the line and getting rejected."

"You're the one leaving in a couple months," I reminded him. "This is all great for now, but once you're back in the real world, with your MBA buddies and the other associates at your daddy's firm…"

Nate blew out a sigh and swatted me on the butt, breaking the spell. "It's my grandpa's firm, and come on. I'm not getting into this argument with you again. You owe me a few more dances if you expect me to put out later."

Something told me the discussion wasn't truly over yet, but for the moment, I felt nothing but relief.

CHAPTER TWENTY-THREE

- Nate -

Olivia and I joined some of my brothers at a bar after the dance. Once we were both blissfully drunk, Olivia insisted I experience my first—and last—bus ride. Back at my apartment, we fooled around until we were both sober and sedate enough to actually sleep. I awoke with a happy, peaceful feeling in my chest as I rolled over to see my first glimpse of Olivia's adorable sleeping face.

Instead, I found I was alone in the bed.

I stretched, hit the bathroom, then trudged to the kitchen, pleasantly surprised to see Olivia fiddling with my Keurig.

"You're still here!" I said.

She peered up slowly, a bemused grin on her beautiful face. "Did you expect me to sneak off?"

I shrugged. Normally, I would've said no, but after my whole admission with the L-word the prior night, I wouldn't have been shocked to see her run.

"You hid my bra somewhere. I'm basically trapped here."

"I don't think you wore one," I said, now vividly recalling the joy of undressing her after the dance. I walked around her and helped myself to some coffee, too, kissing her bare shoulder blade as I passed.

She frowned. "It was strapless, but definitely existed."

I opened the fridge, then shut it again after confirming I really had no edible breakfast options inside. I did have a lot of cereal, though, so it wasn't like we'd starve.

"I hope my car is still there," I said, remembering how she'd convinced me to leave it in the parking lot a block from the bars.

"I'm sure it is. Although, if not, couldn't you just buy a new one?"

Something about her tone gave me pause, but she walked into the living room before I could question her further. I followed once I'd added sufficient sugar to my coffee. Olivia stood beside the coffee table, gesturing to some papers spread out.

"I wasn't trying to snoop, but you left this out. Holy shit that's a lot of money for an intern."

I grimaced. It was the employment contract my dad had sent over. I'd scanned a copy back to him after signing, then just left the original on my coffee table, apparently. It wasn't like I had a lot of guests, so my motivation to pick up in between visits from the cleaning lady was nonexistent.

"Yeah," I said, sliding onto the couch and tugging her down beside me.

"Are you excited?" she asked.

I wrinkled my nose, realizing Olivia was the first person to actually ask me that. It seemed like an odd question. Did anyone get excited about a job? Were there any actual perks to graduating college and entering the real world, where I'd essentially work until the day I died?

"Not really," I finally said.

Olivia pouted. "You've got a lot of big stuff coming up though. Graduation, starting grad school, a new job... I think you're supposed to be excited."

"Am I?" I shrugged, and she laughed.

I leaned forward and picked up the page of the contract detailing the benefits package. "What do you think I'd use the company car for?" I asked, pointing to that line.

"Ooh, maybe to pick up prostitutes? Or just to drive you home from bars when your super hot friend convinces you to do too many shots."

"Friend," I repeated, eyebrow raised.

She didn't take the bait. "What would you do if you didn't have this job lined up?"

"You mean if I had to figure out what to do with my life on my own like all you common folk?"

Her giggle brought a smile to my face.

"I honestly don't know."

Her silence prompted me to think harder.

"Well, I don't want to be a doctor or teacher or lawyer. I'm not cut out for the military, and I'm not talented enough to be a professional athlete or artist of any kind. Definitely not skilled for construction or any trade sort of work either. What else is left?"

She considered the question. "You already got into grad school, right?"

I nodded, although that, too had been a foregone conclusion. For me, even the process of applying was a mere formality.

"There's a ton you can do with an MBA. You don't have to settle for whatever precise job your dad and grandpa did if that's not what excites you. Keep going to school, figure out what you'd actually enjoy, and look for a job in that field."

What she said made sense, and I was almost embarrassed to admit it had never actually occurred to me to really consider what I'd do if I didn't work at Jameson Enterprises. But then I remembered another caveat.

"I already signed the contract. If I don't go to work for them, they won't pay for grad school."

Olivia rolled her eyes. "Get a student loan. That's what normal people do to pay for school. Then when you graduate, you'll pay it off."

"I have a trust fund," I blurted out, oddly ashamed that it was true.

"Of course you do," she said, laughing. "Even better, because I was lying about the ease of the student loan thing. It's awful. They barely give you enough and then you're trapped into settling right away for a job you don't love because the repayment schedule is insane. And then you end up living like a broke college kid well into your thirties."

I swung Olivia's legs over my lap, holding her in place. Since she'd shared her opinions on my financial and career decisions, it seemed fair for me to get to voice the same to her. "You told me your father offered to pay off your student loans. Why don't you let him?"

Her jaw tightened.

"Liv, I'm serious. It's just us now. I want to know."

She sighed. "I hardly know him. It feels wrong to let some stranger buy my affection."

"But he wouldn't be," I pointed out. "You are way too stubborn for that. Even if he pays it off, you're still not going to like him until he proves his worth. You of all people can't be bought. Trust me, I've tried."

"He's only offering because he feels guilty."

"So? He should. Legally, he owed you a ton of money over your childhood and he didn't pay a dime."

"But that isn't exactly his fault. I believe him when he says he really didn't know about me."

"Then let him pay for this and assuage his guilt. It's win-win, Liv. He feels better and you have this huge burden lifted that opens up all these options for you after graduation."

She didn't answer right away, but I guessed from the whimsical look in her eyes that she was actually thinking about her options, or specifically, tennis. Olivia had what it took to play pro, and in my opinion, she could really make it. But I also knew the statistics, and the fact that most professional tennis players barely scraped by, financially-speaking. Endorsement deals and exhibition tournaments were only options for the absolute top players, the ones who were already making enough in prize money to get by. For the majority, it was hardly a lucrative lifestyle.

"It's a lot of money, Nate," she finally said, lowering her voice to a near whisper as she said, "It's close to twenty thousand dollars."

Her tuition was covered by an academic scholarship, so that amount actually did surprise me. But at the same time, twenty grand would be a drop in the bucket for someone like her father. Or me.

"Liv, he can pay that without batting an eye. He'll still have plenty left for his next midlife crisis car and wife and it won't affect whatever he's paying for his other two kids."

She groaned, but I could tell from her expression that she'd at least listened. "I'm out of coffee," she said.

I slid her feet off my lap and reached for her mug then paused. Since I'd already made her uncomfortable, I might as well push my luck. "You know, next week is my last match ever."

Her smile widened. "I know that. I've already begun bedazzling a poster to bring when I cheer you on."

I breathed a laugh. "Right, well, my parents are coming too. It might be a good time to tell them—"

"Nate," she interrupted. "Just get the coffee, please? They already met me and they think we're friends and that is what I'm comfortable with. Okay?"

"Yeah," I mumbled. With everything else going on, that really was okay.

CHAPTER TWENTY-FOUR

- Olivia -

*P*eter came to watch another one of my tennis matches, but aside from waving politely, I barely acknowledged him. During a break between sets though, I couldn't help but notice he and Nate chatting like they were long lost friends. I spent the entire final set trying to guess what they'd been discussing, and if I were the easily distractible type, I would've tanked the last few shots. Thankfully, I wasn't.

When I emerged from the locker room after the game, Nate was lounging at a table under the covered pavilion.

"Where'd your friend go?" I asked.

"Your dad apologized but said he had to run and pick up the boys from someplace."

"Don't call him that. His name is Peter."

Nate raised his eyebrow, but said nothing else.

"You guys seemed pretty chummy. What were you discussing?"

Now he shrugged, slinging his arm around me casually as we started to walk towards the parking lot. I glanced around, but no one was really paying attention to us anyway. "Oh, lots of stuff. Turns out we have a lot in common. Did you know he played tennis?"

I nodded. I also knew that, like Nate, Peter came from family money, went into business, and was in a fraternity. I was basically dating my father, it seemed.

"He, um, seemed to think you and I were more than friends," he said, pausing his gait to gaze at me.

"What gave him that impression?" I asked, not even attempting to minimize the accusation in my tone.

"Reality," he replied with a snarky smirk. "But don't worry, I assured him we were just friends."

"Really?"

He nodded. "Yep. I stuck to the truth, that I really like you and keep asking you out and that you keep shooting me down."

I rolled my eyes at the notion of him calling that the 'truth.'

"I also said we fuck like bunnies, but I'm pretty sure he thought I was kidding."

I glared at him until his laughter confirmed he was joking.

"Thank you. I'll be sure to be every bit as tactful if I run into your parents tomorrow."

He quirked an eyebrow. "You can tell my parents the actual truth. I would love that. We could call it an early birthday present or something."

"Your birthday is in the fall."

"Yeah, so a really early present."

Nate tickled my side until I giggled.

The next day, I greeted his parents warmly, then sat in the row right behind the team bench, thinking I'd be at a safe distance from his parents there. Sadly, though, Mr. and Mrs. Aldridge ended up right behind me. At first, I wasn't sure if they knew I was there, so I could safely observe their casual demeanor.

Jameson Aldridge spent the majority of his time on his phone, answering calls even when his wife was midsentence. He sounded grumpy for the most part, barking orders and verbalizing his disappointment with the caller, but every once in a while he'd laugh or engage in witty banter. During one such call, I felt a presence right behind me.

"Do you play today, Olivia?" Mrs. Aldridge was asking.

I craned my neck to turn towards her. "No, I played yesterday. Just hear to cheer on the guys."

"It's Nathaniel's last game," she continued.

"Oh?" I feigned surprise. "I guess you're right. Wow. Time sure does fly."

I turned back to face forward, but not before catching Jameson's eye. He winked in a friendly, if not a tad creepy, manner, and suddenly I felt self-conscious of the tank top and shorts I'd chosen for the day.

Once the match started, Nate's father continued with his intermittent phone calls, even though most people readily accepted that tennis was *not* one of those sports where the spectators should make noise. When he wasn't on a call, he'd spew commentary under his breath about his son's performance.

I had to agree it wasn't Nate's best game. I wasn't sure if he'd just gotten stuck in his head or what, but his aim was off for sure. The more it progressed, though, the more stressed Nate looked. He had a chance to redeem it all in the last set, but he missed what should've been an easy shot, losing the match.

I cringed, my heart aching at the pain Nate must be feeling. He really wasn't the most competitive person, and he didn't seem to tie his self-worth up on his tennis game, but still...this was his final match, and he lost. Badly.

"Jesus Christ," I heard his dad spit.

"Jameson!" Nate's mom chided her husband, but it was no use.

"What? This is what has been distracting him from class. Why is he spending all this time on tennis, so he can play like this?"

I tried to catch Nate's attention as he shook hands with

his opponent, but he was clearly avoiding eye contact with the entire section of the stands. Watching his face, it was obvious he was already internalizing the loss, and hard. Nate stared at his feet while his coach said something to him, then he sipped his water and stalked off the court as quickly as he could. Nate's expression was so pained that I could practically hear his internal monologue. I knew he was just heading into the locker room so he could beat up on himself in private.

"Shit," I mumbled, standing quickly. I scooted along down the row, careful not to trip over other spectators' feet. As I reached the aisle, I noticed Jameson Aldridge watching me. I smiled politely, then turned away to cringe, certain he knew I was chasing after his son.

Oh well. I'd deal with that problem later. For now, Nate needed me.

I sped up to a jog in hopes of catching Nate before he reached the dressing room, but just when I thought I'd reach him in time, a security guard stopped me.

"Ma'am, it's players and coaches only past here," he said, his voice less stern that you'd expect for someone stopping a trespasser.

"I'm with the team," I said. "I'm a player. Olivia Roberts."

I reached into my purse and tugged out my ID card showing my affiliation with the team.

He nodded and motioned for me to pass.

By that point, Nate was nowhere in sight. I peered around the corner, then planted myself outside the men's locker room. I waited for a moment, then leaned closer to the door. Feeling emboldened, I knocked. No answer. So I pulled the door open an inch.

"Nate?" I called.

No response.

Just as I was working up the courage to march into the men's locker room, the door swung open. It wasn't Nate, though. It was Mason.

He startled at the sight of me, then nodded knowingly.

"He's in a mood," he warned.

"Yeah," I replied. I had figured as much. "Can you tell him to come out?"

Mason disappeared into the room a minute longer, then returned. Alone.

"He's um, he said to tell you he'd catch up with you after the tournament," Mason said, awkwardly avoiding eye contact.

I rolled my eyes then pushed past him, pulling the door open wider.

"Aldridge, you have ten seconds to get out here before I come in there!" I called.

Mason's eyebrows shot up, but he didn't say anything other than to wish me good luck as he sauntered off.

I was starting to think I'd actually have to follow through on my threat when Nate appeared. He looked like shit.

"I'm not in the mood for a lecture," he said.

"A lecture? You think I'm here to lecture you?"

He shrugged. "My last game and I completely blew it."

I sighed. "It wasn't your last game. You and I can play tomorrow and you'll probably take off your shirt or something equally sneaky and I'll be so distracted that you'll beat me. And you hardly blew it. Everyone loses from time to time."

"You don't."

Well, he had me there. "You were distracted. It's not your fault. Why'd you invite your parents anyway?"

"I didn't invite them. That's what parents do, come to cheer on their kids."

I couldn't remember the last time my mom had come to watch me. I wasn't about to point that out, though. Not when Nate still looked so sad.

"I'm supposed to go out to dinner with them later."

"You could blow them off," I suggested.

"They'd hunt me down and find me."

I giggled at that then reached for his fingers.

"Come with us," he asked, his dark eyes staring intently now.

I rose to my toes, pulling his neck down so I could kiss him. It was a short kiss, but hopefully distracted him from his invitation. When we separated, he didn't speak.

"You looked hot out there," I said. "Best butt in the division for sure."

"Why don't they give trophies for that?"

I shrugged. "They should."

I stepped closer, closing the gap between us and gazing up at him. Even sad, he was still ridiculously hot. "I'm a little annoyed that I spent my afternoon watching you play, and all I got was that lousy kiss."

"Lousy? You started it."

I shrugged.

He hesitated before accepting the challenge. His fingers pressed into my waist as he swiveled us around, pressing me against the wall beside the locker room. He paused, staring intently now. I would've smiled, proud at the knowledge that clearly, I'd succeeded in distracting him, but the smoldering look in his eyes now rendered me incapable of any logical responses.

I licked my lips, and he pounced. He leaned forward, pinning me between the wall and his firm torso. Then he cupped my cheek in his hand, running it up towards my hair as he finally pressed his lips against mine. His tongue swept into my mouth, demanding and forceful, and I loved it. He claimed me with his kiss, devoured me, dominated me. I groaned into his mouth and he tightened his hand in my hair, tugging slightly. My hands found his hips, holding him close for a minute before drifting up his sides.

The kiss went on longer than it should have, but not nearly long enough. And when our lips finally separated, Nate leaned his forehead against mine, still clutching my cheek. We were both breathing hard then, and together, we slowed our breathing. He shifted his hand to the wall beside my head, then there was a voice behind us.

I gazed up, locking eyes with Coach Aaron before Nate even seemed to register the presence of anyone else.

Cringing, I ducked under Nate's arm and faced my feet, letting my hair fall over my face. Maybe the Coach hadn't recognized me yet.

"Your father sent me to check on you, Aldridge," the Coach said.

I gazed up to see Nate turn slowly, covering his mouth with his hand.

"I'll let him know you'll be back out soon," he said. Then he paused, opening his mouth as though about to say something else, then simply shook his head and walked off in the direction he'd come from.

Nate reached for my hand, then laughed.

CHAPTER TWENTY-FIVE

- Nate -

I took my time getting ready for dinner with my parents, feeling a little like I was walking into an execution. I already knew what my father would say. I didn't need to hear his critique of my shitty game. I kept myself going by the reminder of Liv's promise, to come and celebrate my final college game properly after I endured dinner with the parents.

Ironically, they took me to the same steakhouse Olivia and I had visited on our first, well, and technically only, real date. In the spirit of reliving that crappy night rather than focus on the current, even crappier one, I selected the same drink I had the last time.

We made small talk until after we'd ordered, my mom filling in whenever my father was interrupted with some inane-sounding yet apparently critical phone call.

When he finally hung up the phone, he turned to me.

"That Roberts girl seemed pretty invested in your match," my father said, watching my expression closely.

"Maybe she had money riding on it," I joked, ripping off the corner of a roll and shoving it in my mouth. Neither of my parents laughed.

"She took off pretty fast after," he continued. "I assume she found you okay?"

I reached for my drink to buy myself time. I didn't think Coach had actually seen us kissing, but he'd definitely seen enough to figure out what was going on, if he hadn't already known. And while I'd like to think he wouldn't rat me out to my own father, I wasn't sure. I decided to play it safe and stick as close to the truth as possible.

"Yeah, she did."

He waited for me to say more, but I sure wasn't volunteering it. Besides, he seemed to enjoy slowly pulling information from people, almost like the psycho dude who tortures spies for a living.

"You two have gotten pretty close?"

I nodded. Then, feeling extra cocky, I decided to kick things up a notch. "Yeah, thanks to you. We've known each other for a while but I honestly didn't really consider her a friend until after that weekend you invited her to the house." I smirked. "Turns out she's a pretty cool girl. Glad to count her as a friend."

"She's quite pretty," my father continued.

My mother shot him a look, but I understood he was goading me, not hitting on a girl half his age.

"Yep," I said. There was no plausible way to disagree with that statement.

"She's got another year though, right?" my mom chimed in, clearly oblivious to the warpath my father was on.

I nodded.

"What are her plans after graduation?" my father continued.

"Why?" I countered, meeting and holding his eye contact even as the waiter arrived with our meals.

"I suppose I just wanted to see how much you actually know about your new girlfriend," he finally said. Then he turned and smiled cordially at the waiter, requested another round of drinks, and asked my mother if her steak was prepared to her liking.

I cut into my food, wondering how quickly I could eat a filet without choking to death. I was about to swallow my fourth bite when my mother spoke up.

"Nathaniel? Your father asked you a question."

He hadn't, actually. At least not with his last statement. He didn't care what Olivia was doing after graduation, anyway. He just wanted me to admit we were dating. "I don't know what you guys want me to say. You've already made your assumptions."

My mom looked confused, but my dad forged on. "Do you know how alimony works? Even with a prenup, do you have any idea how expensive it can be to separate from someone who—"

"Someone who is what, Dad? Exactly what are you implying about Olivia?" I interrupted, my tone sharper than my steak knife.

He smiled, thrilled to have a sparring partner. "I was going to say someone whose assets and income differs from your own."

I rolled my eyes. "No one's getting married."

"Okay then, how about child support? Do you know how that works?"

I glared.

"Let me guess…she's on the pill? Sure. I hear that's super effective, until you need a payday and stop taking it."

He was such a fucking hypocrite. I wondered what form of birth control his slutty secretary used and how that was reliable enough for him. I pushed my chair away from the table. "I'm not even going to sit here if you're…"

My mom reached across the table and squeezed my hand. I didn't think she'd ever undermine my father, but I also sensed she didn't agree with him. And right now, I actually felt sorry for her. Sure, I had to put up with my father on the rare occasions I actually saw him, but she had to live with the guy. She had to put up with the humiliation of my dad's countless indiscretions and deal with his day-to-day jerkiness.

I took a few deep breaths, then returned to my food. "I don't think you researched her very well," I finally said. "She was raised by her mom, but her father is loaded. He's a consultant. Maybe you know him. Peter Wilkerson?" I paused and shrugged like it was no big deal.

Surely the knowledge that she had her own money was adequate proof that she couldn't possibly be after mine. I wasn't even going to consider the implications of my father's assumption that a girl like Olivia couldn't possibly be interested in me for my personality or anything other than my investment portfolio. Admittedly, she had some commitment issues, but her feelings for me were one hundred percent authentic. I was certain.

"Her parents aren't together?" he asked, frowning.

I suppressed a smile at his admission that there was something he didn't know. "No, not since college."

My father cleared his throat. "Then I guess you better hope this isn't a case of like mother, like daughter."

He motioned for the waiter before I even realized I'd just given him more fodder for his battle.

* * *

- Olivia -

*N*ate told me the dinner with his parents was a disaster and that his parents made some comments that suggested they thought we were dating. He assured me he didn't confirm or deny anything, and for some reason, none of it bothered me that much. I decided as long as I was in this new, go-with-the-flow, brave mood, I should talk with Peter again.

We made plans to meet up the following Sunday. I had an out-of-town tennis match Saturday morning, but would be back late

Saturday. I planned to sleep over at Nate's Saturday night and then head up to see Peter around lunch time Sunday. We chose a generic restaurant in a town slightly closer to campus than his house. Even though I'd been nervous the entire way there, I was still surprised at how awkward the first several minutes of small talk were.

"So, how is, um, Stella?" I asked after we ordered. He still wore his ring, so maybe that was a good sign.

His eyes drifted back to the table but he chuckled. "She's good. Still hates me, but…"

"Why?" I asked, not realizing until the word left my mouth how inappropriate and nosy it probably seemed. "I mean, did you cheat on her or something?"

"No," he quickly said. He turned back to his drink and swirled his straw around in the soda. "But I do work too much, and my communication skills suck. And it's possible I'm not the best at expressing my emotions in an open and honest manner."

I giggled at the last part, certain he was quoting his therapist.

"Couples counseling," he said with a half grin, confirming my suspicion.

"Well, maybe I got that from you, then. Mom is constantly expressing her emotions. If she feels it, the whole world knows it. Me, well, I don't really see the point. I mean, emotions are like names. Everyone has 'em. Ignoring the crappy stuff just makes everyone happier."

Peter shrugged. "Yeah. Except sometimes your emotions impact the way you act, and then the people around you start to notice anyway. And the people who actually care, those crazy ones who think they can fix it all if you just open up, they get their feelings hurt when you don't tell them what's going on."

I sipped my drink, shaking my head. "God, Nate and Stella would probably be perfect for each other. She's right around his age too, isn't she?"

He laughed, thankfully not taking offense at the taunt. "She's thirty."

I declined to point out that she was, therefore, just as close in age to Nate as she was to him.

"So this Aldridge boy, he's your boyfriend? I couldn't get a straight answer from him."

"Good. I instructed him to reply that way."

He frowned.

"Look, we've already established I'm not big on discussing my feelings, and I don't think you and I are quite at the point where we openly chat about our love lives."

"You asked about mine," he pointed out.

"That's different. You're still wearing a wedding ring. I'm entitled to ask about my... stepmom."

His eyes widened at the title, but I continued before he could speak.

"Does she know about me?"

He nodded.

That impressed me, although I supposed it probably came out at therapy. "Well, that seems like a good sign, if you're opening up to her about all sorts of personal details about your sordid past coming back to haunt you."

Peter bit back a smile.

"How are the boys?" I asked.

"They're good. Getting excited about school ending, summer camp and all that."

We chatted about the boys a little longer before I got the courage to circle back to my real questions. "Is Carol, um, rich? Or, I mean, was she, before you guys got married?"

He nodded. "We both had our fair share of family money."

That was what I had thought. "And the boys are...okay financially? Like you guys have enough to take care of them and pay for their college and everything?"

Now he outright laughed. "Yeah, the boys are good. Even if I end up having to pay off Stella, they'll be just fine." He paused, cocking his head to the side. "Why the sudden concern about my finances?"

I took a deep breath. "I was thinking about what you'd said earlier, about my student loan debt. Your offer to help out, is it still on the table?"

"Yes, yeah. Of course." Relief filled his eyes. "I'd...really like that, if you'd let me pay for that."

I reached into my purse, pulling out the recent statement that I'd shoved in there to show to him. "I don't have to start making payments for another two years, so there's no rush, if you want to talk it over with your accountant or whoever. And, um, if you just want to help out with a payment or two, that's totally fine."

He took the statement out of my hands as I continued to babble.

"Really anything helps. And if you change your mind, that's okay too. I know I'll get a job after graduation and I'd definitely pay it off eventually, it's just..."

I stopped midsentence as Peter pulled a checkbook from his pocket and began scribbling. He slid the statement and the check across the table to me, but I didn't glance down at either just yet.

"You should confirm there's no prepayment penalty or anything, but um, then you could decide if you want to pay it off at once or stick this in a savings account," he mumbled.

My eyes flitted down to the check, which he'd written for three hundred dollars more than the full amount of the loan. My lips parted.

"I didn't mean—" I began.

"I know, but listen. If I'd known your mom hadn't gotten an abortion, I would've given you money. I can't say I would've been the amazing hands-on father you deserved, because honestly, I didn't really grow up until I was closer to thirty. But I would've at least made sure you had enough money."

I exhaled, forcing the awkwardness out with my breath. I

wedged the loan statement back into my purse and then folded the check into my wallet. "I didn't realize it was possible to just write a check for this amount," I said.

Peter shrugged. "Yeah. They, uh, might hold the funds a day or two while they clear it with me and my bank, but um, generally you can write a check for any amount that's available in your account."

"This is a year's pay for Mom," I said, instantly regretting my words.

He nodded, his expression unreadable.

We both picked at our food in silence for several minutes while I desperately tried to think of some interesting, light-hearted discussion subject.

"Hey, I'm having a little end of the year picnic for the boys. I'd like it if you could come. You could bring your friend Nate if you wanted, or whoever."

I nodded. "Uh, sure. Just text me the date and I'll check my calendar."

"Yeah, will do," he agreed. Then he paused, a wince spreading across his face. "My parents will be there, just so you know."

I had no response for that.

"I told them about you," he added, as if that somehow made it less awkward.

"They treated Mom like dirt," I said.

He shrugged, as if he didn't really disagree. "I don't think they're big fans of hers, but if we're being honest, neither am I. I mean, I'm still pretty miffed that she didn't bother to tell me about you all this time."

I was struggling to understand his point when he continued.

"Me being mad at your mom doesn't have anything to do with how I feel about you. Just like my parents don't hold your mom's actions against you. They're really eager to meet you, actually."

I nodded, forcing my final bite of food down my throat. "Well, yeah, just text me the details. I'll check my calendar."

CHAPTER TWENTY-SIX

- Nate -

*M*y college experience had dragged on for so long, and then somehow, the last month zipped by in the blink of an eye. I aced my last exam, downed copious amounts of booze at my last party, and sweated through my final tennis practice. Then, I walked across the stage to collect the fake diploma that would be replaced with a real one once all grades were verified. It was surreal. As I said goodbye to the guys who'd annoyed me for years, I felt the slightest hint of regret, like I should've joined them for one more drink or one last poker night.

I wasn't moving far away for graduate school, but it would be an entirely different experience nonetheless. When I packed up my bags to head back to my parents' house for a week, a twinge of nostalgia washed over me. It was stupid, really. I'd be back in a week to finish packing everything for the movers. Still, by that time, campus would have emptied out for summer. I gave the place a final once over, then left, unsettled by the weird mix of emotions.

I endured the longest twenty-four hours ever alone with my parents while waiting for Ansley to return back home, and then after a day of just the four of us, I drove to a neighboring suburb to watch Olivia play a match. I shouldn't have been surprised to see her win, but stupidly I'd thought she might actually be distracted by the fact that she was coming back to my parents' house with me after her game.

"Don't take it personally," she told me in the car later. "I don't get distracted."

"Clearly," I said, running my free hand along her thigh.

"No new car?" she asked suddenly.

I frowned, feeling the urge to defend my precious car. It was only a year old and still in pristine condition.

"I thought that was the go-to graduation present for rich people," she quickly explained. "No offense meant towards your car."

I held my other arm towards her, displaying my new Vacheron Constantin watch. I suspected Ansley had helped my parents pick it out, since it was fucking gorgeous.

"They got you a watch? That seems so normal and not excessive." Olivia's shock was adorable.

I chuckled. "This watch cost more than a Honda Civic."

Her expression quickly morphed to one of disgust. Maybe I shouldn't have volunteered that info. I changed the subject.

"Leighton is going to be staying at the house this weekend. Her husband isn't coming to the graduation party because of some business trip and she doesn't like driving after dark." I paused. "Just wanted to give you a heads up."

"Appreciated."

"I'm sure Ansley hasn't said anything about us to her, but now that my parents seem to know..."

"It's fine," Olivia said with a sigh. "They're your family, so you can tell them what you want. It's not my business."

I focused on the drive while unpacking that statement. On the one hand, I really wanted to tell my family about her. Well, not so much *tell* them as not have to continue hiding it. But on the other hand, the fact that Olivia didn't consider it her business seemed wrong.

"I don't need to tell my family anything. We don't have that type of relationship. But I'd love to be able to touch you without worrying about who's nearby. And with Leighton sleeping in her old room, you'd be better off just staying in my room rather than the guest room way down the hall."

I turned to gauge her expression as we rolled up to the stoplight.

"You want me to sleep in your bedroom and have your entire family know it? Maybe we could just embroider the word "slut" on my party dress instead."

I bit back a smile. "How about we just set you up in the guest room?"

Olivia had agreed to stay at the house for four nights, in part for my graduation party the next day and her father's party the day after that. We hadn't really discussed what we would do after that, and I wasn't going to press the issue. We didn't need a plan for everything to work out. Olivia could return to campus while I started my internship, and I'd drive to visit her every weekend. Maybe, once I got my new apartment set up, she'd even stay with me when she didn't have early morning practices. It would be fine.

By some miracle, the house was empty when we arrived. I walked Olivia up to the guestroom and then we changed to head outside for a tennis match.

"You should be way better at the game after growing up with this amazing setup in your back yard," she teased as we took a water break after the second set.

"Ouch," I replied clutching my chest as though deeply offended. She leaned across the net, kissing me slowly. A happy growl escaped my throat. "If I forfeit the rest of this match, could we just head inside and do more of that?" I asked.

Before she could answer, a noise caused us both to jump back. I turned to see my sister Leighton.

"Congratulations!" she called.

I hesitated, momentarily forgetting I'd just graduated and that she wasn't praising my kissing skills. "Thanks. What are you doing here?"

She walked closer. "Mom and I went to pick out some last minute floral arrangements for your party tomorrow. Nice to see you again, Olivia."

Olivia smiled politely.

"Can I watch the rest of your game?" Leighton asked.

I glanced at Olivia, who simply shrugged, so I told my sister it was fine. Even though Olivia had been beating me with ease earlier, she suddenly started missing shots. I thought it was odd that she was letting me win simply for my sister's sake, but as she cast an awkward gaze at the house, I spotted my father. He was on the balcony outside of the master bedroom, sipping what I assumed to be a strong cocktail and staring at us from beyond the railing.

I supposed it was sweet that Olivia was making me look good in front of my dad, but nothing I could possibly achieve would impress him at this point. After the final set, we followed my sister inside and made polite conversation with my mother.

Olivia relaxed as soon as Ansley joined us, but by the time the whole family finished dinner together, it was obvious she was going stir crazy. I talked her into a quick dip in the hot tub, although she wouldn't get within three feet of me while we soaked, and then we hurried straight upstairs. I ducked into my room to grab anything I might need for the night, then snuck down the hall to the guest room.

"What do you think you're doing?" she asked, eying my handful of clothes suspiciously.

"I figured we both need a shower. And then I'm sleeping in here. I'm not about to leave you all alone in this big house."

The delay before her smile appeared dragged on so long that I actually started to worry Olivia didn't want me sleeping in her room. But then she nodded for me to follow her to the shower.

"So why did we spend the night in your room the last time I stayed here?" she asked.

"We wouldn't have had any privacy in Leighton's room," I replied. "Not with how noisy you can be."

"Huh?"

"Something with the layout of her room," I explained. "Noise travels straight from her room down to the sunroom. Back when I was in high school, I could sit in the sunroom and hear every single word of her phone conversations."

"But this room is soundproof?"

"Let's find out," I replied, leaning in to kiss her.

CHAPTER TWENTY-SEVEN

- Olivia -

I slept surprisingly well with Nate by my side. After my coffee, I moved to the tennis court to practice for a couple hours, and then Nate joined me for a run. By the time we got back, a slew of caterers and florists and other service people had overtaken the house, setting up for the graduation party. I couldn't help but try to picture the party my mom would throw for me when I graduated the next year. She'd likely invite me to the diner, where the other waitresses would congratulate me and give me a free milkshake.

Nate, in contrast, was being celebrated by close to two hundred guests. The invitees included his father's business associates, family, friends of the family, and a handful of Nate's friends from school and the tennis team. Once the festivities were underway, I did my best to stick close to Nate's teammates. Nate had told Mason we were involved, but as far as I could tell, he didn't realize I was actually staying at the Aldridge manor that week. And the other guys may have suspected Nate and I were more than friends, but it didn't appear that anyone had confirmed that fact for them. All of that made me feel much more comfortable, although I couldn't pinpoint why.

Nate had given me no reason to doubt his feelings lately. He told me he loved me and his actions were consistent with his words. He wasn't seeing anyone else, and I didn't think he was embarrassed by my background. But other than that, I wasn't so sure about anything.

Seeing Nate surrounded by all the other rich people, I couldn't deny he was in his element. Nate—or Nathaniel as everyone at the party called him—may have fit in just fine on campus too, but *these* were his people. Nathan would be in his element at any country club in the nation. He knew how to dress for oddly formal graduation parties. He knew what to say and how to talk with people whose watches cost more than I spent on rent in a year.

I, however, did not. I could smile politely and shake hands, and I even could feign interest in short discussions when standing at Nate's side, but I didn't know how to respond to these people. I couldn't relate to their concerns about changes in coast guard regulations for their stupid yachts or which stocks did what overnight. I had no preference between the U.S. Virgin Islands or British Virgin Islands, and I'd probably never travel to Hawaii or New Zealand. All of the vivid shows of money left me itchy and unsettled. I would never fit into this world, and surely Nate saw that, too.

He didn't kiss me during the party, didn't even hold my hand, although our fingers brushed together multiple times. And while I could interpret that to mean he was embarrassed by our relationship, it could just have easily have been something he did for me, since he knew I wasn't eager to flaunt our involvement. But the fact remained that there had been no mention of a future between us.

Over the past few weeks, Nate had fleetingly mentioned different cities he'd like to visit with me or activities we should pursue together, but it was always in the vague and generic way, like, oh this would be fun. There had been no concrete invitations, and not even a cursory discussion of how he'd ever find time for me between his MBA program and his internship at his father's company.

Besides, we'd be living in separate towns. Logically, he had no intention of us staying together after summer.

"Are you having a nice time?"

I jumped, practically spilling my iced tea at the sound of the deep, smooth voice. How I hadn't noticed Jameson Aldridge sauntering up beside me was a mystery.

"I am. Thank you. You throw a lovely party," I replied, regaining my composure quickly.

He chuckled and then raised his glass to his lips. "I can't take the credit. That's all Jackie. Well, and the staff of sixty that she makes do all the real work."

I mustered a smile, hoping it covered up my surprise at the fact that he—and many other guests—were actually drinking martinis, complete with green olives on a spear, from an actual breakable martini glass at an outdoor mid-afternoon party. I felt like I was trapped in some James Bond warp zone.

"You look beautiful, by the way," he added, although I wished he hadn't. "I may not agree with all of my son's decisions, but he certainly has excellent taste in women."

I turned away, clenching my teeth together and desperately trying to think of an excuse to walk away. Unfortunately, nothing came to me.

"Do you have a job lined up over the summer?"

The abrupt transition in topic threw me, but I welcomed it. "I'm training year-round now, but I teach tennis clinics and private lessons still."

Mr. Aldridge smiled. "I bet you're an excellent teacher. Your students are lucky." His words seemed kind enough, but then he threw in a wink that rubbed me the wrong way. Before I could vomit, he squeezed my shoulder then gazed past me. "Excuse me. I think it's almost time for my speech."

I watched in confusion as he strolled off, whispering something to Nate before joining his wife near the DJ stand.

The rest of the party dragged on, and I was happy when the final guests departed. Mr. and Mrs. Aldridge disappeared into the house the moment the official gathering concluded, but a couple of Nate's closer friends from school remained. The caterers and other uniformed staff were cleaning up, but we all sat at one of the round tables off to the side.

Nate kissed the side of my head. "That was exhausting."

I nodded my agreement.

"We could go somewhere to get a real drink," Mason suggested.

"But it's all free here," Nate replied, making us all laugh.

We hung out with the group for over an hour before I excused myself to head inside. It wasn't a reasonable bed time yet, but I was worn out. Besides, Nate surely could use some time alone with his friends.

I was toying with treating myself to a relaxing bath when there was a knock at the door. I was still dressed, so I went to the door, praying it was Ansley or Nate and not Mr. or Mrs. Aldridge.

"Hey," Nate greeted me, his rich eyes filled with concern. "Everything okay?"

I nodded and explained that I was giving him some time with his friends.

"I'd rather have time with you. Do you want me to send them home? It's getting late anyway."

"No! It's your day, and it's early. Don't be ridiculous. You should celebrate."

He hesitated, clearly still concerned that something was wrong.

"I'll be back down soon," I finally promised. "I just need a few minutes of quiet."

"You're not panicking about the party at your dad's tomorrow, are you?"

I hadn't been, but now that it was on my mind, I surely would be. Especially if I was alone. I might as well join Nate back downstairs. I plastered a smile to my face and walked to the door. "Come on. Let's not keep everyone waiting."

* * *

- Nate -

*O*livia fidgeted with her skirt the entire time we drove to her dad's. I reached for her hand, squeezing it to show my support, but then she just busied her right hand.

"You've already met him and your half-brothers. Everyone loves you. You have nothing to be nervous about," I reminded her.

She turned towards the window, obscuring my view of her expression. "I haven't met Peter's parents."

"Well, like I said. Everyone likes you. They're no exception."

"They might be."

"So what? You don't need their approval. You've made it twenty-one years without doting grandparents."

Olivia gazed towards me, working her bottom lip with her teeth. "That's true," she finally agreed. "But what if they *do* like me and I just can't forgive them?"

I didn't have an easy solution for that and frankly, that was a much more likely scenario. Olivia was amazing in so many ways, but her ability to forgive wasn't exactly high on that list. She had an innate dislike of most people before she even met them, and if it was hard to overcome her disdain when you'd done nothing to deserve it, it would be damn near impossible if you actually wronged the woman who'd raised her.

"That one's it," she said, pointing to a stately house on the right.

I was surprised when she actually let me hold her hand walking up to the door. We rang the bell, and a moment later, a woman who didn't look much older than us answered.

The woman smiled. "You must be Olivia. I'm Stella."

I caught the flicker of confusion in Olivia's eyes before her lips curled upwards. "So nice to meet you. This is Nate."

I shook her hand, and then she accepted the gifts we were holding while spouting the requisite crap about it being unnecessary. She motioned for us to make our way through the house to the back yard. I gripped Olivia's hand firmly, but she stopped abruptly as we reached the back patio.

I guessed without seeing her face that she must have located her grandparents. "Just get it over with," I whispered through gritted teeth. "But be civil. It's a kid party."

Olivia swiveled her head around to grimace at me. I shrugged. I stood behind my warning. I knew her well enough to realize the reminder was warranted.

She started straight towards them, but just before we reached them, her dad jumped in front of us.

"Olivia! Nate. So glad you both could make it. Have you seen the boys yet? They'll be excited to see you," he said.

Peter was clearly nervous about the direction in which Olivia was headed, but his parents had already spotted us anyway. Peter awkwardly made the introductions. I held my breath, certain the next few minutes were crucial to the life of their relationship.

Olivia's grandma's smile was genuine as she pulled Olivia close for a hug. Her grandfather stuck with a simple handshake, but he, too, seemed truly delighted to meet her. After a few minutes, Olivia seemed comfortable enough for me to leave to grab drinks for all of us.

"I'll help," her grandpa offered.

We made our way over to the drink station, where I was delighted but a tad surprised, to see beer and wine offered alongside the kid-appropriate selections.

"So Peter mentioned you live nearby," Mr. Wilkerson said.

"My parents do. It's about a half hour."

"I think Peter told me your father was the head of some business. What's his name again?"

"Jameson Aldridge," I replied.

Mr. Wilkerson looked neither surprised nor repulsed by this. "I think we might have done some business together at some point," he finally said. "Small world."

I nodded and smiled politely as we carried the drinks back to Olivia and her grandma. The two of them seemed to be getting along, with Olivia explaining how the tennis rankings worked nowadays. Mr. Wilkerson asked me more about my internship and my father, so we chatted away. I held my drink in one hand, but kept my other palm gently pressed against Olivia's lower back. She seemed comfortable at the moment, but I didn't want her to forget that I was there for her, both literally and figuratively. Her family struck me as friendly and welcoming, but Olivia had a much harder time seeing people that way. And with her history, I didn't blame her for being hesitant.

CHAPTER TWENTY-EIGHT

- Olivia -

J would never admit it to Nate, but he was right. The party for my half-brothers was perfectly pleasant. I didn't exactly feel like family yet, but there was definitely a connection, something positive brewing. Something I was pretty sure I'd been missing thus far in life. Meeting my grandparents was surreal. I hadn't known how exactly they'd react to me or how I'd respond in turn, but I'd been certain there would be drama. Instead, everything was calm and easy, like a sitcom.

Not wanting to press my luck, I excused myself from the conversation with them to introduce Nate to Logan and Noah. They were predictably quiet, still unsure how to act around me, let alone third parties I brought to meet them. Besides, they were in the middle of a party with their friends.

Just as we were about to move on to say hello to Peter before tactfully sneaking off, Nate's phone rang. His forehead tensed when he checked the caller ID.

"It's my father," he said, already starting to walk off. "It's the third time he's called. I should take this."

I nodded, hanging back until the person talking to Peter walked off, leaving him free.

"It's a great party. The boys seem like they're having fun," I said.

He bobbed his head in agreement. "I saw you talking with my parents earlier. Sorry. I would've stuck around to help you get to know them, but…"

"It's fine," I interrupted. I nearly said I'd wanted to get it over with, but stopped myself in time. Just then, a hand pressed into the dip between my shoulder and neck.

"I'm so sorry, Liv, but there's some emergency and the office and my dad needs me to meet him there," Nate said.

"Oh. Well, okay. Let's go."

He hesitated. "I don't want to drag you to the office. It's the other direction, and it might be some confidential stuff."

"I'll get a cab. It's fine," I insisted.

Nate frowned again. "I'll text Ansley the address and she'll come get you shortly."

Before I could refuse, he kissed my cheek then turned to Peter. "Sorry to run. Thank you for having us." Then he dashed out of the yard.

Peter and I turned back to each other, both of us suddenly shy. I didn't want to talk to him too long, or people would start to ask who I was. But I also felt bad darting away, especially when I really had no one else to talk to.

"I never had any graduation parties," I blurted out. "Especially not for third or fifth grade."

To my relief, Peter's smile was genuine. He hadn't taken my rambling as criticism.

"Kids these days celebrate everything, but divorced kids really get spoiled. It wasn't that great when their mom and I were together, but now we both go out of our way to show them they aren't missing out on anything." He paused for a beat. "Although fifth grade graduation is pretty big stuff. He'll be in middle school next year."

I supposed that made sense. We spoke for a few more minutes before he scurried off to help some of the kids with some over-sized water balloon gun they were yielding. I watched for a few minutes, until I got a text from Ansley saying she was fifteen minutes out.

I said my goodbyes to the boys, then went to thank Stella. We hadn't really spoken much, but the fact that she was at the house seemed to be a good sign for her and Peter.

I politely complimented the house and the party, then gazed around to find Peter.

"I think your grandparents are inside," Stella offered.

"Thanks." I supposed I should say goodbye to them, as well. "It was lovely meeting you, and hopefully we'll have a chance to get to know each other soon," I said, nearly cringing at how easily the words flowed. Maybe I'd been to too many fancy events lately, because the polite, meaningless phrases just fell out of my mouth now.

Stella leaned forward to envelop me in an awkward hug, then released me to go find Peter and his parents. I crossed the patio, then stepped into the bright, yet cool kitchen. Eerie silence greeted me. I paused, suddenly questioning whether anyone actually was inside, but then I heard a voice coming from the den. I tiptoed, not wanting to track any mud from the yard across the hardwood floors. Then I froze when I heard the discussion.

"Peter, we're only saying you should insist on a paternity test," a woman's voice said.

"Especially before you give her any more money," a man chipped in.

I was certain the voices belonged to Mr. and Mrs. Wilkerson, the blood relatives who'd pretended to be doting grandparents. I squeezed my eyes shut, praying Peter would speak up.

"Did you see she's with Jameson Aldridge's boy?" my grandfather continued. "The apple doesn't fall far from the tree."

"What does that even mean?" Peter asked.

"Maybe she's angling to get a huge payday from his parents too," my grandmother said.

I swallowed, trying to force bile back down my throat.

"You're think you're too smart to be scammed, but having money means you've got a target on your back. And how do you know her mother didn't put her up to it? She could've had a baby with someone else right after aborting your child. Are you really going to support that kid just out of guilt?"

That was enough. I'd hit my limit. I took a breath, silently prayed that I wouldn't trip and fall as I barged into the den. Their eyes all widened as they saw me.

"I just wanted to thank you for a lovely party. I had also planned to tell you it was nice to meet you, but…" I turned to Mr. and Mrs. Wilkerson and made a sour face before swiveling back to Peter.

"Also, they're right. You should get a paternity test. Here," I said, reaching up and tugging a hair from my head. I placed it gently on his desk. "I haven't spent a dime of your money yet, so I'll mail a check back to you Monday. If this is what money does to people, I don't want anything to do it."

I scowled at them all a minute longer, then marched out the front door. Relief flooded my system as I saw Ansley pull up right then. I flew into her car, begged her to drive fast, then burst into tears.

I was still sobbing when we returned to the Aldridge house. I wasn't normally a crier, but apparently, I'd hit my max. I texted Nate but got no response, and not seeing his car, I felt even more alone. I hurried through the house and up to the guest room, relieved to finally be alone.

A few minutes later, there was a tap at the door.

"Come in," I whispered, hoping it was Nate. It was Ansley.

"You sure you don't want to talk?"

I shook my head. "Thanks, but no."

She nodded, apparently having assumed I'd refuse. Then she held out her hand and deposited four small pills into my palm. There were two round white pills, a yellow oval-shaped one, and a slightly larger blue oval. "If you want to feel better fast, take these."

"What are they?"

She shrugged. "Nothing illegal. Just overpriced prescription stuff. Sleep aids, but they help with anxiety and just really relax you. Take those three together and you'll sleep great and feel better tomorrow."

"Thanks," I mumbled, not really paying attention to which of the pills she'd gestured.

She smiled shyly and left me alone. I shoved the pills into my pocket, not needing anything else to go wrong today.

* * *

- Nate -

My dad's office "emergency" wasted nearly three hours of my day, and it wasn't the sort of thing I truly needed to be involved in. I got the impression he really just wanted me to know that my internship wasn't merely a title on a piece of paper. If I wanted to collect that ridiculous salary, I'd have to work. Occasionally. Or at least show up.

I called Olivia on my way back, but she didn't answer, so I assumed she was on the courts. It wasn't until I got home and ran into Ansley that I even realized something had happened. Ansley told me Olivia had been really upset and had gone to bed early.

I rushed upstairs to check on Olivia and the guest room was empty. I tried her cell phone again, but it went to voice mail. I checked the tennis courts as a last-ditch effort, but she wasn't there, either.

I pounded on Ansley's door. "You really have no idea where she went?" I asked as soon as she opened the door. But no sooner than I spoke, I figured it out. She hadn't taken her stuff and she wouldn't pay for a cab somewhere unnecessarily. The only possibility was that she'd left on foot. And knowing Olivia, it made perfect sense that she had decided to go for a jog until she felt better.

Ansley shrugged. "I assumed she'd be asleep by now."

"It's eight forty-five."

"I gave her something to relax her."

"What?"

Now my sister shook her head dismissively. "Geez it wasn't heroine. Just some anxiety meds and sleeping pills. I showed her which ones she could take together and it's totally safe."

"Why would she want sleeping pills?"

"She didn't tell me what happened, but she was really upset."

"How do you know if she wouldn't tell you?"

"I'm psychic," she said, deadpanned. Then she rolled her eyes. "She was crying, Nathaniel. A lot."

I blew out a sigh. Olivia was not a crier. If she was crying, whatever had happened must have been bad. Especially if she cried in front of my sister.

"Thanks," I mumbled, starting off to my own room. I wasn't in the mood for a jog, but if Olivia was out there somewhere, I should at least try to find her before she got lost. I stripped off my slacks and collared shirt and grabbed a pair of athletic shorts I'd worn for a quick round on the courts earlier in the day. I stepped into my shoes, not bothering to tie them before dashing down the hall.

I went out the back door, about to take off down the driveway, but thankfully I cast one last glance towards the back yard.

A small figure was seated on the bench alongside the tennis court. I heaved a sigh of relief and hurried towards her.

She glanced up as I reached her, visibly relieved to see it was me. But then she quickly dropped her head back towards the darkened clay court. "You're back," she said, her voice cracking. "How did it go?"

"Liv." I reached for her hand and squeezed it. "Ansley said you were upset. What happened?"

She took her time answering. She carefully tucked a strand of hair that had escaped her ponytail back behind her ear then raised her shoulders in a slow, choppy motion. "I really don't know, honestly. I guess I just realized that people are almost always exactly the way I think they'll be."

I hesitated, unsure of how to respond to that.

"When I have zero expectations of others, they can't disappoint me. But when I start to hope… well, then I have no one but myself to blame. I should've known better. I did know better."

"I have no idea what you're talking about."

She gazed up at me and this time, there was an inkling of a sincere smile, just in the corner of her mouth. "Did you solve the emergency?"

I knew Olivia's M.O. The sooner I gave in and accepted that she wasn't just going to open up, the sooner she'd end up confiding in me. "It wasn't a true emergency. I think my dad just wanted to show me who's the boss or something."

Olivia giggled. "I mean, he is literally the boss, isn't he?"

I nodded. "Yeah. Where'd you run?"

"Who knows? All these McMansions are identical."

"These are actual mansions, Liv, not McMansions."

That time, when she smiled, her dimples showed.

"How far did you go?"

She glanced at her watch. "Three and change. I would've gone longer, but I didn't want to get lost."

"Smart call." I agreed. Olivia had already worked out that

morning, so if she ran more than three miles and still wasn't feeling better, the situation was even more serious than I'd thought. But still, she wasn't going to open up to me until I earned it. I had to be smart. If someone disappointed her, it had to have been her father. So, I'd beat around that bush.

"Let me guess. Your dad's ex-wife's new boyfriend made a pass at you?"

Her eyebrow lifted. "Carol?"

"I meant Stella's. I should've said soon-to-be-ex-wife."

Olivia shrugged. "They might be getting back together. Hard to say. But no boyfriends that I'm aware of. In fact, no one sexually harassed me all day."

"We could change that," I teased.

She narrowed her gaze.

"Seriously, we can head back to my room, get you a shower, and I'll harass the crap out of you. As many times as it takes to cheer you up."

Olivia hesitated, then nodded. She stood first, tugging me towards her.

A heaviness washed over me as I realized I might have misplayed my cards and would never find out what had really happened. But as we walked to the house, I decided maybe that was for the best. Olivia would feel better later, and then maybe she'd tell me everything. Until then, I'd just keep doing my best to distract her.

CHAPTER TWENTY-NINE

- Olivia -

*N*ate followed through on his promise to shower with me. But as I lowered myself to the aptly-positioned bench in his giant shower, gripping his hips in my hands while I took him in my mouth, I was the one in control of the harassment. He protested for a moment, insisting he'd wanted to pleasure me and not the other way around, but this was what I wanted. What I needed.

Watching him turn to putty at my touch reminded me of my power. Nathaniel Jameson Aldridge the Third was wealthier, stronger, and by far had more clout in the world, but I was in control now. And as his fingers clenched my shoulders, his lips moaning my name, his hot seed spilling into my mouth, I finally felt at peace with my day.

"Babe, you didn't have to..."

"I wanted to," I interrupted, rising to my feet and pressing a finger to his lips to shush him.

He stared intently for a moment, then stepped around me, dropping to the bench where I'd been positioned a minute before. He tugged me closer, kissing my abdomen once before parting my legs with his hands and licking me roughly where they met.

I moaned unintentionally, certain I wasn't actually in the mood for him to return the favor. But as his tongue stroked me again and again, my hands drifted to his hair, my hips arching towards his face.

The water was still warm when he finished devouring me, and the steam from the room combined with the intensity of my orgasm made me dizzy.

Nate shut off the water and grabbed a towel, draping it around me before reaching a second towel for himself. "If you're still not ready to talk, I'm going to have to make love to you."

I laughed, too sleepy to envision talking or lovemaking.

"I should sleep in my room," I said.

He shook his head, and I didn't have the energy or desire to protest.

"Fine, then make love to me," I said. I wondered if either of us was actually ready to go again, but shouldn't have been surprised that we were. Stress—and beautifully sculpted men—did crazy things to my libido. Plus, it was the lazy kind of lovemaking that went on and on, building slowly like a fire without enough kindling. But once we got going, the climax was every bit as explosive as ever.

I settled my head against his chest, pleased to hear Nate's rapid heartbeat. He didn't say anything, but between his pulse and his occasional twitches, I knew he wasn't anywhere close to sleep.

"I was right about my grandparents," I finally said. "They're judgmental evil assholes, just like I predicted."

"Hmm," was his reply.

"What does that mean, hmm?"

"I don't know. What was I supposed to say? Good for you?"

"Well, no."

"Sorry."

"Me too. I've had a lifetime to accept that they're jerks, and I shouldn't have thrown that all away on five minutes of pleasant conversation. Am I that starved for praise and affection that I assume someone cares about me just because they make it through small talk without insulting me?"

"I mean, you did just go down on me in the shower, so…" he teased, tilting his head so I'd see his cheeky grin.

I shook my head. "Don't you want to know what they did?"

"Let me guess. Your grandma made a pass at the soon-to-be-ex-wife's new boyfriend?"

"I overheard them telling Peter he should get a paternity test. They thought it was fishy that I just accepted his money. I gave them a hair sample and said I'd return the money."

"Don't do that. They'll still be assholes whether or not you keep the money."

"I've been fine without money for twenty-one years. I don't need it now, certainly not if they're going to think they can treat me like dirt if I take it."

He was quiet for a moment.

"They brought you up, too," I added. "They actually said I was just like my mother, going after some rich guy. I wouldn't be surprised if you get a text warning you to crush up a morning-after pill into my daily coffee."

Nate made a face. "Shit. I spoke to your grandpa some about my dad's company. I bet this is all my fault."

I pressed up to my elbow beside him. "It's not your fault that they're jerks. I've known my whole life that I was better off without a dad or grandparents and it was stupid for me to decide otherwise all of a sudden. Besides, it's not like they didn't realize you were rich before you mentioned your dad."

"What do you mean?"

"I don't know. You just give off that vibe. It's obvious."

"I smell rich?"

"Your watch cost more than my childhood home. People make assumptions. Okay?"

Nate sighed loudly, then slid his arm behind his head. My eyes drifted down to his pecs, which were flexed due to his position. It was a good reminder that this was just for fun. Nate was way too hot—and to rich, for that matter—for this to be anything but a fling.

"I'm going to talk to them tomorrow," he said.

"No, you're not."

"Yeah I am. I'm going to let them know they can't treat you that way."

"I don't need you to fight my battles for me."

"I didn't say you did, but just because you don't need something doesn't mean I don't want to do it anyway."

I frowned, working my bottom lip between my teeth. After a moment, we both laughed softly, apparently simultaneously reaching the conclusion that his statement was incoherent.

"My point is that I want to stand up for you," he finally said.

"No," I replied firmly. "I appreciate the gesture, but this isn't your problem. I don't want you involved."

"I can't just let someone talk badly about you."

I raised my hands. "Too bad. It's not your call."

"Seriously? If someone talks shit, I'm not allowed to defend you?"

"No. You're not. Because I'm a big girl and I can handle things on my own." I waited until his expression changed, signaling that he'd heard and maybe even accepted my words.

He was slow to speak, but he pressed a kiss to my forehead. "I love you," he whispered.

I curled into the nook between his arm and chest, squeezing my eyes shut in hopes of putting the terrible day behind me as quickly as possible. I wanted to simply believe him, and to believe that was enough, that I didn't need a father or grandparents as long as I had the love of a man like Nate.

But I couldn't help replaying Nate's final words in my mind and wondering if Peter had ever said the same thing to my mother.

* * *

- Nate -

I awoke to an empty bed. Olivia's pillow was cold, leaving me to wonder if she'd slept beside me at all or retreated to the guest room once I'd fallen asleep. I rubbed my eyes, taking my time to fully rouse before dragging myself to the bathroom. I brushed my teeth, splashed cold water on my face, and debated shaving. Deciding against it, I reached for a pair of athletic shorts and a tee shirt.

The door to the guest room was shut, but opened when I tried the handle. Olivia was nowhere to be seen and the bed was still pristinely made. So, she *had* spent the night with me. Well, either that or she hadn't slept at all. I trudged down the stairs, expecting to find her in the kitchen with her hands curled around a mug of hot coffee, but instead the only person I found was Leighton.

"She's on the courts," my sister explained, nodding her head towards the door.

I followed her gaze outside, where I could make out a figure practicing her serves on the court.

"Does she ever stop practicing?" she asked.

"No."

Leighton made a face, as if there were some possible downside to being a dedicated athlete.

Before she could voice a snarky comment to go with the look, I slid open the back door and went to chat with Olivia. She didn't acknowledge me as I made my way to the court, but that wasn't surprising. I couldn't be offended by her focus. When she ran out of balls, though, I grabbed the hopper and began to collect the scattered ones from the other side of the net.

"Did you sleep any?" I asked.

"Uh huh."

"Are you okay?"

"Uh huh."

I sighed, collected the rest of the balls, then walked around the court to meet her. Finally, she smiled. Her hair was pulled back into a braided ponytail, her eyes were bright, and her skin was glossy. By comparison, I looked like I'd slept in my car.

"For someone who didn't sleep much, you sure look alert today," I told her.

"Alert? Wow, now that's a complement."

I swatted her butt in response.

"I thought I'd go for a run before it gets hot," she said.

I guessed it was already upwards of seventy, but it would only get worse as the day went on. "I need to grab some shoes first," I said. "And eat something." As much as Olivia thrived with only coffee in the morning, I was certain I'd collapse if I ran without something substantial in my stomach.

"Actually, I'd rather go alone if that's okay with you. I need some time to think."

I stared at her, trying to gauge her mood before nodding. "Yeah, okay. Call if you get lost?"

She nodded then slapped her palm on my shoulder like I was just another of the guys.

The kitchen, thankfully, was empty when I returned, letting me enjoy a peaceful breakfast. I tried to get motivated to accomplish something productive after eating, but instead, I wound up poolside. It was after noon by the time Olivia returned, and somehow, I convinced her to join Ansley and I by the pool after she showered and ate.

I appreciated Ansley's laidback demeanor, since she was clearly the only person in my family who didn't make Olivia uncomfortable. But when she finally left me alone with Olivia mid-afternoon, I didn't complain. Olivia seemed fine, but she hadn't said much all day. We needed a chance to talk. Besides, seeing Olivia lounging poolside in her tiny, black bikini, I was struggling not to ogle her. Or touch her.

I crooked my finger at Olivia in what I thought was a sexy 'come hither' type motion. She grimaced.

"Join me for a swim," I said.

She smiled, but shook her head. "I should practice a little more."

"Or you could cool off in the pool and then practice after dinner when it's a bit cooler."

"A little heat never hurt anyone."

It was tempting to tell her that actually, excessive temperatures hurt and even killed people. Lots of people. But instead, I walked over and reached for her hand.

"I can seduce you right here, in the wide-open patio, or you can join me in the water for a few minutes," I said.

She rolled her eyes but stood and followed me to the edge of the pool, shrieking as I dove in. Olivia perched on the edge, dipping her toes into the cool water.

I shook my head, feeling like a dog shaking the water off its fur. Olivia giggled.

"It's not that bad. It actually feels good," I said. "And once you've cooled off, you'll play much better."

Olivia licked her lips and slowly lowered herself into the water, cringing as it hit her bare stomach. I playfully dove down and grabbed at her ankles, hearing her shriek from underwater. When I came back up for air, she stepped closer, grinning.

"How many girls have you flirted with in this pool?"

My brain flashed back to high school, when my parties tended to attract a fair number of attendees. "None that were as hot as you," I finally said.

Olivia rolled her eyes dramatically, but let me kiss her.

She stayed in the pool with me for over an hour, happily letting me distract her from her drive to practice. When she finally climbed out and dried off, I was ready to head inside, too. We walked upstairs together, both of us avoiding the judgmental glare from Leighton. I didn't know what her problem was anyway. It was Sunday. Why did she care if we were relaxing? And why was she still here anyway?

"Need another shower?" I asked Olivia, wiggling my eyebrows eagerly.

"Not before I go hit balls," she replied. "You could join me though."

I considered that, but opted to talk to continue my laziness instead. Now that my competitive tennis days were behind me, there was no reason for me to suffer through crazy summer heat to practice.

"Nope. You go. Maybe I'll join you later."

She smiled, then ducked into her room to change. I went ahead with my shower, then took my time lounging around my room and texting some friends. I switched into dry shorts, then started back into the hall, nearly slamming into Leighton.

CHAPTER THIRTY

- Olivia -

*a*fter the refreshing swim, I figured I could handle a couple hours on the court before overheating. My hair was still damp, which kept my head and shoulders cool even after I secured it with an elastic band. I only practiced my serve for about fifteen minutes when I felt thirsty. Somehow, in my eagerness to get back outside while still cool from the dip in the pool, I'd forgotten to grab a water.

I finished hitting the balls from the basket I was using, then collected them all and grabbed my racket to start back to the house. I felt silly carrying my racket with me, but still did it. It was habit, never to leave my prized belongings—or a mess—on the court, but also, I generally practiced on courts where others could steal anything I left out. Obviously, that wasn't a concern here, in the middle of the Aldridge estate. But it also didn't feel like appropriate guest behavior to leave my crap on their courts, either.

I entered the house through the sunroom, and went straight

up to the guest room. I grabbed my water bottle then peeked my head into Nate's room. It was empty.

"Nate?" I called.

Silence ensued.

I trudged back to the sunroom with my water bottle, determined to enjoy a few minutes of air conditioning before returning to the court. I sipped my water, then bent to tie the laces on my left sneaker. I froze when I heard Nate's voice.

"Why are you still here anyway?" he snapped.

I startled. It sounded like he was right behind me. But when I turned, no one was there.

"Shouldn't you be home with your husband?" he continued.

I cringed, realizing the voice was coming from above me. I remembered him telling me the sound traveled well from his sister's room above the sunroom. Clearly, he hadn't been exaggerating.

"He's still traveling," Leighton barked back.

"Seems like your loyal husband is gone an awful lot. Maybe there's something you're not telling us," Nate retorted.

I clenched my teeth together and started to the door. I'd never heard Nate speak so harshly to someone, but the conversation was clearly not my business.

Well, until it was.

"Don't change the subject. We're talking about your relationship, not mine," Leighton said, her voice carrying even more loudly than Nathan's.

"I'm not discussing Olivia with you," Nate said, stopping me in my tracks.

"Who said anything about discussing? You don't have to say anything. I'll do the talking." Leighton paused before continuing. "You're not in college anymore, Nathaniel. It's time to grow up. You can't just play around."

"I have a job and I'm going to grad school. That's hardly playing."

"I saw you two, making out in the pool all day. What are you thinking?"

There was a muffled sound before Nate replied.

"She's hot. I bet you could guess what I was thinking."

"You can't just sleep with random girls. You are an Aldridge. You're supposed to take over the family business someday. You need to act respectably."

"I can kiss whoever I want at my house. It's not like we were fooling around at a press junket."

"What if she gets pregnant? Have you considered that?"

"I know how babies are made, Sis. You don't need to worry."

"Really? Because I'm pretty sure her father would've said the same damn thing, and now look at him. Forty years old and still paying for a mistake he made twenty-one years ago with some cheap hussy who threw herself at him at a party. Don't even act like you don't see the parallels here."

I swallowed repeatedly, trying in vain to force down the lump in my throat. Why didn't Nate say something? Why wasn't he arguing with her?

"Olivia's not like that," he finally said.

Okay, that wasn't exactly the defense I'd hoped for, but it was something at least.

"Sure. They never are until you're meeting with the company lawyers sorting out the payoffs. God, you're such a cliché."

Nate mumbled something else, but I couldn't make out his words.

"Do you even hear yourself Nathaniel? How do you see this working? Are you going to marry her and live happily ever after? I'm sure she'll fit in really well at the country club with those tennis skills. But what exactly is she going to discuss with all the other wives? And do you seriously think mom and dad will even consider going through with your inheritance if you're still involved with someone like her?"

There was a pause, then Leighton continued her rant. "This is bullshit. I have a business degree too, and I'm the oldest. I should be the one in line for the family business, not you. But I supported you because everyone liked the tradition of the oldest son carrying on. And you finally had a chance to prove to us that you were actually capable of this job, that it wasn't all just a big joke to you. But now you're going to throw it all away on...what, some skank who looks good in a tennis skirt?"

I held my breath, not even sure how I wanted him to respond. Part of me wanted to run up there and slap her myself, but my feet were glued to the ground where I stood.

"God, Leighton, chill out. You don't need to get so worked up over this. Nobody is talking marriage. We always use condoms, and it's not even serious. It's just for fun. I don't know how you thought you saw me looking at her, but we're not even involved. It's just sex."

My teeth clenched so hard together that it actually hurt. And then, I saw a shadow just behind me. I turned slightly, jumping as I realized I wasn't alone.

"Didn't mean to startle you," Jameson Aldridge said, his eyes wandering up my body in that creepy, slow way they always did. "Sound travels really well here. I apologize if you overheard something you didn't want to hear..."

"I didn't hear anything," I mumbled, dropping my gaze to my feet and willing them to work. I shook my head and brushed past him before I burst into tears. "Excuse me."

I dashed up the stairs, then froze at the top. I wasn't about to confront Nate or his sister, so what was my plan exactly? I was inside his house. There was no place for me to run and hide.

I tiptoed to the guest room, quietly pulling the door shut. I scurried into the bathroom, quickly changing out of my tennis gear into the first thing I found—the outfit I'd worn the night before. I began tossing all of my things into a bag, focusing on the work to avoid crying. Then I glanced around the room one last time to checked I hadn't left anything. I poked my head into the hall, confirmed the coast was still clear, then dashed back down the hall.

Relief filled my bones as I stepped onto the front porch without seeing anyone, but then I realized I didn't have my tennis racket. My lucky racket.

I braced myself, then cut through the house, making it all the way to my racket and almost back to the front of the house without running into anyone. But when I got back to the porch, Jameson was there. He scratched his eyebrow, frowning at my bags.

"I, um, I just got a text, and um, I need to head back to campus today. My roommate um, she needs…" I stopped talking, realizing how stupid it all sounded. We both knew why I was leaving and more importantly, we both knew he was glad to see me go. Jameson Aldridge didn't like me any more than I liked him, at least not as a partner for his son. Clearly, Leighton felt the same way.

"I'm going to take a cab back," I said finally. "Thanks so much for letting me stay with you all. You have a lovely house."

Unsure of what else to say, I started off the steps and down the ridiculously long, gravel driveway. The heat was oppressive now, particularly with all of my stuff, but I at least needed to make it past the front gate before I stopped to call a cab. I didn't dare think about what I'd do if I couldn't get a car fast enough. Or if Nate found me before my ride arrived. There was no way I could even look at him after how he'd betrayed me.

God, I was so stupid. How many times was I going to let people prove me right before I started trusting my instincts?

Nate was hot. We had fun together. The sex was good. Too good, apparently. Because somewhere along the line, I'd gotten it in my mind that our chemistry in the bedroom meant something more than it did. Somehow, I'd lost track of my goals. I'd lost myself. I'd lost track of the reality where he was nothing more than a fun, short-term fling.

I ducked around the gate and dropped my bags at my feet. Leaning against the brick pillar, I scrolled along my phone to try to find my best bet for a quick ride out of the suburban prison. I was about to finalize the ride share request when the gate buzzed loudly behind me.

I drew in a sharp breath and scooted to the side, wishing I could make myself invisible. I felt like a toddler standing behind a small flower while playing hide and seek, closing my eyes in hopes that my inability to see the seeker would prevent them from seeing me. I heard the gravel crunch as a car slid to a stop in the mouth of the gate.

Slowly, I opened one eye then another.

It was Jameson, not Nate.

"Do you need a ride?" he asked, his expression a mixture of confusion and disdain.

I shook my head and held up my phone as though he could psychically infer that I was arranging my own ride. "I called for one," I lied.

"I'm headed into the city. You're welcome to come with me. You'll be able to get a ride back to campus quicker from there." He paused and glanced down the empty tree-lined street. "I think you might be waiting a while here, and it's pretty hot…"

I really didn't want to be alone with Jameson Aldridge, but I also didn't want to risk seeing Nate. My desire to avoid Nate was stronger, apparently, so I slowly nodded. I dumped my bags and racket in the back seat of the car then climbed in.

CHAPTER THIRTY-ONE

- Olivia -

*M*r. Aldridge smiled as if the scenario weren't painful and awkward, then he shifted back into gear and took off. I watched in the side mirror as the massive house grew smaller and smaller, exhaling with relief at the absence of any Nate sighting.

I was about to switch off my phone when it buzzed with a text. I glanced down, bracing myself for some pathetic apology from Nate.

Instead, it was Peter.

I cringed, aware that he'd called a couple times and left two voice mails, but I hadn't listened to either. In retrospect, I should have ignored the text, too. Nothing Peter had to say mattered. His words would not dictate my feelings about him, his parents, or myself. He didn't deserve to have any control over my emotions. Or anything, for that matter.

But I needed a distraction from the awkward silence of the car ride with Jameson, so I clicked on the lengthy text to reveal the full message. I braced myself with a deep breath, then read.

"Not sure if you listened to my voice mail or if you'll read this, but I feel terrible about yesterday so I figured I had to try. I don't know how much you overheard, but I'm sorry. My parents are assholes and I should've warned you. The truth is I have no idea what I'm doing. I'm not a great father to my boys and I don't really know what you need from me. I'm not cut out to be a father, especially not to someone who is already grown up. I've enjoyed getting to know you and I feel bad about what you overheard, but if I try to be a parent, I'll just screw it up again. I'd really like to be your friend though."

I stared at my phone, slackjawed. *Friends?* My father just sent me the traditional breakup text. The let's-be-friends text. My *father*. Someone with a biological fucking connection to me wanted to be 'just friends.'

I clenched my phone in my fist, trying to refrain from chucking it out the window, when it buzzed again. Against my better judgment, I glanced down again.

"Also, I don't want a paternity test and I don't think you're scamming me for money. My parents might think that, but I don't care. I want you to keep the money. I already feel bad enough and it's really the only thing I can do for you, so please. Keep it."

I swallowed the lump in my throat and squeezed the power button on my phone to turn it off. I dropped the phone into my purse then squeezed my eyes shut.

"Everything okay?" Jameson asked awkwardly.

I glared at him, annoyed at the ridiculousness of the question. Obviously, everything was not okay. In fact, nothing was okay.

"Super," I mumbled, turning back to the window. I reached into my pocket in hopes of finding a tissue, but instead my fingers brushed against what felt like tiny candies. I carefully pulled out the items, almost laughing as I realized it was the collection of pills Ansley had offered me. I wondered if Jameson knew his youngest was a walking, talking pharmacy. *God*, he probably funded the damn enterprise.

Normally, I wasn't a big fan of medication to soothe the pain. I knew it wasn't healthy, and more importantly, it wasn't something I could control. And I hated not being in control. But at the moment, I didn't have any chance of improving my thoughts on my own. My boyfriend and my father both let me down. They both just wanted to be my friend. My grandparents were judgmental assholes, and my mother had lied to me my entire life about some major things.

Literally, everyone who mattered in my life had betrayed me. Anything I could do to escape that knowledge, even for only a few hours, seemed like a good opportunity. I placed the pills on my tongue and washed them down with a large swig from my water bottle, then I relaxed back against the leather seat.

Jameson cleared his throat, casting repeated sideways glances in my direction. Apparently, he felt he should say something, but I wasn't sure I wanted to hear it any more than he wanted to say it. I turned to the window, trying to signal that I was fine with silence.

"You know, I could just drive you to campus. I don't have any other plans, and it's a nice day for a drive anyway.

"That's not necessary. I don't want to inconvenience you," I said, already dreading an extended time in the car with him. Although, even as I said it, I started to mentally calculate the cost of a ride from the city back to campus. There was surely a bus, but...

"I insist. It's the least I can do after my son—"

At that precise moment, his phone rang, sparing Mr. Aldridge from trying to explain exactly what his son had done.

Jameson pressed some button on the steering wheel, then quickly popped an earpiece into his left ear and answered the call. It was impossible to avoid eavesdropping on his end of the conversation, although I couldn't hear anything the caller said. It seemed to be a work call. After a minute, Jameson clicked something on the stereo, but he didn't remove his earpiece.

"I'm so sorry," he said, disconnecting the call. "I have to pick up some papers that are at my apartment before I can take you to campus. It should only take a few minutes. I can fax them from the apartment."

I already felt bad enough about inconveniencing him. I could think of nothing more mortifying than hitching a ride with the father of my jerky would-be boyfriend, but I'd had no other options. I had to get away when I did.

"No, it's fine. I don't have anywhere to go anyway," I said. I meant for it to make him feel less bad for dragging me along on his errand, but it came out sounding pretty pathetic.

Jameson gazed at me out of the corner of his eye, but didn't say anything. Instead, he flipped on some music. The sound system in his car was amazing, so I actually felt moderately better while the tunes distracted me. I suspected it was actually just that the pills I'd taken were finally kicking it, but I'd rather credit music over pharmaceuticals for my mood.

As we neared the city, Jameson lowered the stereo volume.

"I'm sorry about my son," he said, clearing his throat awkwardly. "He's, um…well, not as mature as we'd like."

"No shit," I mumbled. Then I cringed, remembering I was talking to his father. "I'm sorry. I didn't mean… Well, it's not your fault anyway. He is his own person."

"That he is," he said with a sigh. "I feel that I should have warned you though."

"Warned me?"

"I've seen how he is, I recognize his pattern. I could've told you he wasn't ready for anything serious."

"You hardly can blame yourself for that. You didn't even know we were…involved."

He made a face. "I did though. I mean, I suspected as much.

LIZA MALLOY

You're exactly his type, and I saw the way he was around you. Like a lost little puppy dog."

I didn't have any response for that.

"You could do better than him, you know. You're a smart girl, hard-working, undefeated on the courts..." he turned to me and smiled.

"Thank you."

"You're gorgeous too," he added. "I hope you don't mind me saying that. Not trying to be the creepy older man. Actually, I'm not that much older."

He paused, but I didn't bother to do the math. He *was* that much older.

"Anyway, I just mean on an objective level. You *are* beautiful. I bet you could find some modeling offers if you have any time between the busy tennis schedule."

I tuned him out as he started to list former tennis pros who had appeared on various magazine covers or modeled different gear for ads. I was well aware of the options after I graduated, but I hadn't worked my ass off the last decade so that I could get by on my looks.

"Here we are," he said, gesturing to a tall building. I still thought it was odd that Jameson had his own apartment in the city, but Nate had explained that a lot of executives did that. He claimed it was helpful when they worked late and didn't have time to deal with the commute. Nate had also told me it gave his dad the perfect place to engage in his multitude of extra-marital affairs.

"You might as well come up. I'll be quick, but make yourself at home."

I would've rather sat in the car alone, but he was already pulling towards the curb and handing the keys to a valet.

My legs felt jiggly, so it was probably good for me to walk anyway. Maybe the movement would help metabolize the pills I'd downed.

"You okay?" Mr. Aldridge turned to me.

I nodded and picked up the pace. I didn't want to be what kept him from getting his papers faxed on time. When we stepped onto the elevator, I half expected him to key the button for the penthouse, but apparently, he wasn't that rich. Although, when he did swing open the door to his "little bachelor pad," as he called it, I was impressed. For a place Jameson only used to crash in a couple nights a week, it was roomy.

He flipped on the lights and turned towards a desk near the far wall. As if suddenly remembering I was there, he glanced back. "Sorry. I'll just be a moment. Make yourself at home."

"No rush, Mr. Aldridge," I said.

He made a face. "Please, call me Jameson. Mr. Aldridge is my father." He chuckled as he strode to his desk.

I gazed around at the apartment. We had entered into a small foyer, which opened directly into a large seating area and a kitchen. Everything was light and airy. The kitchen counters and cabinets were white, the appliances sleek stainless steel. The living room furniture was mostly white, with some dark blue accents scattered throughout. A large wall of windows looked out on the city below.

Just past the desk area where Mr. Aldridge, er, Jameson, was flipping through papers was another hallway. I assumed it led to a bathroom and bedroom. Suddenly, I was curious.

"Could I use the restroom?" I asked.

He turned and nodded, pointing down the hall I'd suspected. "First door on your right."

I went in the first room, but counted two doors past it. Clearly there was a master bedroom—probably with its own bath—and a guest room. I couldn't even imagine how much this place cost. And for what? Just so Jameson had a place to take his girl-friends without his wife walking in on them?

I sipped some water from the faucet, touched up my makeup,

and finger combed my hair. Then I just stood there looking at myself in the mirror.

I didn't get it.

Everyone seemed to agree I was pretty. And I *knew* I was phenomenal at tennis, and I earned decent grades, too. So why did I only attract dirtbags? What exactly made me so unworthy of love? Obviously, there was something. Even my own father didn't even love me.

Maybe, I was too cranky, or too intense. I could never just shut up when I should, I always had to keep going and tell everyone exactly what I thought. I was boring and too serious and altogether selfish.

It was no wonder everyone hated me. I didn't even like myself.

I reached for my wrist, pressing my thumbnail against my flesh until it drew blood. I focused on the slight sting, the new physical mark I'd made. That pain was real. The shit in my head? It wasn't. I should be able to let that go in an instant.

Except I couldn't.

The more I tried to focus on my arm, the more I felt the sting of rejection. How could I have been so dumb? I'd realized all along that Nate and I weren't meant to be. He was too good to be true from the start, and I knew it. Yet still, somehow, I'd fooled myself into thinking our relationship could succeed. That I was good enough for him. That I could make him love me.

It had been the same with Peter. My dad. Stupidly, I thought it was working, that he could love me like a father. That he could somehow someday actually be proud of me. Maybe that he'd even defend me when people called me trash. *God*, and those people— my grandparents? *Ugh*. How was I even related to such monsters? And why did I assume that something as meaningless as a biological connection could ever overcome our circumstances?

I was a fool. I was gullible. Stupid. Worthless.

I clutched a hand over my mouth, certain I was about to be sick, but instead, I started crying. Big heaving sobs that I could barely catch my breath in between. I sunk onto the lid of the toilet and covered my face with my hands and cried harder than I ever had before.

I lost track of the passage of time while I sobbed in the bathroom, but the knock on the door startled me. I jumped up, having completely forgotten where I was. I grabbed a tissue for my nose, then took another to dab at my eyes.

"Olivia? Are you alright?"

Jameson sounded so concerned that it actually made me feel worse. I didn't deserve sympathy from a stranger. I was worthless, a nobody. Even my own mother didn't think I deserved a father. My own father didn't want me enough to fight for me. The man I thought I loved was just using me for sex.

I opened the door, painfully aware that no reasonable amount of time would make me any more presentable. I tried to speak some sort of apology, but before I could say anything, I stumbled forward a little.

Jameson caught me in his arms and held me in a comforting hug. "Oh, sweetheart. I'm so sorry. Don't cry over him."

I let him hold me for a minute before realizing how incredibly awkward this had to be for him. I pulled back, wiping my eyes again. "I'm so sorry. I, um, I can get a cab."

"A cab? Are you headed back to campus? I faxed my papers, so I can drive you."

"I've already inconvenienced you enough," I said. "I'll just…" I started towards the door, but I stumbled and nearly fell.

He rushed to my side again. "Okay, hang on. You're not going anywhere like this." Jameson walked me to the couch and deposited me on the side. "Sit down," he said in a voice one would use with a dog.

I did. He went to the kitchen and filled a glass with water and brought it over to me. I accepted it and sipped obediently. He sat beside me on the couch, a respectable distance away.

"I'm so sorry about Nate. He's an idiot, if it makes you feel any better. He's always been self-absorbed and he uses people."

I finished the water and Jameson immediately popped up with the glass.

"More water?" he asked. There was a pause, and then he added, "Or something stronger?"

Alcohol actually could make me feel better. Or at least make me numb. "That would be nice," I said.

Jameson disappeared into the kitchen then returned a moment later with a bottle of whiskey and two crystal high ball glasses. He poured some amber liquid into each glass then offered one to me before raising his own in the air.

"Cheers," he said with a wink.

"Cheers," I mumbled, swallowing the bitter liquid and welcoming the burn that traced the path of the drink down my throat and into my abdomen.

As Jameson smiled and refilled our glasses, I realized I was already starting to feel a little bit better.

CHAPTER THIRTY-TWO

- Nate -

I stormed out of Leighton's room, desperate for a drink. It was almost dinner time, anyway. I headed straight to the back yard to see how much longer Olivia planned to practice, but the courts were empty. I turned to go back upstairs, curious how I could've missed seeing her in the guest room when I left Leighton's.

I slammed right into Ansley. "Sorry," I mumbled, patting her bicep as I started around her.

"What did you do?"

I raised an eyebrow.

"Olivia's stuff is all gone."

"What?" I didn't wait for her to answer. I pushed past my sister and jogged to the second floor, taking the steps two at a time. Sure enough, the guest room was empty. I glanced down at my phone to confirm I didn't have any missed calls from Olivia, then checked my own room in case she'd moved her things in there.

Instead, there was no sign of Olivia.

I sat on the bed and dialed her number, but it went straight to voice mail.

"Did you guys have a fight?" Ansley asked as I hung up.

"No. We were great. She was just out playing tennis." I grinned thinking about the fun we'd had in the pool that morning, and we'd definitely had fun the night before. Hell, we'd had fun twice. Surely Olivia was still upset about what happened with her grandparents, but she didn't blame me for that. She would've told me if she was leaving.

"Are you okay?" I texted Olivia, clicking send before typing a second message, simply asking, "where are you?"

I blew out a sigh and turned back to my younger sister. "I don't know. I guess something must have come up, because she wasn't planning on leaving until tomorrow. And she's not answering her phone now, so—"

"Oh good. You're both in here," Leighton said, popping her head into my room. "I'm heading out now. Just wanted to say goodbye."

The moment I saw Leighton, it all snapped into place. "Shit."

My sisters both turned to me expectantly. I rose to my feet, glaring at Leighton. "I hope you're happy. Olivia overheard everything you said about her and now she's taken off."

I didn't wait for my sisters to answer before heading downstairs. If I was right, if Olivia had overheard, she wasn't going to accept my calls or read my texts. I'd have to find her in person to make her listen. I jogged to my car.

I spent the entire drive to campus trying to ignore the visions of the future I'd now ruined. God, I'd been so stupid. I'd acted like I was fine with the casual relationship Olivia pretended to want, but it was all a lie. I needed Olivia, needed her more than air. I couldn't imagine my life without her kisses, her sassy quips, or her sarcastic jokes. I couldn't live without hearing her laughter, seeing her smile, tasting the salty sweet tang of her skin after a long match.

I wanted a life with Olivia more than I wanted anything else. Spending nearly every minute with her over the last several days showed me that I was happiest by her side. I was in the midst of so many big changes, what with moving and starting my internship, yet nothing mattered more than finding Olivia and making sure she understood.

I didn't want just sex with her. I didn't want friends with benefits. When it came to Olivia, I wanted it all.

* * *

- Olivia -

*T*he throbbing headache greeted me before I even opened my eyes. I briefly considered trying to fall back asleep, but the pain was too intense to sleep through. I needed Ibuprofen. I tried to recall why my head hurt so badly, and the first thing that came to mind was whiskey. With... *oh shit.*

My eyes flew open as terror flooded me. The first thing my eyes settled on was the other half of a bed. Thankfully, that half of the bed was empty, aside from a pillow and jumble of sheets. I turned my head slowly, praying the rest of the room was similarly vacant. Once I confirmed that it was, I slowly sat upright.

Nausea swirled throughout me, but I forced it back down, focusing on my breathing. I gazed down at my body, somewhat relieved to find that I still wore my panties and bra. My shorts were on the floor next to the bed, so I slipped them on. Then I stood, studying my surroundings more closely in hopes of finding my shirt.

The room was swathed in gray, with sparse but modern furnishings. If not for the attached bathroom and walk-in closet, I would've assumed it to be a guest room since it didn't appear someone lived there full time. Except, I realized, no one did. Mr. Aldridge was only at his apartment occasionally. He just dropped by whenever he needed a quickie with whatever floozy crossed his path.

I caught a glimpse of myself in the mirror, my hair matted and my eyes puffy, and my stomach churned again.

I dashed into the bathroom, emptying the sparse contents of my stomach in the pristine toilet and then rinsing my face and mouth with cool tap water. Still not having located my shirt, I grabbed the robe hanging beside the shadow and wrapped it tightly around myself. As much as I hated the thought of wearing Jameson Aldridge's bathrobe, picturing him seeing me topless was even more disturbing.

Of course, he probably already had seen that— and more. I lunged back towards the toilet, but there was nothing left to throw up. Steeling myself for an awkward encounter, I slowly opened the bedroom door. As I crept into the excessively bright living area, silence greeted me. Glancing around, I confirmed there was no sign of Jameson, or anyone else for that matter.

The aroma of freshly brewed coffee overpowered my weak stomach and I turned, seeing an empty mug in the sink. On the counter beside the sink was a note.

"Had to leave for work. Brought your stuff inside. Here's money for cab to campus."

The note wasn't signed, but only one person could've written it.

On the plus side, I was alone. But really, that was the only positive. Every single other aspect of my current situation, and my life in general, was absolute and complete shit.

I spotted my bags and rifled through them, retrieving a shirt. And then, I located a clean mug and poured myself a cup of coffee. Hopefully, warm liquid would settle my stomach. I couldn't actually recall how much I'd drank the previous night, but I'd definitely finished at least three shots of whiskey. On an empty stomach, that was more than enough to deliver a nasty hangover in someone my size.

God. Why had I drank so much without eating dinner?

Before I could even finish chastising myself for overindulging in whisky, I remembered Ansley's pills. *Crap.* Maybe that was why I couldn't remember anything after the third drink.

I supposed it didn't matter. I didn't have to be a genius to figure out what I'd done. Waking up half naked—and in Mr. Aldridge's bed—was a pretty big clue. It was what I always did—I took a shitty situation and fucked it up even more.

I felt dirty. I raised my arm to my nose and sniffed it, as though I'd still be able to smell him on my skin. Just the thought of his slimy hands on my body made me gag again. I scratched at my arms, truly understanding the expression that something could make my skin crawl.

I needed a shower, with all the soap in the world. I reached into my purse for my phone, switching it on to call for a ride, then cringed as the series of missed calls and voice mails popped up. Another wave of nausea hit me, so I returned to the bathroom. Jameson was gone for the day anyway, so I might as well shower.

I waited for the water to heat up, then climbed in, immediately reaching for the soap. I lathered my body and rubbed all over my skin until it was raw. I felt a bit better, but not necessarily cleaner. I wrapped my arms around myself, shivering despite the hot water pounding into my skin. Then I pressed my nails firmly against my bare flesh again and again, focusing on the vivid red spots that would appear. After a moment, I stepped back into the spray of the water, turning my head towards the drain to watch as the blood dribbled down.

I dried quickly, then put on fresh clothes and briskly wound my hair into a single braid down my back. I searched one last time for my old shirt, then gave up. I wedged my phone into my purse then glared at the two one-hundred-dollar bills Jameson had left on the counter beside his note. Was he trying to make me feel like a prostitute? Or maybe was the money just to shut me up?

I shivered with disgust, then ripped his note to shreds. Leaving the cash untouched, I grabbed my stuff and let myself out, confirming the lock clicked shut behind me. I rode the elevator down to the lobby and then used my phone to arrange for a ride back to campus.

CHAPTER THIRTY-THREE

- Nate -

Olivia wasn't at her apartment and she wasn't at the tennis courts. I wasn't sure where else to go. She wasn't answering my calls and neither Mia nor her roommate had any idea where she might be, either. I considered trying Olivia's mom, except I didn't have a number to reach Laurie Roberts, and I suspected she and her daughter weren't on speaking terms at the moment anyway.

Without any other options, I drove back to Olivia's apartment and sat on the front step. Not exactly what I'd planned for my last day as a free man before my wretched nine-to-five working life had begun, but however long I had to wait, I owed it to Olivia. I had been a colossal ass.

I hunched over and rest my head in my hands. I'd actually dozed off when the slam of a car door woke me. I opened my eyes and saw Olivia scurrying away from an older Prius.

She looked terrible. Her eyes were red and swollen and her complexion was pale, like she was sick. I instantly felt a hundred times worse than I had before. *I* had done this to her.

"Liv, I'm so sorry," I said, rushing towards her.

She jumped back as though frightened, then held her ground.

I tried to take her duffel bag off her shoulder but Olivia shook her head. "You can't come in," she said.

I couldn't blame her for that. "I'm so sorry," I repeated. "I wasn't thinking about anything my sister was saying. I've gotten into the habit of tuning her out and agreeing just to get her to shut up. Leighton can be a total bitch and she's the most stubborn person I know. There's no point in arguing with her when she gets an idea in her head. I don't agree with any of that stuff she said about you, and once I started paying attention to her, I did stand up for you. I should've done it sooner, should've said more, but I just haven't known how to handle things as long as we're keeping it a secret."

Olivia squeezed her eyes shut, and the duffel slid down her shoulder. I grabbed it and set it on the ground beside us, taking the opportunity to step closer.

"Leighton is wrong about you, and I told her as much. I also told her that I'm in love with you," I said.

Olivia's eyes flew open. "You shouldn't have done that. She's your family. Just…forget about it."

"I can't forget about it. The things she said—that was horrible. And I hope you know I really don't think of you that way. I never did, honestly."

She shook her head. "You were right. I'm not good enough for you. We don't belong together."

"What?" I screeched. I hadn't meant to yell, but her words caught me off guard. "I screwed up and I know it. And I'm sorry. I can't lose you over this. I love you, Olivia."

She slumped down to the steps and pressed her hands over her face. Her shoulders shook as she sobbed.

I sat beside Olivia and wrapped an arm around her, trying to rub her biceps to soothe her. Instead, all I did was knock her thin shirt off her shoulders. I started to tug the top back into place when I spotted them—the small, half-moon shaped red marks on her arms. It was along her biceps mostly, but I suspected if I looked at her forearms I'd see them there, too. It was the distinct mark from her own fingernails, cutting into her skin. I remembered everything she'd confessed to me months ago about her depressing high school years.

A wave of nausea washed over me at the knowledge that I'd made her feel that awful. Because of me, the woman I loved had actually resorted to hurting herself. "Baby, no. Liv, come on." I kissed the marks along her arms, wishing I could actually make her better with a simple kiss. She tried to shrug me off, but I kept going. After a moment, I realized my own eyes were getting damp.

"Liv, please. Let's go inside. Let me help you clean up. You need something to eat, sleep, and we can talk."

"Stop touching me!" Olivia shouted, brushing me away.

The tenor of her voice caused a couple of strangers passing by to turn and stare. I inched away, complying with Olivia's request even though it pained me.

"I will do whatever it takes for you to forgive me, Olivia. Whatever I have to do to earn your trust again. I blew it and I'm so sorry. You have to know how much you mean to me." I paused. I was painfully aware I was bordering on pathetic, but how else should I sound? I was desperate. I knew without a shadow of a doubt that Olivia was the woman for me. And not only had I killed my chances of a future with her, but I'd also hurt the person I cared most about.

"Olivia, for years I've pictured my future and never have I envisioned any version of my adult life where I'm happy. Until now. The last couple months, with you, that's all changed. I don't care what's going on with my family, what I'm doing for work, as long as you're with me, I'll be happy. And I know I can make you happy. I promise I will."

Olivia pressed one hand to her mouth as if she were about to be sick. Then she held the other hand up to shush me.

"Nate, please. Just go home. There is no future for us."

I felt like she'd hit me. Part of me knew the dignified thing to do would be to accept defeat and leave. Later, or maybe in a few days, I could apologize again, and maybe she'd take me back.

But a bigger part of me knew I couldn't last even a few more hours without making things right with Olivia.

"I'm not leaving. You can yell at me, throw things, go inside and ditch me out here. Whatever. But I'm standing right here until you agree to at least let me make it up to you."

She wiped her eye on her sleeve and then stared straight at me. "There's no point."

I didn't budge.

Olivia winced. "Ask me where I was last night, Nate."

I shook my head. It didn't matter.

She pressed on. "Ask me who I was with. You must've realized I wasn't here. Surely you're curious."

Well, I *was* curious.

I'd assumed she'd stayed with a friend, but after how I'd behaved, I also figured I had no right to know. Something was off with the tone of her voice, though. Olivia didn't really want me to ask. She was trying to tell me something. Something about where she'd spent the night.

Where she'd spent the night after I broke her heart.

Shit.

The thought of her with another man killed me. A pang of jealousy ripped through me every time I saw her even talk to other guys, so the idea that she had spent an entire night with someone else... I clenched my fists together, squeezed my eyes shut, then turned to face her again.

"It doesn't matter, Olivia. Whatever you did last night, you did it because of what I said, how I treated you. It's all forgivable. It doesn't change anything between us." I told myself that was the truth. I couldn't be upset when I'd driven her into another man's arms. I would make myself get over it. We'd both been with other people before, and none of that mattered. What mattered is that we would be each other's last partners.

"Ask. Me." she repeated, her tone firm.

I rolled my eyes. "Fine. Where were you last night?"

Her bold blue eyes resembled cut glass as she spoke, her tone unnaturally calm and her words uncharacteristically formal. "I went to an apartment in Manhattan last night. With Jameson Aldridge."

Olivia stopped talking, but I still didn't fully appreciate what she was saying. I'd assumed she was with another man, so the fact that she just had my father drive her someplace seemed better. Olivia waited for me to figure it out, but after a minute, she continued.

"I spent the night with your father, Nate."

Olivia held my gaze for a moment, but as I felt the weight of her words hit me, she turned away, a small sob escaping her lips.

"What do you mean, spent the night?" I asked.

She didn't answer, so I stepped closer, gripping her arms in my hands.

"What are you saying, Olivia?"

She was crying harder now, but she still tried to look me in the eye. "I don't know. Ansley had given me some pills, and then we were drinking. I don't remember anything that happened last night, but when I woke up this morning, I was in his bed. And my clothes were gone."

I dropped her arms like they were burning my hands. I stared at Olivia for a moment, trying to make sense of what she'd just said, but it was futile.

She was right. There was no future for us.

Lashing out because she was upset, that was forgivable. Even hooking up with some random guy was forgivable, under the circumstances. But fucking my father?

That was not something I could forgive. And definitely not something I'd forget.

I turned and walked off down the street without another word.

CHAPTER THIRTY-FOUR

- Olivia -

*W*atching Nate walk away hurt even more than I'd expected. I had assumed that once I came clean, once I told him that he was right, that I was a worthless, cheap, piece of trash, that I'd feel better. I had anticipated him yelling, maybe even throwing or kicking something. Anger, I was prepared for.

That crippling look of pain in his eyes—that was unexpected. So was the fact that he walked away without a single word. Nate —the boy who never shut up—was actually rendered speechless by my horrific and unforgiveable conduct.

I couldn't blame him.

I went inside my apartment and stared at my surroundings. Addie was gone for the summer, and since I, too, had been gone for several days, the room was hot, stuffy, and dark. I adjusted the air conditioning, left the blinds shut, and made my way into the kitchen. I had no fresh food, but luckily an unopened box of cereal remained on the shelf. I poured myself a bowl, ate it dry, then washed it down with a glass of water and some ibuprofen.

Then I crawled under the covers of my bed and slept.

When I woke, it was evening. I ate another bowl of cereal, swallowed more pills, and returned to bed.

In the morning, I felt better, but only physically. As soon as I stood, I remembered the horror of everything I'd done. The onslaught of emotions hit me and tears welled up in my eyes. I held off as long as I could, but once I began crying, I couldn't stop.

I dropped to the floor in the center of my living room, sobbing until my tears ran dry and my muscles spasmed from the sheer exhaustion of bawling so hard and so long. Then I dragged myself to the couch, pulling a blanket over my head and squeezing my eyes shut. For the next several hours, I stayed there, feeling safely sheltered by reality by the blanket. I got up only to fetch tissues and use the bathroom.

When the doorbell rang, I had no intention of answering. But then my phone chimed with a text from my Coach.

"OPEN YOUR DOOR," it read.

I groaned and tugged a sweatshirt over my head before heading to the door. Since I'd laid down immediately after my shower, my hair was still damp, and I had no bra. I wasn't sure why she was here, but I assumed it had something to do with me missing practice. Still, that didn't really seem like a big deal. It was literally the first practice I'd missed in three years on the team. It wasn't like we had any critical skills to go over today, and I was entitled to a break.

I opened the door, wincing at the assault of light.

Coach Katelyn stared at me, her a mixture a combination of annoyance and concern. She'd clearly come straight from practice. Her whistle still hung proudly around her neck.

"You missed practice," she said.

"I'm sick," I said, gesturing to my attire. I was more than confident I looked ill. After my shower, my eyes were still sunken in and puffy. "And I sent a text."

"It's not like you to miss a practice. You still showed up once when you had that stomach bug."

I grimaced, distinctly recalling that horrible day. I'd thought I was going to die on the court, but I hadn't puked during practice. "We had a tournament to prepare for then."

"Well, you have some pro matches later this summer, so you need to stay sharp. Remember?"

I refrained from rolling my eyes. Obviously I had not forgotten that I was slated to play in a couple professional tournaments over the summer. Only the top college players were ever invited. Since college tennis was largely inactive over summer, the timing was perfect to offer some of us collegiate players a chance to dip our toes in the professional world.

Coach Katelyn brushed past me, inviting herself into the apartment. She peered around as though searching for something. Heat rushed to my cheeks as I realized this was the first time she'd seen my apartment, and it was a total mess. I wasn't normally a complete slob, but I hadn't exactly picked up after myself the past twenty-four hours. Tissues decorated the floor around the sofa, and I'd left a trail of them leading the way to the kitchen.

"You missed practice for a cold?" she asked, staring pointedly.

Uncomfortable with the eye contact, I turned, grabbed a waste basket, and began collecting my tissues. "I'm allowed to miss one practice," I said, in lieu of directly answering her question.

"You're right, but it's unlike you to miss practice so I thought I'd check on you. Is everything okay?"

"Just dandy," I replied, shoving a blanket to the foot of the couch so I could retrieve the tissues stuffed between the cushions. When I thought I'd collected them all, I plopped down the trash can and went into the kitchen to wash my hands.

When I came back, Coach Katelyn was sitting on the chair adjacent to the couch. "Have you seen a doctor?" she asked.

"Not necessary." I plunked onto the couch.

"Will you be at practice tomorrow?"

I considered that. I really wanted to curl up under the covers at the foot of my bed and stay there until I died. But assuming I couldn't actually do that, practice might be a good distraction. Except…would it? Tennis reminded me of Nate.

Then again, everything reminded me of Nate.

"Probably," I finally said.

Coach nodded. An awkward silence ensued. Just as I wondered if I should've offered her a drink or something, she spoke again. "I was surprised when you introduced me to your dad at the last game," she said. "Not that I'm snooping into your personal life, but it's hard not to notice that you never had a dad listed on any of your releases or emergency contact papers. And I don't recall seeing him at earlier games. Does he live far away?"

"No. He's maybe a half hour from campus."

"Oh, wow." She didn't bother to hide her surprise.

"I didn't know he was my father until recently. Apparently, I had to start winning big tournaments for him to claim me," I said, my voice dripping with misdirected bitterness.

"I'm sorry. That must be hard. For the record though, you've always won more than you've lost."

I supposed that was true.

"Have you considered talking to anyone about your father's sudden appearance in your life?"

"Like a private investigator or something?"

She laughed. "No, I mean a therapist. That's a lot to deal with, and I know your mom doesn't live nearby. Talking through things can help."

I shook my head. "Honestly I don't think it's necessary. It's not…ideal, finding out I do in fact have a father when I'm basically all grown up, but it is what it is. And I'm fine."

"You're not fine. You missed practice and you've obviously been crying all weekend."

I probably should've been mortified that my mounds of tissues appeared to be three days' worth and not just one night, but I didn't have the energy to care. "I'm fine," I repeated.

Coach Katelyn rubbed her forehead like I was the frustrating one out of us. "Olivia, if you're fine, why am I getting concerned messages from your boyfriend asking me to check on you?"

My stomach tightened. "He called you?"

"He texted. Yesterday. I planned to talk to you this morning at practice, but you didn't show, so then I was just worried. You're such a private person and for as long as you've played for me, I really don't know much about you. But I do care about you. A lot. And I want you to know I'm here whenever you need me, even if it isn't tennis-related. It has to be hard with Nate moving away…"

"He's not my boyfriend," I interrupted.

She sighed. "Olivia, it's fine. We've known for months. The whole team knows. I would never recommend you date another player, but you're adults, and it's not really my business. You're actually a cute couple."

"He's not my boyfriend," I repeated, hoping if I enunciated the words more clearly, she'd understand what I was telling her. I couldn't stomach the thought of saying we broke up. Saying it out loud would make it too real.

Her eyebrows raised, but she took her time answering. "Oh. Well, I'm sorry to hear that. So this…" she motioned around the messy room. "Is because of Nate and not your dad?"

I gave the slightest of nods in response.

For once, it appeared Coach Katelyn had nothing to say.

"I'll be fine, though. You don't have to check on me."

She hesitated. "He seemed really worried is all. And I don't feel like I know you well enough to say with confidence that you're alright. Would you tell me if you weren't okay?"

I gritted my teeth together, grinding back and forth, focusing on the slight twinge of pain in my jaw as I moved. "I've dealt with shit before. I'm strong. It won't kill me."

Coach mustered a half smile. "You are strong. I would kill for an ounce of your resolve or focus. But it's okay to admit you need help sometimes."

"I know."

She stood then hesitated. "I'd like you to check in later today. And you need to be at practice tomorrow morning."

I nodded.

"You have my number. Please call if you need to talk. I was twenty-one once too. I remember how hard it was, and I had a much broader support system than you."

I walked her to the door, eager to be alone so I could overanalyze what it meant that Nate texted my coach. Probably that he never wanted to see me anymore but would feel guilty if I offed myself. Not that he actually cared. After what I did, how could he ever care again?

I locked the door behind her, grabbed a new box of tissues, and crawled back under the covers in bed.

CHAPTER THIRTY-FIVE

- Nate -

I needed to cool off before confronting my father, but no amount of time would truly calm me down. When I reached the office, the doorman greeted me by name, as always. Only this time, my stomach churned at the sound of the Aldridge moniker. I rode the elevator straight up to the office, storming past the receptionist before I could lose my nerve.

I spotted my father in the smaller of the conference rooms, seated at the head of an otherwise empty table, hunched over his laptop. I knocked on the door, then barged right in.

My father flew back in his seat at the sudden interruption, revealing a woman sitting adjacent to him. I hadn't seen her from the window I'd peered through a moment before. Judging from her age and demeanor, I guessed she was an intern or secretary. I also assumed my father was sleeping with her.

"We need to talk," I said.

"I'm in a meeting," my father replied, scowling.

"I'll be quick. What did you do to Olivia?"

He sighed and turned to the woman. "Please excuse the interruption. This will only take a few minutes."

My father waited as the woman folded her laptop and grabbed her notepad, pen, and coffee mug. Time seemed to move in slow motion as she crept out of the conference room, closing the door behind her. The door didn't offer much privacy, thanks to the wall of windows facing the main hallway of the office, but I didn't care.

When my father finally turned back to me, his expression held a familiar mixture of disappointment and disgust. He'd been scowling at me like that since childhood, when I protested taking the training wheels off my bike and when I couldn't hit the right notes on the piano. He'd offered me the same grimace when I didn't make the football team and when I wasn't accepted to college until he called and offered copious donations to the business department.

I was accustomed to being a failure in his eyes. But now, it was his turn.

I stepped forward. "Did you sleep with Olivia?" I asked, pleased that my voice didn't falter.

The bastard laughed.

"Is that what you think?" He shook his head, still chuckling. "Christ. She's the same age as your sister. You think I just screw anyone who looks my way? Like I'd be dumb enough to subject myself to some bullshit sexual assault charge or ridiculous claim that I fathered some illegitimate piece of shit? I'm not an idiot."

I interpreted his answer as a no, but he continued before I could feel too much relief.

"The little hussy threw herself at me, then passed out drunk. She vomited all over her shirt and started stripping, so I left her in my bedroom and slept in a different room. I didn't touch her."

For the briefest of moments, I was happy. My father wasn't as evil as I'd thought, and Olivia hadn't done something that I'd probably never move past. The situation wasn't nearly as dire as I'd assumed.

But of course, Jameson Nathaniel the Second just couldn't shut up.

"I don't know why you brought home that piece of trash anyway," he said.

I flew forward without a second thought. I registered the pain radiating from my knuckles before I even realized I'd actually punched my father.

From the look in his eyes, my father was even more surprised than I was, although strangely enough, I could've sworn I saw a hint of pride on his face.

Another middle-aged man in a suit burst into the conference room. "We need security!" he belted over his shoulder. He rushed at me, pushing me off my father.

My father raised his hand to his cheekbone, confirming I hadn't drawn blood. He waited a moment, then shook his head. "It's fine, Fred. Just a misunderstanding. Leave us and cancel security. He's calm now." He turned to me. "Right Nathan?"

I recoiled. No one called me Nathan. To my entire family, I was Nathaniel. To my friends and classmates, I was Nate. Inventing a new moniker for me now, in my twenties, seemed cruel. It was almost like my own father had simply forgotten my actual name.

"Yep. I'm good now," I said.

We both watched as the other man left.

"You know she's an alcoholic," my father said.

"She's not," I replied.

What I knew was that she'd drank more than a sip of alcohol maybe twice in the last six months. The first time was the night we'd first hooked up, and that time, she'd been distraught. Olivia only drank to excess when she faced some emotional trauma she didn't think she could handle. She had zero tolerance for alcohol, probably in part because she never drank and in part because she had such an athletic build. I didn't doubt that she'd passed out at my dad's, but I wasn't about to waste my breath convincing him it wasn't from alcoholism.

My father continued in his lecturing voice. "Everything she heard you and Leighton saying was true. That girl is different from me and you. She's going to ruin your good name, take all your money, and leave you."

I snorted. "My 'good name' as you call it is an embarrassment. And Olivia is different from you and me, but not in a bad way. She has integrity and grit. Olivia is a better person than you'll ever be."

My father replied with a sardonic laugh. "We all like to slum it every once in a while. I guess it's good that you're getting it out of your system now."

I stepped closer, gritting my teeth together so hard that pain radiated along my jaw. "If you're not going to shut up, you may need security after all."

My father rolled his eyes but said nothing else.

After a moment, I eased back. I'd said what I needed to say. I'd confirmed what I'd suspected—that nothing had actually happened between Olivia and my prick of a father. Now, I could go.

My father apparently sensed the same and relaxed.

We both glared at each other for another moment before he spoke.

"Obviously, you're fired," he said.

"Obviously," I agreed, having forgotten I intended to quit anyway. I had been fooling myself, thinking I could tolerate an entire summer working under his controlling thumb. "You can mail my unemployment comp along with my trust fund payments."

I backed away and turned towards the door, wincing as I noticed at least a dozen of the office employees had gathered to watch the drama unfold.

"Your grandfather would be so ashamed of you," my father added.

I was sure my father meant that as the worst insult he could possibly muster. To him, my grandfather was a genius. He'd built a company from scratch, forged a name in an industry that was already competitive, and essentially launched an empire. But from everything I saw, my grandfather was also a greedy, demanding asshole, much like my own father. My grandfather's approval meant even less to me than my own father's.

"Then I must be doing something right," I mumbled, yanking the door open and storming out.

I ambled around the city for close to an hour, trying to figure out where to go, or what to do. I didn't want to go back to my new apartment. It didn't feel like home. And I certainly wasn't going to go to my childhood home, even if I knew neither my father nor Leighton would be there. Ironically, what appealed to me most was hitting some balls on the court, but there were no outdoor courts nearby.

So, I just kept walking. Now that I had no job, and no girlfriend, there was no place I needed to be anyway.

CHAPTER THIRTY-SIX

- Nate -

*A*s I walked, it hit me. For the first time in my life, I didn't have anything planned. No job, no school, no sports, no travels, no social life. My future—both the immediate and long-term—was a blank slate. Well, I supposed I was still registered to start my MBA program in the fall, but frankly, I wasn't sure that would happen anyway. Without my internship, I'd probably have to pay for the degree myself. And as much as I liked the idea of being back in school, I didn't want to fund an education I wasn't certain I'd ever use.

I thought about Olivia, and the time she'd tried to get me to confess what I'd do with my life if I weren't destined to take over the family business. She'd thought I was being coy when I didn't tell her, but really, I just didn't know. Since the day I was born, there'd been a plan for my life. And before Olivia came along, I'd never had the balls to even consider straying from that plan.

Now, I had options. Thanks to her, I could choose what my future would hold.

Olivia had made it clear that she wanted nothing to do with

me. But when she said that, she still believed she'd spent the night with my father. And while I believed nothing had happened between her and my dad, I still wasn't sure where that left me and Olivia. At a minimum, we both needed some space. The image of her near my father still made my stomach churn, and she surely still resented me for the shit she'd overheard my sister and me say.

But I was worried about her. Olivia was always harder on herself than anyone else would be, so when I'd been angry at her, she must have been even more furious at herself.

I'd seen the marks on her arms. I didn't know if it was what she'd heard me say to Leighton or what she thought she had done with my father that drove her to hurt herself, but it didn't matter. I needed to make sure she was okay. Over and over, Olivia had told me it wasn't my job to protect her, but she was wrong. Just because she could fight her own battles didn't mean I should let her. Especially since I was the one who brought my wretched family into her life, it was my job to keep her safe from their manipulative tricks. And now, I'd let her down.

I doubted I'd be able to repair the damage to our relationship, but that wasn't my priority anyway. I told myself I'd eventually move on without Olivia, that I could survive even if she spent the rest of her life hating me. But I couldn't live with myself if she also hated herself, especially over an act she hadn't actually committed. Besides, Olivia deserved to know the truth about what happened with my father. It was up to me to tell her the truth, to clear the air.

I wasn't the slightest bit surprised when no one answered the door at her apartment. I drove straight to the tennis courts, parking at the far end of the lot and walking up slowly. There wasn't a doubt in my mind that the lone figure on the courts was Olivia.

Even from a distance, I could tell her eyes were closed. Other- wise, she would've seen me coming, and possibly would've beaten me with her racket. I watched her for a moment, admiring her grace and the quiet fluidity of her movements. Olivia had the sort of serve coaches would film and show to students. She was that good. That controlled. That perfect. Even while her world was crumbling, Olivia still played like nothing existed past the faint white lines of the court.

Someone as talented as Olivia should have an ego the size of Texas. Olivia should see herself like the rest of the world did, as an icon, an athletic genius. She should know how uniquely wonderful she was, not just on the courts but in every aspect of life.

But she didn't, and in part that was my fault.

Olivia had told me from the start that I would hurt her, and she was right. And while part of me figured I'd run in the other direction if I truly loved her, to let her live her life without my negative influence, I just couldn't. I wasn't even sure I could survive another day without her in my life. Even breathing proved harder without her by my side.

I wasn't okay, but surely neither was Olivia. We needed each other, even if Olivia didn't yet realize it.

A lump rose in my throat as I watched the muscles from her calves up to her hip ripple in a line as she swung the racket down. I wondered why she hadn't braided her hair, but I loved the way the locks swayed with her movements, cascading around her angelic face like a shimmering waterfall.

My eyes fell to her long, delicate fingers, and I shivered at the memory of her hands skimming my body. I craved her touch like it was a desert oasis. I needed it. Needed her.

"Hasn't anyone ever told you it's not safe to practice all alone in the dark out here?" I called.

Olivia heard me—the slight pause before her next serve told me that. But she didn't reply. Instead, she kept hitting balls. With every serve she delivered perfectly into the corner of the court, I ventured another step closer. When I was close enough to touch her, she lowered her racket to her side.

Standing behind Olivia, I couldn't tell if her eyes were still closed, and I supposed it didn't matter. I wanted to see her, to peer into her vivid cerulean sea, but I knew better than to try to do this any way other than on her terms. She'd turn when she was ready.

Well, either that or she'd pummel me with her racket.

"I'm sorry," I began. "I shouldn't have walked off when I did, but…it was a lot to process. I needed to talk to my father, to think about what you'd said." I winced, hating that it sounded like I was making excuses. I wanted to be able to tell her it wouldn't have mattered either way, but I couldn't do that, in good faith. Truthfully, I'd never know. "I screwed up. I'm sorry."

Even in the dim lighting, I could see her shoulders rise and fall as she took long, deep breaths.

"Nothing happened with my father," I continued. "But if it had, it would've been my fault, not yours. Anyway, I talked with him. He's…well, he's not a good man, or not the kind of man I want to be, anyway. But I'm certain he's telling the truth about this. You were upset, you hadn't eaten anything, and you drank too much," I began. I remembered her mentioning something about pills from my sister too, but that didn't seem relevant at the moment. Olivia just needed to know how she ended up in his bed. She didn't say anything, so I continued.

"Your clothes were dirty. You…got sick on them. You went to bed in his room and he slept in the living room. Nothing else happened. Nothing."

I paused, letting my words soak in, hoping she felt some relief over this revelation, praying she'd let go of her guilt. "I had a…candid talk with my father. I'm not working for him anymore. I'm not even speaking with him at the moment. Maybe someday we'll get back to a place where we can be cordial to each other, but I don't know."

I inhaled sharply, wishing Olivia would say something, anything to rescue me from my ramblings, but she didn't, so my jumbled thoughts kept pouring out of me. "Right now, I really don't care what happens with my father. All my life I've been trying to please him and I don't know why. His life is not what I want for myself. I don't want to take over the family business. I don't even know if I want to get my MBA. He's the one who came up with this stupid plan for my life, and I never even thought to question it before. If you hadn't come along and made me think about what I actually wanted to do, I could've been stuck in a life I never even wanted. You're the only person who ever believed I could do something meaningful with my life."

I paused to catch my breath. My heart thumped erratically, but all I could do was wait, praying she'd forgive me…or at a minimum, that she'd speak up and put me out of my misery.

CHAPTER THIRTY-SEVEN

- Olivia -

*A*s Nate spoke to me, I clutched my racket tightly. With the amount of tension building in my body with every word he expressed, I needed something to squeeze, needed some outlet for the emotion flowing through me.

What he said about his father brought me immeasurable relief. Not just because I'd never intentionally do anything with Mr. Aldridge, and not just because it was horrifying to even think I could fool around with someone and not remember the act. I was relieved because the thought of having done something that would hurt Nate that much literally made me sick. I couldn't breathe, couldn't eat, could barely even move with the crushing pain of thinking I'd betrayed him so cruelly.

I wasn't sure how to feel about Nate's confession that he and his father were now on the outs. I agreed his father was a dick. And I knew Nate would be happier long-term carving out his own path in life rather than constantly disappointing his family. But I didn't want to be the cause of that chasm in his life. Family was important to Nate, and he needed them, even if they didn't act the way he wanted them to.

I focused on Nate's deep, soothing voice as he continued, remembering all the times that voice had lulled me to sleep, and all the times that simply hearing his voice had offered a reassurance I hadn't known I needed.

"I don't know why I was so concerned about what my family thought for so long," he continued. "Honestly, I didn't really realize how much their opinions mattered to me until recently. And now, well, I don't care if they disapprove. My father is not the person I want to please with my choices." Nate paused, swallowing loudly.

"You are the only person whose opinions matter to me. I want to live my life in a way that makes you proud. I need your approval, Olivia," Nate said, his voice strong but soft.

I dug my teeth into my lip, squeezing my eyes shut tighter in hopes of keeping the tears at bay. It was futile.

"I still mean everything I said to you before. I'm so, so sorry for how I behaved with my sister. I didn't mean any of what you overheard. I could never be embarrassed by you. You are too good for me. I have a feeling I will never be good enough to deserve you, but that won't stop me. I'm going to get up every day and try to be the man you need me to be."

I held my breath, feeling myself unable to resist the sway of his words. The racket slipped from my hands, hitting the court with a high-pitched clank. Nate's fingers slipped around my own, gently entwining themselves. His touch was so simple, so innocent, and yet I felt it so deeply. With Nate's hands on mine, I felt safe. I felt whole.

He stepped closer as he continued talking. I could feel the heat from his breath on the back of my neck, felt the firmness of his chest lightly pressing against my back. "I've been miserable being apart from you, Olivia. I can't sleep without you in my arms. I can't focus without seeing your smile and hearing your laugh." He chuckled softly. "I can't even dress myself without you there, mocking my outfits."

His free hand wrapped around me, tugging me firmly against his chest as he rest his forehead on the crown of my head. "I love you so much, Olivia. I want the world to know it. I want you." Nate paused. "I will always want you."

I lifted my hand to stroke his forearm that clutched around my abdomen, leaning into him and feeling the full support of his embrace before turning towards him. I buried my face against his chest, inhaling his familiar sporty scent and relishing the sound of his heartbeat. I felt his lips press against the top of my head and just like that, I could think of nothing but those lips. How I'd missed touching them, tasting them, God, even just seeing them.

I pulled back enough to tilt my head upwards. Nate cupped my cheeks in his hands, gazing at me with his bold brown eyes.

"I love you so much," he whispered.

I shushed him by bringing my mouth to his. Warmth flooded my body at the contact, and even though the kiss started gently, it quickly intensified. My mind swirled with the flurry of everything he'd told me, and then my thoughts stilled as his tongue brushed past mine. Kissing Nate settled me. His kiss filled me with a calmness I barely recognized.

Nate had confessed so much to me, apologized for so many things that, really, weren't even his fault. I hadn't said a word. And despite that, he was more than ready to proclaim his love for me. Somehow, the most caring and handsome man I'd ever met, the one who'd shattered every stereotype I'd believed, the one who was just as perfect in real life as on paper, the one who could have any woman he wanted... somehow that man chose me.

Somehow, Nate loved me despite my many faults. Even more than that, though, he knew me. Nate knew what I felt in my heart but couldn't say aloud in that moment, and he knew exactly what I needed.

We made out like a couple of teenagers, like we had that first night he'd surprised me on the darkened courts. And just like that night, the lights popped on suddenly, well before we were ready to end our kiss.

Our mouths flew apart at the onslaught of light, but Nate wrapped his arms around me so tightly around me that I couldn't have pulled away completely, even if I'd unlinked my own arms from behind his neck.

"Definitely a timer," he said with a laugh. Nate pressed a final kiss to my forehead then released me. "So, are we gonna play here or what?" he asked, walking to the other side of the net.

I was smiling so hard my cheeks hurt, but I scooted back to the line, raised the ball in the air, and got ready to swing.

"Love-all," I called.

The End

EPILOGUE

- Olivia -

*T*he next six months flew by in a whirlwind. I played in a few professional tournaments over the summer, and while I lost enough matches to keep me humble, I won enough of the games to attract some serious attention. With no intention of leaving school early anyway, I still had time to improve my game and to decide if I truly wanted to play professionally after graduation. My coaches and Nate were all encouraging me to give it a try for a few years.

Peter had insisted I keep his check, so I'd paid off my student loans. He'd also given my mother a hefty check, which she of course accepted. Peter and I still weren't exactly best friends, and we certainly didn't have a normal father-daughter relationship, but that was okay. We exchanged text messages on occasion, and he'd bring the boys to watch me play when his schedule permitted. Someday, maybe we'd attempt a traditional Thanksgiving dinner together, but we weren't there yet.

I'd struggled with forgiving my mom, but Nate had really convinced me to think of the situation from her perspective. She hadn't lied about my father to hurt me, and at the end of the day, I couldn't even say whether I would've been better off knowing the truth about my dad from the start. Meeting Peter's parents certainly helped me sympathize with my mom, and I understood how hard it must have been for her to face their judgment and raise me alone.

Nate bought her a plane ticket to watch me play in a tournament, and the two of them truly hit it off. My mom instantly picked up on his wealth, but unlike me, she actually formed her first impression based off his personality. She laughed at all his jokes and actually listened to his advice about investing the money Peter gave her. When the three of us went out to eat, I ended up feeling like the third wheel because of how well Nate and my mom got along.

As for his own family, Nate made some progress. Neither he nor his father ever apologized, but his sister did. Leighton explained that she and her husband had separated. Instead of telling the family about her situation, she'd focused on Nate's drama. She apologized to both of us, actually, and it sounded sincere. I didn't foresee myself ever becoming as close to Leighton as Ansley, but we were at least friendly.

After meeting with one of his finance professors early in the summer, Nate decided to go ahead with the MBA program. He still didn't want to follow in his father's footsteps, but the careers that interested him would all benefit from an advanced business degree. Besides, his trust fund more than covered his tuition, housing, and expenses, especially since he ended up renting his old college apartment another year instead of moving closer to the city.

He had a commute once school started in the fall, but not a bad one, and since he was still on campus, I was able to move in with him. Once I graduated, we could find a place closer to Nate's new school together.

Not one for wasting free time, Nate had spent the summer

before grad school setting up his own non-profit organization to help low income families invest wisely. He credited me with the idea, saying he loved advising my mother. According to Nate, the ability to invest in the market was what helped the rich get richer while ensuring the poor stayed poor. I didn't disagree, nor did I hate seeing his father's reaction when he learned his family's money was going to help the "trash" of the world.

Nate started small with the Aldridge Organization, as he called it. He had a few helpful investors from both of our families, including his sister and Peter. When it was time for him to start school, Nate installed his sister as the CEO of the new organization. She had the perfect credentials and was eager to show the world—or at least her own husband and father—that she could run a business just as well as any man. I also thought Jackie Aldridge was pleased to see her children working together and forging a new association with the family name.

As for myself, I'd never been happier. My world consisted of tennis, school, and Nate, and that was just perfect. Whenever I thought about that fateful day when Nate had challenged me to a tennis match, I smiled. At the time, I'd been mortified that I actually threw a game just to lose a bet so I could date a boy. But looking back, I had no regrets.

I would bet on Nate any day.

* * *

- Nate -

I watched as Olivia effortlessly won the point. One more game, and this set would be hers, ending the match. It wasn't a crucial game for her, and she was playing a junior who didn't have a hope in the world of winning. But still, I could tell Olivia was completely focused. Part of me hoped she'd remain that way, but part of me really wanted to see if I could actually fluster the unwavering Olivia Roberts.

I was seated in the third row of the stands, but well within Olivia's line of vision. She'd glanced over at me a couple times, so I prayed my timing worked and she actually looked my way when I needed her to.

Taking a deep breath, I raised the sign above my head. At first, I held it directly in front of me, covering my face. But then, I didn't want any confusion messing up my moment, so I ducked my head around to the side.

"She's ready to serve," the announcer said. "This could be the game point. If Roberts scores on this serve, she wins the match."

The crowd fell quiet as Olivia bounced the ball and then tapped it against her racket before raising her racket in the air. Then she paused, lowering her racket to her side.

"Hold on," the announcer said. "She's pausing for…what is…"

Olivia burst into laughter, then covered her face with her racket.

"She seems to be distracted by a sign in the stands," the announcer continued. "Can you read that?"

The second announcer laughed. "It looks like it says 'Winner Marries Me.' I wonder if this is just a fan, or a true contender."

Olivia cast me another gaze, smiled, then turned back to the court, nodding to her opponent.

I stopped listening to the announcers as she tossed the ball and served. To my surprise, her opponent actually returned the ball, but missed it on the third volley. I kept my sign on display, watching as Olivia shook hands with her opponent, laughed at something the girl said, then turned to me.

A few of the spectators had already started to file down their rows, but the majority were still seated, pointing and staring at me. I hadn't expected that level of attention, and suddenly I felt dizzy.

Excitement buzzed loudly in the stands, and Coach Katelyn turned to me.

"Aldridge, get down here!" she shouted.

I climbed down the stands, making my way onto the court.

"You're lucky you're not on the team anymore or I'd make sure your coach had you running laps for weeks after that stunt," she said. Her broad smile told me she wasn't too upset.

Olivia walked to the side of the court, and when she peered up to me, I held up the sign one last time. As she walked towards me, Olivia bit back a smile, like she was still wondering if it was a joke.

I took a deep breath, reached into my pocket, then pulled out the ring box. Dropping to my knee, I extended the jewelry box towards her.

The fans went wild, but I didn't even care anymore. I couldn't take my eyes off my beautiful Olivia. She dropped her racket and clutched both hands over her mouth. She stopped walking towards me and shook her head, but it was her chastising head shake and not an actual "no."

I crooked my finger towards her and motioned for her to come closer. Thankfully, she did.

"It looks like you're the winner," I said.

Olivia cast a glance to her opponent, who was watching us with an amused smile. I felt a moment of relief that the poor girl hadn't taken offensive to my antics. "It looks that way," she said.

"So…what do you say? Will you marry me so I can get a front row seat at the NCAA Championship match?"

Olivia giggled and wiped a tear from her eye. "That's your proposal?"

"I mean, I could tell you that I've loved you since the moment I saw you. Or that I don't want to even imagine a life where you're not mine. Or maybe that you are the most talented, passionate, brilliant and stubborn woman I've ever met." I paused. "But that all seems a tad personal for this space."

Her smile widened, then she glanced down at the ring. Her expression altered instantly, suggesting I'd maybe gone a tad overboard on the ring. Olivia looked back at me.

"I love you," she whispered, raising her hand to her mouth again.

"So…is that a yes then?" I asked.

Olivia laughed and nodded. "Yes, you romantic fool. Now get up and put that ring on my finger."

She didn't have to tell me twice. The ring slid smoothly into place and looked even more impressive on her hand than it had in the box. We both stared at it for a moment, and then she threw her arms around me, practically knocking me backwards with the force of her kiss. I held her tightly. I was reassured that everything had gone according to plan, and utterly shocked that the woman who'd been so adamant about hiding our relationship—was now happily making out with me in front of a live crowd and televised audience.

We might just be okay after all.

If you enjoyed this story, please leave a review!

SNEAK PEEK OF MAFIOSA
PRINCESS

Mafiosa Princess is a steamy mafia romance series. If you haven't yet begun this series, here's a sneak peak of the first book in the series. After you finish Mafiosa Princess, you'll move on to Mafiosa Princess- Sacrifice, Mafiosa Princess- Honor, Mafiosa Princess- Trust, then Mafiosa Princess Omertà. Look for two more books in the series in 2023!

Chapter 1

I peered into the trunk again, surveying my collection of bags. Maybe I had overpacked for my winter break trip, but in my defense, we'd spent over three weeks in Italy. That sort of trip demanded lots of outfits and accessories, and I'd come home with even more thanks to a shopping spree in Milan. My heart thumped harder as my eyes landed on the suitcase filled with all of my new fashion nestled beside my brother Angelo's singular suitcase.

I tapped my foot, casting yet another glance across the tiny courtyard. Angelo showed no signs of nearing the end of his heated phone call and our driver stood behind him, seemingly chiming in on the discussion. I suspected they would not appreciate my eagerness, but my fingers were already stiff beneath my cashmere-lambskin gloves. Besides, there was no reason to wait for them to complete a task I could handle on my own.

I retrieved my duffel bag and backpack with ease, then braced myself as I lugged the larger of my two suitcases out of the trunk and onto the luggage cart. The muscles along my forearm twitched as I grabbed my garment bags and the smaller suitcase.

I reached into my coat pocket and untangled my rosary from my cell phone before checking if my roommate Gabriella had texted to announce her arrival yet. I was dying to catch up with her. She'd spent part of her break with her boyfriend, which seemed infinitely more exciting than my travels with my mom, two brothers who rarely got off their phones, and a father who could only spare a few days away from his business to catch up with the family. Not that I'd ever complain about a trip to Italy, but having someone other than my mother to talk with would've been nice.

Confirming my chaperones were still oblivious, I began to steer the luggage cart towards the building. The front left wheel spun listlessly, forcing the entire contraption to veer to the side. I braced my foot against the wheel, brushed my hair behind my shoulders, then used my hip to ram the cart in the other direction. I was panting by the time I reached the covered entrance to my apartment building.

I paused by the building, appreciating the protection from the wind and the fleeting rush of warmth that blew my way whenever someone else opened the door to leave. No matter how many winters I spent in New England, I'd never adjust to the painful frigidness that settled in by November each year.

I was debating heading inside when a gust of wind hit the cart at just the right angle, causing it to lurch back down the ramp. Visions of a collision ricocheting my precious clothes across the alley flashed before my eyes. I lunged for the cart, but it rolled just out of my reach.

Suddenly, it stopped with a jolt.

"Thank you," I said, relief flooding my system.

I stepped around the cart to see the hero who'd saved my stuff. Heat rushed to my face as I realized it was *him*. The hunky guy Gabriella and I affectionately referred to as Baby Blues. Admittedly, it wasn't the sexiest nickname for the guy, but since he had the bluest eyes I'd ever seen, the moniker fit. Plus, based on the frequency with which he visited the criminal justice building, I assumed he was studying to be in law enforcement. With broad shoulders, a tall muscular frame, and a butt that belonged in underwear ads, he sure looked like a cop.

"I really appreciate you catching my runaway cart."

"No problem," he replied with a wink. Up close, his eyes were even more mesmerizing. Their cerulean blue contrasted nicely with the dismal grey sky above us. He steered the cart back to the door and angled it away from the sloped sidewalk. "You moving in?"

"Returning from vacation," I said, appreciating the effort he made not to laugh at this response. "It's possible I overpacked."

"No, not at all," he teased, his smile revealing symmetrical dimples.

"Do you live here?" I asked, nearly positive from my stalking that he didn't.

"No, but I'm studying criminal justice, so I spend a lot of time next door," he said, gesturing at the building.

"Ah, studying to be an officer of the law?"

He laughed, revealing straight white teeth. "An officer of the court actually," he said, adding, "A lawyer."

"Oh. Wow. Fancy," I said. "I'm Giada Conti, and I do live here." My heart thumped harder once I knew he wasn't going to be a cop. I had nothing against police, but my father thought they were all self-dealing liars. And not that I'd let my father dictate who I'd date, but…

"Adrian," he said, jolting me out of my thoughts.

I extended my hand towards him, wishing we were gloveless so I could touch his skin. "Do you have a last name?"

"Patras."

"Nice to meet you. I feel like I owe you a coffee to thank you for rescuing my stuff." Out of the corner of my eye, I spotted a dark sedan roll up beside Angelo and Enzo. My brother climbed into the sedan without even so much as a glance in my direction, leaving Enzo alone on the sidewalk. It sure looked shady, but that was nothing new with Angelo. He had long since mastered the art of being creepy and mysterious.

"Hang on," I said as Enzo approached. He paused by his car, closed the trunk, then shook his head at me.

"Stubborn, impatient…" he began lecturing, his tone light.

"Independent and capable?" I proffered. "Angelo didn't want to say goodbye to his favorite sister?"

Enzo held his hands in the air. "He's got fires to put out."

I rolled my eyes. My brother was training to take over the family business, but as far as I could tell, he was hardly essential to the current operations. Not that anyone ever told me anything about the family business.

"You okay to get all this inside?" he nodded towards my luggage.

"Of course." As much as I wanted to catch up with Enzo, having not seen him much since summer, I really wanted to get back to flirting with Adrian.

Enzo appeared skeptical, but nodded. "It was good seeing you, Princess."

"You too," I said. I threw my arms around him as he squeezed me so tightly that my feet lifted off the ground. It was the hug I'd wanted to give him earlier, when he met us at the airport, but I figured Angelo would've pitched a fit over me touching the help.

Enzo lowered me to the ground slowly, then stared at me for a moment before winking again and turning around. I watched him stroll back to the car then remembered the cute guy standing beside me.

"Sorry," I mumbled. "Where were we?"

He licked his lips and furrowed his brows. "You had offered to buy me coffee, and I was about to suggest I take you to dinner instead, but…"

My heart pounded erratically. "But?"

He gestured to Enzo's car as it drove off. "Isn't that your boyfriend?"

I bit back a smile. "No. That would be my driver."

"Um, I've had my fair share of rides and my drivers never hug me like that. You must be a great tipper."

I couldn't help but giggle at that. "Lorenzo works full time for my family. He has for years. I mean, yeah, he's hot, but he's twenty-six and he treats me like a little sister."

Adrian shook his head slowly. "I'm trying to ask you out and you just called another guy hot. Can we just push this cart back into oncoming traffic and start over?"

"I'd rather start over at dinner this week," I said, acting bold despite the flutters in my belly.

His grin widened as he reached into his back pocket. "What's your number, Giada Conti?"

I rattled off the digits and let him push the luggage cart into the building for me. I wasn't entirely positive I'd be able to maneuver it off the elevator on my own, but I was so giddy at the moment that I really didn't care.

Click here to order Mafiosa Princess

ACKNOWLEDGEMENTS

*L*ots of people helped bring this fun story together... I especially appreciate my cover artist, who went through many different designs before creating the beautiful cover on this book. As always, I'm grateful to my family who supported me during the writing and editing of this book. Last but certainly not least, thank you to all of my readers. Your support means so much to me. And if you've read this far, please please please leave a review for this book so others can help find my stories too!

ABOUT THE AUTHOR

Liza Malloy writes contemporary romance and women's fiction. She's a sucker for alpha males, bad boys, dimples, and muscles, and she can't resist a man in uniform. Liza loves creating worlds where her heroine discovers her own strength and finds her Happily Ever After. When Liza isn't reading or writing torrid love stories, she's a practicing attorney. Her other passions include gummy bears, jelly beans, and the occasional marathon. She lives in the Midwest with her four daughters and her own Prince Charming.

Visit her website at www.LizaMalloy.com

Join her email list at http://eepurl.com/gnuROD

facebook.com/authorlizam
twitter.com/authorlizam
instagram.com/authorlizam
amazon.com/author/lizamalloy
bookbub.com/profile/liza-malloy
pinterest.com/lizamalloy
tiktok.com/@authorlizamalloy

ALSO BY LIZA MALLOY

CPSIA information can be obtained
at www.ICGtesting.com
Printed in the USA
BVHW031211240123
656976BV00004B/57

9 781950 478378